Bluff

Jeremy Leland comes from an old Anglo–Irish family whose French ancestors fled to Ireland to escape the Huguenot pogroms in the sixteenth century. His forbears include the Senior Fellow of Trinity College, Dublin, Dr Thomas Leland, who wrote a definitive history of Ireland in 1773. After studying painting at the Slade School in London, he farmed a small estate north of Dublin, and it was here that he began to write; the writing has persisted through various occupations. After several years as a textile designer, he now works as a voluntary Citizen's Advice Bureau Advisor, is a landlord to university students, and lives with another designer and her Great Dane in Norwich. Ireland, however, is still the context of his writing.

JEREMY LELAND

Bluff

A Methuen Paperback

To Liz and Dan the Dane

A Methuen Paperback

BLUFF

British Library Cataloguing in Publication Data

Leland, Jeremy
Bluff.
I. Title
823'.914[F]   PR6062.E47

ISBN 0–413–17620–7

First published in Great Britain 1987
by Victor Gollancz Limited
This edition published 1988
by Methuen London Ltd
11 New Fetter Lane, London EC4P 4EE
Copyright © Jeremy Leland 1987

Printed and bound in Great Britain
by Cox & Wyman Ltd, Reading

Two ravens flew along the bluff in the late afternoon, high above him, their dispassionate croaks a mild tut-tutting at his intrusion into their realm; although in terms of real estate the valley and its mountainous sides were his. Yet that wasn't strictly true either. Conor de Burgh might be the name on the title-deeds, but they lay as security in the belly of the Bank of Ireland, a creature so fat with paper land that if disturbed it might vomit up half the country.

Set in its huge stony landscape among long grey hills crouching like limestone dinosaurs, a small pocket of green, a cleft in the strata, lined with ash trees and hazel, smeared with grass that grew on the débris deposited in its basin, Conor's valley was a private world of its own. No one ever came there save the occasional tourist or university botanist from the Galway University field-station, for rare pre-ice-age plants grew here. In extravagant mood he saw himself as sharing it with the wild creatures—badgers up in the ash wood on the steep southern slopes, pine martens in the fir trees behind the bluff, squirrels in the hazels that grew like weeds everywhere, hares, ravens, kestrels, summer swallows, whitears and so on. He saw the valley as an ark bearing this bounty of wildlife through the seasons; a verdant hull ribbed with stone walls, all around an Atlantic landscape heaving its limestone waves, moving an inch a year. And he a sort of helmsman.

The reality was not so romantic: he no more than herdsman, the valley often a bowl of mud and stones and wet dripping trees. About it he stumbled and slithered in greasy boots, to

5

round up straying sheep, elusive goats, suspicious cattle, his small flocks, whose lambs, calves and goat's milk enabled him to ease the bank's digestion, and buy himself the sustaining bacon, bread and cans of Guinness. He was not a farmer by birth. He had inherited the valley from a bachelor uncle, and there were times when he felt trapped—trapped by the struggle to survive in a barren, stony world. It was a basis of his chronic rage with the world that nothing ever seemed to go right.

Those sanctimonious pricks from the Inland Revenue daring to suggest he must be concealing profits, and they with their fancy salaries and shiny cars and bungalows with bay windows, kitchens like spacecraft lined with gadgets to cook the food and wash the clothes, all at the touch of a button, while he had to saw logs for the old cracked Esse, boil his shirts in a black pot, stand on cold flagstones to wash at the sink, and spend half-an-hour twiddling stumps of knobs on the geriatric television to get a fuzzy picture of a man telling him diesel was to go up another tenpence and the rates a quid an acre.

But you have over four hundred acres, wrote the rates collector.

Dear Mr Gogarty, Certainly there's 483 acres of stone beauty here, but there's no market for limestone, it's hard to chew, and much of it's so vertical you might hang wallpaper on it. The only new article I've purchased in five years is a lavatory, where my bowels can squirt their daily anxiety as to how am I going to meet the bills that the postman insists on bringing with the monotony of a weaver's shuttle. The few leathery beasts that struggle to survive on the miserable fifty acres of reasonable grazing mostly belong to the bank. If there was any justice the government would be paying me to preserve the land as a heritage for tourists. Yours, indigently.

The valley was actually in two parts. The wester, higher end was known as the glen. Originally this had been a separate farm, and the ruins of a small stone farmhouse and crumbling sheds, overgrown with moss, brambles and nettles, lay olive-dark beneath a clump of ash trees. In the part of the valley hidden from the longer eastern section, lay a dense slope of copse and mature wood rising to a monumental crag at the western end of the bluff. As he stood checking the chocolate-brown forms of his contentedly munching cattle in the small fields that surrounded the ruined farmhouse, his eyes were drawn to the wood. Rising out of the centre was a thin column of smoke.

There must be someone in there, he thought, surprised.

A solitary grey crow flapped across the glen. The smoke was white where it emerged from trees. He felt alarmed and angry at the intrusion. The wood was a mile from the road, and the nearest inhabited farm was three miles away, apart from his friends and neighbours, the Riordans.

Could there be tourists up there? he thought. Have to go up and investigate. He gripped the old uncle's ashplant tightly and looked round for the dog.

When acting as his shadow Belle could be irritating. But when working, she was his wholly admirable assistant: a small black border collie who twice daily set off into the hills to find the goats and bring them down for milking.

There she was, over in the next field, approaching the trees, sniffing. She knew something was odd. When she looked back, he raised a hand for her to wait for him. A whitehead cow with a brown monocle about one eye lifted her head to watch him pass. A small silky calf ran after him, then stopped. He crossed a wall, the stone grinding as his thigh rested on the top. At other times he might have vaulted the wall, enjoying the physical exertion. But now he was concentrating on moving quietly, as if stalking his prey.

When he came up to Belle, she gave one wag of her tail, then stood waiting for his command, ears pricked. He felt slightly sick with apprehension, climbing up past the first trees, entering the leafy chambering of their intertwining branches. He moved cautiously, pausing to peer ahead every few paces, self-conscious of every sound, resting a hand on tree trunks, curling the fingers of his other hand firmly round the handle of the ashplant as if expecting to be leaped on at any moment.

Who would want to burn a fire? Travelling people never came to these parts, the hills were too remote for them, they preferred the more populous lowlands where they could find plenty of scrap to deal in, plenty of palms to cross with silver. And it was a long way off the road for campers, even those bronzed young Germans with towering rucksacks who pitched small orange tents thin as nylon tights, and hung up washing-lines between saplings to dry extraordinary numbers of socks and little paisley-patterned underpants. But they, with their

7

plastic boxes for rubbish, for keeping butter cool, for protecting their radios from the rain, were always correct, always came to ask permission. Nobody else would light a fire. The tourists were car people, staying in hotels or rented cottages. They wandered over the land, exclaiming like delighted children, calling to each other as they found gentians, hellebores and orchids. Then they would return to their cars to drive a little further, to explore one of the old round forts that were the fortified farms of the dark ages, or peer under the slabs of a dolmen or a wedge grave. It was too remote for children to be mitching from school.

He paused. There was the scent of roasting meat. Quite distinct. He glanced back at Belle, who was following quietly, nose raised and eyes half-closed in ecstasy. But when she saw him look at her she dropped her head guiltily and pretended to be industriously sniffing the ground. He could rarely afford roast meat himself, though there was the time a calf fell off the rocks and broke its neck, and he and the Riordans who owned a freezer had feasted royally for weeks. Often he would be invited to the Riordans for Sunday dinner. Mrs Riordan was a generous woman and would have had him eating there every evening. But he would only allow himself to accept her invitation if he had been giving them a hand with the cattle, or the hay, or the shearing. He was up there helping more often recently, since Sean had died. And no day was quite the same if he didn't have a sight of Nuala. Even if he hated to admit to himself that she had no time for him.

The leaves of the trees rustled above him with the persistent hiss of surf. The aroma of the cooking meat was extremely appetising. Someone preparing food does not suggest a terrible threat, and he stepped forward, no longer cautious.

The first object he saw in the clearing was the dead lamb. In quick succession his eyes darted from the bloody hacked-off haunch to a well-browned leg on a makeshift spit over a fire, then back to the green mark on the lamb's fleece. His mark. And then on to the real surprise, a young woman licking fat off her lips, still chewing, a knife in one hand, her eyes wide with shock at his sudden appearance. She'd killed one of his lambs, he thought, pain rising behind his ears, clouds narrowing his vision as his anger swelled up through his body and into his temples.

He could hardly breathe. Vomit in his throat, sharp as acid. The ground was rushing up fast, too fast, he couldn't lift the nose, it wouldn't respond, this was a nightmare happening. The trees charged towards him like green Zulus shaking their assegai branches. Too late the plane began to lift. He felt the fuselage ripping as if his own ribs were being torn from his chest. And it was all his own fault. That Lyn was dead. And here was Nuala Riordan, dark-eyes and high-coloured, in through the door, breathless. Can you drive Sean to Ennis? He's taken bad again and the car's not back from the garage. I'll go with you. Hurtling through the black tunnel of the night, hurling hedgerows over his shoulders. If I had a plane we'd be there in five minutes, he exclaimed. You live too much in the past, Conor. You're a dreamer, always what might be. But this is the here and now, and if you don't have a care, you'll have us all in the ditch and dead. But Sean isn't going to die? he cried. But he did.

'That's my lamb you've killed,' he exclaimed, the words igniting him to action, sweeping him forward, the ashplant raised.

The girl leaped backwards, waving the knife at him. 'Keep off,' she shouted in alarm.

But he struck the knife from her hand, cannoning into her in his rush, knocking her to the ground. 'You bloody thief, you bloody killer,' he cried, lifting her up, shaking her. 'One of my best lambs.'

'Christ, fuck off,' she shouted, struggling to free herself.

Belle bounced round them, barking. As the woman clawed at his face, tried to kick him in the groin, he pinioned her arms, pushed her down on to the ground. 'My god, I'll deal with you,' he cried, so angry he could barely tell what he was doing. With one hand inside the waistband of her jeans, he gave a great yank so that they tore away, pants and all, revealing her buttocks like the white segments of a peach. And then he began to beat them. The action drained away his anger, and suddenly he was aware of her cries, of the red marks he was making on her flesh, and he stopped, aghast. 'Jesus,' he exclaimed, backing away from where she lay sobbing on the ground. He turned, nausea and fear clogging his throat, tripped over the body of the lamb and stumbled away through the trees, hurling the ashplant from him.

9

Halfway across the second field he stopped, looked back at the wood. Smoke still hung above the trees. He looked at his hands, felt the scratches on his face, listened for any sounds. Belle was waiting for him at the wall.

He wanted to shut what had happened out of his mind. But there it was inside his skull, flapping about like a bird in a cage, beating its wings at the wire bars. He put his hands up to his head as if to wrench it open, let it free so the pounding would cease. It was blocking his mind, choking it from thinking. He took great gulps of air, afraid he was on the verge of convulsions that would throw him down, paralyse him.

The pain inside his mind did not seem to rise from inside his battered body in the wreckage of the fuselage, the aluminium bones and rent metal glinting in the brilliant sunlight burning down on him. They were all dead, the others. Smashed into meat. The wings, engines and body had been ripped off by the trees, allowing the cockpit to detach and escape the worst mangling. The pain was because she was still beside him. But dead, too, her neck broken. The white-hot sun burned right down inside his skull, melted the colloidal gimbals of his equanimity, all the pent-up anger of his entire life came pouring out like all the meals he had ever been poisoned with, and he yelled in that desolate place till he felt his head must burst. His rage at this senseless annihilation, at his own stupidity, at fate, at all the people he could blame, blew through him like a hurricane that would not go away, but continued to shake and blast and circle back in a trail of carnage, and he knew that life would always go wrong, that he was a marked man.

He must get back to the house. He began to run again. Then found he was heading in the wrong direction. This was stupid, he must take a grip on himself. He was panting, his chest hurt, he slowed to a walk. Whatever had possessed him? Maybe he should go back, make sure she was all right.

He was just about to enter the yard when he heard running footsteps behind him. He spun round quickly.

It was her. She slowed down about ten paces away, came a few steps nearer. She was carrying a large shoulder-bag slung diagonally across her back. One hand was holding the strap, the other was clutching at her waist. 'I'll pay you,' she panted. 'I'll pay you for the lamb. I hadn't eaten for five days.'

The contradiction in her last remark struck him at once. He was suspicious. She seemed to realise this, too, that what she had said did not add up. 'I could work for you,' she said. 'Pay it off that way.'

He had not taken in her appearance before. Only her tangled, shoulder-length hair the hue of brown beer bottle. She had a pale intelligent face, a small but fat-lipped mouth, and large eyes. He was embarrassed when he saw her clutching at her waist to keep her jeans up. 'Could you let me stay somewhere?' she asked. 'In a shed maybe? I'll be no trouble.'

It could be a trick, he thought nervously. To lull him so that when he was off his guard, she could take her revenge. He could see her face stiffening as if to ward off his expected rejection, the inevitable rebuttal. 'I shouldn't have lost my temper,' he said. 'I'm sorry.'

She brightened up at this, shook herself. 'I just wish you hadn't found me. How did you know?'

'The smoke.'

'I should have thought.' She smote her forehead with the palm of her hand. 'I broke the rules.'

He frowned, wondering if she might be on the run. 'Are you from the north?'

She nodded. He looked round, up the lane, back down the valley. 'You'd best come in. I'll make you a cup of tea.'

He lived in the kitchen much as his uncle had done. It was a large room with a stained matchboard ceiling, an old sofa beside the Esse, a big scrubbed table in the centre. Building a concrete cistern and diverting the stream through it had enabled him to install running water, so the stone sink now supported a cold tap. He'd brought a fridge and a Kosangas cooker, and a TV sat on an old dresser.

He plugged in the electric kettle and motioned her to sit down at the table. 'You must be hungry,' he said, fetching bread from the bin and butter from the fridge. He was trembling with tension as he brought plates and mugs. 'I interrupted your meal.'

She grimaced as she unhitched her bag and put it down. She licked her lips. 'I could eat a horse.' She glanced uneasily at him at the allusion to eating an animal. 'I was at a wedding the day before I left. I kept a piece of cake in my bag. That's all I had to eat these last three days. I suppose it must be four now,' she added.

She was looking round as she began to sit down, suddenly winced and jerked back upwards. Then she lowered herself carefully, tilting forwards to perch on her thighs. He noticed and blushed with embarrassment.

'Do you live on your own?' she asked, seizing a slice of bread, smearing a slab of butter on it and devouring it ravenously.

'I suppose it must show,' he replied. He made a pot of tea, then seeing her hunger, broke a couple of eggs in the pan to fry and cut some slices of cold bacon.

She waved a hand at the fireplace, 'I like that,' she said.

When he moved the Esse, he had found behind the plaster a stone mantelpiece with a great chamfered bressummer of limestone protruding over carved supports, now restored as a feature in the room. One of the Galway botanists had reckoned it to be early seventeenth century.

He was pleased by her appreciation. He poured a cup of tea out for her. 'How did you manage . . . to kill the lamb?'

'Couldn't have managed without the knife.' She spoke thickly between mouthfuls. 'Found it stuck in a bale of twine. In a yard I spent a night in. Somewhere near Killashandra. Didn't think I could do it, all the same. Lucky it was lame. I never knew what terrible things hunger can do to you. And not speaking to anybody for days. I was going a little crazy.' Thirstily she gulped mouthfuls of hot tea. 'Is that goat's milk in the tea? I like the flavour. You're very kind,' she said as he put a plate of eggs and bacon in front of her. 'I thought this valley was deserted, you know, seeing the ruined farmhouse. I'd heard livestock was run on these hills by people who have farms round Ennis and Gort. So I thought I was safe.'

He was about to ask, safe from what? When there was a clatter outside, a shovel falling, a bucket being knocked over, the patter of feet on cobbles. She looked up, startled. 'What's that?'

He nodded to the window. 'Take a look.'

Fork in one hand, the other hand across her bulging mouth, she crossed cautiously to look out of the window. Then she laughed. 'A deputation of village elders. What do they want?'

'The dog's just brought them in for milking.'

'D'you want a hand?' she asked as he collected a couple of buckets covered in cloths from beneath the sink.

He was still wary of her. It was difficult to gauge her friendliness. 'I've only five in milk at present, they won't take me long. Then I have to take the milk up to the neighbours, collect theirs and deliver it to the cheese factory a couple of miles away. You finish your meal. There's fruit in the bowl on the dresser.'

'You won't mention me, will you?'

'Not if that's what you want.'

*

When he came in half an hour later to pour the milk into a churn, he found the girl asleep on the sofa, lying on her side, her mouth slightly ajar. He crept out quietly, hoping the clatter of the Landrover's diesel wouldn't wake her. In all the time he'd lived in the house, nobody had even slept on that sofa. He sensed that it was safe to leave her there, though he could not have expressed any exact reasons for his trust. The image of her lying curled up, an ear protruding through her hair, her feet bare, remained before him as he drove up to Riordan's long thatched farmhouse.

'You're late this evening, Conor,' said Mrs Riordan. She was an ample woman with a turban of white hair and the pink complexion of an overblown rose.

'The goats were up on the long hill.'

'Nuala's away to Corofin,' she said as he followed her to collect the churns from the dairy. 'The man in the museum has some rugs she wants to see. She was looking for a loan of your camera, but you weren't in.'

He cursed beneath his breath the intrusion of fate. Opportunities to please Nuala were few.

'Thought you'd forgotten,' said Vaun, daughter number four, already lugging a churn. She was seventeen and had the same rose complexion as her mother, together with dark hair and a plump puppy-limbed body that made her flop and flounder. Her real name was Siobhan. 'Thought maybe you were tapping away at your old typewriter thinking it was our turn to take the milk. Like the time we came down and all the goats were in the kitchen, licking out the saucepans, chewing up the cushions and eating your rates demands, while you had your head down in the back room, making sparks fly out of the old machine.'

'He barely needs reminding,' said her mother as they lifted

13

the churns into the back of the Landrover. 'The stains are in the lino to this day.'

He remembered that letter.

Sir, If the national language is said to be a dead duck, is it not right that it should be properly stuffed and preserved in the dodo category, for all to appreciate what once roamed the land, to mourn what we have lost through our materialist obsessions to acquire the lifestyles and ape our erstwhile masters across the channel? But if it is not dead, then why are the Gaeltachts run like lingual taxidermist's shops? If the damned thing won't regenerate of its own accord, is it worth stuffing it down the throats of fledgelings whose prospects are tied up with uncle USA or our cousin Europe? Identity, they cry, we must retain our national identity. Bring out the harp, skip to the fiddle, and whistle a dirge to our lost heritage, whatever that was, and lament the millions who died in the struggle for freedom. To hell with the old language. What about a new one? Yours, etc.

'I'm coming with you,' said Vaun, climbing into the Landrover. 'I want a lift to Davoren's. Nuala said she'd pick me up on the way home.'

'And listen,' said Mrs Riordan, sticking her head through the window. 'Are you coming with us the Sunday after? The mass for Sean? It's a year gone.'

'If you don't mind a heathen at the feast?'

'Get away with you,' she exclaimed, stepping back. 'You're a shocking man.'

Vaun sprawled over the two passenger seats, scrutinising Conor with uncomfortable intensity as they drove down the narrow lanes, through the wild stone-strewn landscape. He often felt uneasy the way she devoured him with her eyes. 'What's on at Davoren's?' he asked, his vision once again filled with the image of the girl from the north, lying asleep on the old brown sofa in his kitchen. She might be rummaging through the place this very instant, to see what she might steal, before slipping away. 'I thought young Niall was gone for a job in Limerick?'

'Niall?' she exlaimed, lifting her eyes heavenwards. 'He's a fascist. He should join the army. D'you know?' she said, moving close to him. 'He really believes women have brains half the size of men's?'

'You mean it isn't true?'

'I like you, Conor.' She still gazed intently at him. 'Niall's got a sense of humour the size of a rabbit dropping. Would you take me to a dance one night?'

'I've told you, Vaun, I find dancing a boring activity making an unnecessary exhibition of oneself.'

'I know, I know,' she said crossly. 'You get all the exercise you need running up and down the hills after your stupid sheep.' She couldn't help letting out a deep sigh.

'I thought you liked farming?'

'I do,' she snapped, rolling her eyes hotly over him. Then she flung herself back in her seat. 'But there are times when it turns in my throat like the milk going off. I'll have no stake in the place when Nuala marries. She'll get the farm.' She scowled. 'She'll never marry you, you know.'

'So you keep telling me.' He changed down as they came to a steep climb, the diesel roaring.

'She says you've no ambition, that you're a wet. But Mam keeps singing your praises, saying what a hard worker you are and the two farms together would make a grand enterprise. I could crown her.'

Conor couldn't help laughing. When he drew up outside Davoren's new house on the edge of the village she put a hand deliberately on his thigh. 'Give us a kiss,' she urged.

'Get away with you. You're under age. What would Father Devenney say?'

'I hate you,' she cried, slamming the door. She ran between the Moorish arches of the Davoren's brand-new bungalow to the gleaming mahogany front-door set in the crazy-paved stonework of the façade illuminated by imitation coach-lamps, and rang the chimes.

He shook his head and drove on to deliver the churns.

Nuala's face came and floated on the windscreen between him and the distant Ailwee mountain. The same rose complexion as all the Riordans, the same dark hair, but while the rest were easy-going, she was thin and sharp, quick and forceful, impatient when anything went wrong. She was even angry with Sean for dying. 'If he hadn't abused himself with the drink and if he'd taken his responsibilities seriously, the cancer might never have struck. Might never have left me saddled with the bloody farm.' But she was not going to be diverted. She combined the two, making the hills support exotic sheep and goats for her wools, for the rugs she designed and made.

He watched her face endlessly, hungry for a smile. How he envied some kitten or calf that delighted her. Or her elder sister Marie, to whom she was very attached. Marie had qualified as a doctor and was now an intern at the Mater in Dublin. There was even laughter when she came down for a visit.

If only she would see that he shared that inner burning anger. If only he could make love to her, he imagined he could mellow her. But he could not touch her. She seemed to relegate all men to the level of dogs or chickens, creatures with limited use.

Earlier women in his life were remote now, against this wild bony landscape, this pocket charnel-house of history. The numbers of castle keeps, ring forts and stone graves suggested a once substantial society. The bared limestone strata suggested they must have overworked and exhausted its fertility. Perhaps people did the same with their relationships, not realising that fertility is a balance of nature that has to be maintained. Sometimes it seemed to him that he had just crumpled them up and thrown them away.

Four men had died in that crash. As well as Lynn. He squeezed his eyes shut, gripped the steering-wheel tight till his knuckles cracked like walnuts. Lynn had shone steadily like a globe of electric light, as if her sole purpose was to illuminate enigmatic possibilities that stretched his imagination endlessly to try and comprehend. She had loved him as if it was part of a natural evolution of intentions he could never devise. In the midst of this ever-tantalising enigma, he had destroyed her, in a trivial oversight. And four other men. His conscience was so blackened and charred by this, that the very touch of its memory made him feel ill, heavy, disinclined to function. 'For Christ's sake put it behind you,' Nuala would say. Why are you taking the blame if you don't do something about it? Guilt isn't supposed to be a negative pressure. When sins are understood and regretted, God washes them away. But I don't believe it was your fault at all. You just want to burden yourself with it, so that you can blame every other failure on it.'

16

Sometimes he hoped that her attacks on him indicated that she cared a little.

God, he was forgetting all about the girl sleeping on his sofa. He put his foot down and the old Landrover slowly gathered speed, lurching over the uneven lane, the empty churns rattling about in the back. He was a fool to have left her there on her own. She'd probably have the place burned to the ground by now.

The light was beginning to fade, so that the greying of the greens toned with the stone hues, making the landscape a vast monochromatic cyclorama beneath a silver sky. If it hadn't been for his anxiety he would have stopped. He liked to measure his puniness against the scale of nature, revel in its everchanging breathtaking beauty. It was something he never ceased to draw pleasure from. This was his only advantage over the locals. They might be more phlegmatic over its hard-ships than he, but they viewed it as miners might see with jaded eyes a seam of coal they had to dig.

The kitchen window was a rectangle of light as he drove into the yard. His chest was tight with apprehension as he approached the back-door. First he noticed the glass every-where steamed up, then the appetising smells, then all the noise as if the room was crowded with people. He could not have described, had someone asked him for the truth of his first reaction, whether he felt alarm at the take-over threatened by this improbable scene of domesticity, or pleasure at the unexpected, especially the delicious aroma of cooking food.

'It's ready,' she exclaimed, whirling round, an old pinafore knotted round her waist that his uncle used to wear when boiling an egg or opening a tin of baked beans. She rushed across to turn off the chattering television. 'I'll serve it up while you wash your hands.'

'I didn't expect this,' he said, and then his reactions stuck in his throat, unable to go up or down. From the oven she was lifting a roast leg of lamb.

She saw his expression. 'No point in pretending it didn't happen, keeping it like something we can't talk about. It was half-cooked already, so I took a plastic sheet I found in the shed to cover up the rest. Is that all right?'

'No point in wasting it,' he agreed. Was this all to lull him into complacency? he wondered, scooping water from the tap and refreshing his face. Could she have poisoned the food?

17

Taken some weedkiller from the barn? Or was it more likely that she was trying to soften him up, make him sleep heavily so that she could put a kitchen knife through him in the middle of the night?

She put a bowl of steaming potatoes, a bowl of carrots and cauliflower and a jug of gravy beside the roast. He picked up the carving knife, then noticed she had put out two plates. 'Still hungry then?'

She pursed her lips. 'I wouldn't miss it, not after what I went through.'

He concentrated on slicing the meat. 'We don't even know each other's names.'

'I have the advantage there,' she said, wagging her head knowingly. 'I've seen your name written on a couple of envelopes. Conor de Burgh. I'm Maggie McSweeney. Though if anybody asks for me you've never heard of me.'

'Why did you do all this?' he asked, gesticulating at the meal and all the washing-up and cleaning he could see she had done.

He fetched two cans of Guinness from the dresser while she sat tilted on the edge of her chair, helping herself to vegetables. 'My mum told me that after any time my dad tanned my backside when I was a kid, I'd become unbelievably helpful about the home. She could never understand the psychology. And here you are acting towards me as a figure of authority and I'm responding by behaving like an anxious-to-please child.' She waved her fork in the air. 'Anyone would have thought it more natural, before you say so yourself, that I would have been furious and resentful, going off and planning some revenge at least. Maybe I have a strong sense of expiation. Once a good catholic. And I did kill your lamb.'

Conor was chewing on a mouthful of that lamb. 'When I was a child I remember being conscious of injustice. Nobody would listen, grown-ups were always right, they were always determined to exercise their authority.'

She put her head on one side. 'You seem to have inherited that?'

He frowned. 'That lamb was worth fifty quid.'

'If there'd been time to explain that I was starving, that I was willing to pay, would that have stopped you?'

'I'm sure . . .' He looked down at his plate. 'I am sorry . . .'

She waved a hand dismissively. 'My sore arse'll mend.' She

18

brushed a fallen strand of hair from her eyes. 'I felt far worse killing the lamb. I made myself do it by convincing myself it was him or me. When you, the indignant owner burst in on me, I felt caught red-handed, guilty as hell. But I am getting pragmatic these days, which is a help. I've been a practising lawyer, learning to erase the old instincts, appreciating that justice is often dependent on the state of the judge's stomach. I've learned that authority is merely the rotten tool of whatever rotten rules are upheld by whatever rotten group is in power.'

Her face is like soft leather, he thought as he ate, watching her as she talked. A small pouch of animation. Not unattractive.

'I've been up to my armpits these last five years,' she said. 'Defending our people. In the early days I was scared shitless I was a marked target for the UDR and the UVF and all the other little prod assassination squads. Mark you, it was twelve of them and a dozen of us, it's a dirty business. Once I went down to eight stone. I'd rashes on my face made it look like a well-used dartboard. It's been part of my life since I can remember. I was a baby when it all began, and all those years of simmering boiled over, when we thought the Brits were there to help us. Perfidious Albion per usual. At school we played games of catholics and prods like our parents played cowboys and Indians. Now the baddies are the Brits.'

'Ours used to be the Russians.'

'This could be a hundred years war,' she said. 'We'll never love a prod. The trouble is the splits in our own ranks. I got into some bother with INLA. It was a case where I should have got an informer off so they could lay their hands on him, and somebody mislaid the evidence so he stayed safely inside. Then somebody else carelessly left some information lying about, and a number of their members were rounded up. The INLA council decided as I'd been doing a lot for work for Sinn Fein, I was to blame. Once they get their knife in they're as fixated as ducklings following the first thing they see after they're hatched. I was tipped-off two men with duffle-bags were looking for me.'

He offered her more meat. 'So that's why you took off?'

She nodded. 'I'd been under a lot of strain. It's not an easy life rubbing shoulders with incipient hostility. The law courts used to be a brotherhood and they didn't mind sisters, but not any more. Anyway I panicked, threw a few things in a bag and slipped away. A friend suggested going south, gave me a few addresses. Don't show your face, they'll be looking out for you, he said. That really put the shits up me. I decided I'd better do it properly and really disappear, but it's not easy trying to be invisible.'

He raised his eyebrows. 'Practically impossible I would have thought. If you can't go into shops for food, stealing soon gets noticed.'

She smiled wryly. 'You don't think of that when you start off. In the farmyard where I found the knife, there was a dish of milk left out for the cats. It was half-sour and filthy. The next day was the first time I stole. A bottle of milk off a float. I was going to leave 20p, but thought, no, he might mention it to someone, whereas if I just nick it he won't notice he's one short till he gets back, and he won't known where it happened. See the way a crazy fugitive's mind works?'

'Maybe you should have stuck it out, enlisted some protection or proved it wasn't you?'

'Are you joking? Violence is in the brickwork up there. Any complaints, you don't write letters. And once you've watched the RUC at play, you know that nothing anybody else does'll ever match those sadistic blockheads. Besides, who'd help me? I've always avoided belonging to any specific ideology. I prefer free-range. If you commit yourself to one lot, you're supposed to agree with every feather-brained bit of crap they come up with, every bloody-minded little farce.' She took a long drink, then sighed. 'It's so quiet here, so far away from all the madness. But how will I know where I'll really be safe? For all I know you could be an INLA sympathiser, letting me talk away, taking notes ready to get on the phone in an hour or so.'

Conor laughed uneasily. 'Especially since I've already behaved like a sadistic blockhead.'

She frowned. 'There is something about you that doesn't quite fit.'

He fetched two more cans of Guinness. 'If you'd known my background you'd have run a mile first. I was once in the dreaded Albion's armed forces.' He felt alarmed at the ease with which his confession slipped out, studied her face for her reaction.

She swallowed as the information sank in but her expression remained unchanged. 'It's that clean-cut look. And the way you fold clothes.'

'It was a long time ago.'

She narrowed her eyes. 'What about that picture in your bedroom of the grand mansion?'

'Been snooping, have you?'

'I was looking for the bathroom.' She laughed. 'That's a great room. Lovely white walls, and all those lengths of copper and plastic piping going nowhere, except to a shiny white lavatory like an alabaster sculpture all alone. It works a treat. But do you have to wash in it as well?'

He nodded at the kitchen sink with its solitary tap. 'There was no water at all when I came. I'm making progress slowly.'

'A bit different from the big house?'

He shrugged. 'I was only there as a child. It's all gone now, pulled down with the dry rot. My mother lived there with her mother, on their own. My father looked after the horses. His name was Casey, and his brother was the uncle who left me this farm. Anyway, my mother and he were lovers in the haylofts and the back of the horsebox. When she became pregnant he was sent away, a euphemism for being sacked. When I was six my grandmother died of cancer, and the house and estate had to be sold as it was entailed to a distant cousin in England who had no interest in it. So there was my mother with two hunters, a horsebox, a few sticks of Sheraton furniture and a small bastard of six and nowhere to go. She was walking down the centre of Mallow one morning when she bumped into this bronzed man in leather breeches and a fine pair of boots. . . .'

'Don't tell me. It was your father?'

He nodded. 'Turned out he'd never married, had this job as head-groom to a flourishing stud, living in a fine stone cottage in the grounds. So he threw out the woman he'd been living with and installed my mother and me instead. And soon afterwards they were married, and my mother had twin girls and a year later a boy. That meant a lot of babies about, and it was how I came to be sent here to stay with my bachelor uncle and give her a break. I would have starved if it hadn't been for Mrs Riordan next door. But I loved it here.'

'I don't blame you, it is beautiful.'

'It was coming here that made me want to fly. All this space where you could climb up and look down on so much pre-history in a matter of seconds, vast rolls of molten rock that had cooled and set, been scarred by glaciers, eroded by weather, colonised by nature, depleted by man. I saw the ravens patrolling along the bluff, looking down at me, and envied them. The valley's always been full of swallows, they were masters of the air, they could go anywhere, and I wanted that power over my environment. I used to have countless dreams where I could just hold out my arms and skim under the ceiling, dip out through the open window and soar up into the sky. I even read the bible to see how to become an angel. I tried to overcome gravity on my own account, making wings out of wood and plastic and old umbrellas. Broke an arm and a leg. . . .'

'Didn't you ever think of trying an aeroplane?'

He laughed. 'Of course. I made models, hung around clubs hoping for flights, bored people frantic with my questions, read every book ever written about flying. My grandmother had left some money for me to be educated at an English public school, providing I kept the name de Burgh. The school had an Air Force Cadet unit. I lived in it. I was obsessed. I had a pilot's licence at seventeen.'

She sighed. 'So it was inevitable you'd end up in the RAF.'

'But I didn't enjoy it. It was too restrictive. Life according to the rule-book and the notice-board. I was posted to a Phantom squadron in Germany. They were fast but heavy. You couldn't dodge about in them, only take long parabolic curves. And every mission was minutely pre-arranged, so that the air was no longer my medium of expression. Then I had a spell in England with a squadron of obsolescent Hunters. One day on solo patrol I got carried away, rediscovering the mastery of the air, and spent half-an-hour looping and spiralling about the heavens. For that I was grounded and court-martialled. "You are not the calibre of officer material suitable for the reliable defence of Her Majesty's realm". . . .'

She grinned. 'And out you went on your ear?'

'I knew that'd please you.'

'Was that when you came here?'

'I got a job as a crop-sprayer out in Australia. The stench of those bloody pesticides. I was helping create deserts of corn. Nothing lived after the pink clouds settled, just fatheads of wheat. All other life died. It took me a while to realise what I was doing. I'd already handed in my notice when I was ferrying four other pilots and my girlfriend, and we ran out of fuel and fell into some eucalyptus trees. I was the only survivor. They exonerated me at the enquiry. By the rules it was my fault, every pilot should check his gauges. But I'd taken over at the last minute when the ferry pilot fell ill; and I didn't know the gauge was faulty.'

She stared at him. 'That was tough on you.'

He nodded. 'I never want to go through anything like that again. I had a breakdown. My whole life was without purpose, utterly pointless. I haven't flown since then. A year later my uncle died and left me this farm. So I came back. Sometimes it can be like the Garden of Eden. Sometimes I wonder what on earth I'm doing here.'

All the time he had been talking he had been regarding her, often locked into her eyes, and they in turn had been looking unwaveringly back. But during the last few minutes her pupils had begun to film over and her head to nod. The clock registered midnight. 'I've been waffling on,' he said.

'No you haven't,' she said. 'But I haven't had a good night's sleep in days.' There came a musical yawn from Belle, who had stood up in anticipation of their moving. Maggie yawned in turn, went over to stroke her. 'What a patient undemanding creature she is.'

The femaleness of the figure bent down to fondle the dog aroused in Conor a sudden lurch of sexual desire.

'Could I sleep on the sofa?' she asked, standing up.

He turned quickly to hide his feelings. 'There's a bed in the back-room. You'd be more comfortable there. I'll get some bedding out.'

The farmhouse was single-storey, a traditional stone building, originally of two large rooms, gradually extended so that now there was a passage at the back and two more rooms. One of these he had been converting into a bathroom, the other was full of suitcases, paraffin heaters, boxes of books, a huge Victorian cathedral of a dressing-table with terraces of drawers, pinnacles and pillars, and a gothic mirror with carved tracery across its peak. And there was a bed piled high with blankets, pillows, towels, old eiderdowns. He began to shift them on to the floor. 'I hope it's not too damp,' he said.

'It's paradise after the places I've been kipping in. Have you ever woken up in the middle of the night with rain pounding your face?'

'No, but I've been woken up by ants chewing my feet and a kangaroo stealing my breakfast.'

She smiled.

'Sleep well,' he said, closing the door after him as he went out.

He stood in the kitchen surveying the tableau of empty plates and glasses, the knuckle of bone protruding from the half-carved leg of what had been a living lamb that morning. Belle whined at the door to be let out, and he opened it. The night was cool, black and silent.

Sir, Does a woman feel herself unattractive if a man does not make a pass at her? Who can forget those first dates after school with girls who expected a necking session as part of the evening out? Any failure to conform to this code of conduct offended them. As if to be mauled and groped was essential to their self-esteem. Perhaps a woman endangers herself by piling on the allure and stepping into the company of wolves, not so much because she half-longs to be raped, but because she enjoys the potential, because she is made to feel female by the glinting eyes, the licking lips and the snarling flattery as they prance around her. In the way that admiration is always essential to the ego. But speaking as a male, who wants to be such a basic beast? Yours, etc.

Belle scratched to be let in. He cut a hunk off the lamb and threw it to her, put the rest away in the fridge.

*

The next morning he was up early and out of the house, fed the stock and milked the goats out on the lane. It was a high day, peeled mint-fresh from the night. In the hazel copse beside him leaves doffed and blinked as dunnocks, chaffinches and blue-tits flitted through the branches. The pure notes sung by the thrushes and blackbirds echoed down the valley as if a group of instrument-makers were testing their flutes, clarinets and whistles before the din of rush-hour.

He carried the two pails of milk to the back door, pushed it open, paused momentarily, then spun round, slopping milk over his boots, and went out again. He crossed over to the barn and put the pails inside, took a hoe off a hook on the wall and went through the small gate into the garden at the back. He began to weed and thin a line of carrots.

As he stared down at the dark soil, at the groundsel and chickweed he was drawing into limp heaps, he saw again the back view of a woman standing naked before the kitchen sink washing herself. It had been like reading a magazine in a crowded train compartment, turning a page and revealing an unexpected nude. Embarrassment made him flip the page over quickly lest anyone should notice.

One arm had been raised as she soaped an armpit. Water was splashing onto the stone flags. Like one of those intimate Dégas scenes. When had a woman last stood like that in the kitchen? Perhaps never. She had tied a ribbon to lift her hair, so that her ears stuck out. Across her buttocks were dark bruises. The hoe slipped and savaged a number of healthy carrots. It was terrible to think he had done that. In the bathroom at school boys had displayed such stripes on their behinds like medal-ribbons. The more they had the more they were admired as heroes, those who had suffered wounds from the conflict with adults. It had all been taken for granted, as in a war, nobody fussed or talked of cruelty, as if it was the old 'baptism of fire' to make men of them, toughening for the real world as if they were to become terrorists rather than stockbrokers. Never show emotion, crying's sissy, keep a cool head, and if you're pleased, say three cheers. Everything was either jolly or bloody. How his ego soared if anyone said, well done de Burgh. Collecting those little words was important. what does your father do, de Burgh? He's a head-groom. I say, how bloody. He knew he should have described him as a racehorse-trainer. They had come once to take him out to lunch in a horse-box, one somewhat more luxurious than the one he had been conceived in. They were on the way back from racing a prize colt in the 2000 Guineas. The horsebox had Co Cork number plates. You're not bloody Irish, are you, de Burgh? How bloody. Well, French, actually. About nine hundred years ago. Listen to the cock-crow.

'What do you eat for breakfast?' asked a voice. 'Or don't you bother with it?'

'Eggs, toast, coffee. What about you?'

'Coffee's all I can usually manage. Give me ten minutes.'

She has a lot of hair, he thought as she disappeared round the corner of the house. Surprising it doesn't catch on things.

When he came in, she had the table laid and put a plate

before him with two fried eggs on a piece of toast, then brought the coffee-pot. 'You actually have real coffee.'

'So you didn't leave?' he said, sitting down.

'Did you expect me to?'

He shook his head.

'There's something special about this place,' she said, pouring out the coffee. She was still careful how she sat down.

He nodded. 'None of the locals can ever understand why I rave about it.'

She put her head on one side. 'Maybe because it's womb-shaped?'

He laughed. 'The valley is primeval. It does cause me to speculate on my origins and the purpose of life.'

She sipped her coffee. 'Would it be all right if I stayed here a few days? I could try and pay my way?'

He nodded even before he'd considered the consequences.

'But I don't want anybody to know I'm here. What about your neighbours?'

He considered this. 'I could say you're the sister of a friend from Australia. Can you do the accent?'

She's got so much hair, he thought. It falls into her coffee, it gets in the butter, it could do with a wash. 'Why don't you cut your hair short? It might alter your appearance so people wouldn't recognise you so easily.'

She stared at him, put a hand up and stroked it.

'How did you manage to wear a wig in court?'

'I used a hairnet.'

Memories of his mother, her fair hair gathered like meat in a sausage-skin, settling her velvet-domed cap on. She wore a tight-waisted black jacket, thighs encased in cream jodhpurs, and in her white stock a gold pin with a fox's head that had rubies for eyes. He dreaded when she went off to a meet that she might have a fall and never come back. In those days he feared horses, great engines of sweating muscle.

She frowned. 'How can I get some money out of the bank without giving where I am away?'

'Banks are only interested in credit-worthiness. If you like I'll drive you to somewhere like Loughrea or Galway.'

'I don't want to involve you.' Her eyes narrowed. 'You don't know what it's like up there now. It's getting like Sicily and Chicago. Racketeers getting rich, killings getting paid for, shops being bombed because they didn't up the ante. It may still look like politics and sectarianism on the outside, but it's getting carved up on the inside by Mafia-type thugs with hides forty times thicker than Paisley.'

'I must get the milk up to Riordans,' he said, getting up. He gathered plates and cups, took them to the sink, filled the kettle.

'I'll do that,' she said.

'You're very keen on the woman's role.'

'And you're a sarcastic bugger. I don't know anything else in a place like this. I want to be helpful.'

His mother's voice was always reasonable, never commanding, with a ringing note to it like an out-of-tune piano. Be a dear and help me find my reading-glasses, I'm sure they're in here somewhere. I'm busy, he'd say, intent on sticking an aileron on to a wing. Give us a hand clearing the table, dear, she'd say. And he would slip away through the door, melting out of sight and earshot, going out into the garden or up into his room. He could remember this strong aversion to being helpful as if it would undermine his need for independence, limit his free-flying in the restricted space of adult domination. They made all the decisions, when to have meals, when he should change his clothes, when he should go to bed, when they would leave him alone. There was a dry ditch at the bottom of the garden behind the tool-shed, and he built a hide there, hidden by nettles, roofed with old bits of timber crawling with woodlice and earwigs, and put a rusty sheet of corrugated-iron on top. He'd take some bread and an apple and pretend he was the only survivor of a shipwreck. Conor, he'd hear them calling. Conor? My name's Oliver, he hissed to himself, crouching at the back of the hide. He'd always wanted to be called Oliver.

'We'd better settle who you are,' he said. 'In case somebody comes, or you're seen around.'

She chewed her lips. 'But if you tell the Riordans, won't they think it strange if they don't meet me?'

'Then we'd best make up a story.'

When he took the milk up to Riordans the first person he saw was Nuala. The sight pierced him like an arrow, all his emotions pinned fluttering within his chest. That short black hair and those sparkling eyes. Her brilliant complexion that other women might spend hours painting to achieve the same effect, she got out of bed with. He felt a touch of guilt, as if he had been unfaithful to her.

She was unloading some cones of wool from the boot of her Datsun. 'I ran out and had to buy some in Loughrea,' she said. 'I hope it never gets around.'

'You must have been up with the larks.' All the electric currents were lighting up with gladness to be speaking with her, yet he always felt awkward with her, words and feelings turning to twigs and pebbles. 'I'll bring the other one,' he said, lifting the second box of cones.

She had converted an old cow-byre into a weaving-shed. Lifting the roof and fitting a skylight with the aid of a grant from the Arts Council after she had won a design competition. Conor had been the carpenter to keep the costs down. Now the two looms, one smaller than the other, filled most of the space like great square harps that clacked. The walls were lined with racks of spools and cones of wools of different hue rather than colour, as her designs used earth tones. Beside it was the dye room where she experimented with lengths of yarn dipped in beakers, then plunged specially wound spools into vats of inky liquid and pressure-cooked them. This room seemed to have little connection with the controlled delicacy of the finished rugs, it was like entering a marbled madness of brilliant colour spilled and splashed by the frenzy of a concocting cook. Conor considered her real gift was in colouring. The designs she played safe with, culling them from sources like the Book of Kells, and muting and obscuring them. She was already making quite a name for herself.

'What d'you think?' she asked, pausing before the three-quarters completed rug on the small loom.

It was in greens and olives and greys, a maze of interlocking ribbons. 'You know what I think, Nuala. You never put a foot wrong.'

'If only everyone were as easily pleased as you,' she muttered tartly.

He was reminded of the existence of his rival. A certain Niall McCarthy, who appeared in aluminium-grey suits tailored to the last lapel, with brandysnap hair and gold rings that spread his knuckles apart like claws, and who kept saying, absolutely great, absolutely great, and took her off in his sky-blue Mercedes. Officially he was her agent, owned the Persimmon Gallery in Galway city. When Conor had been up a ladder in tattered jeans and covered in sawdust, building the weaving-house roof, he would appear, a silk and biscuity Apollo, and briefly nod to the yokel stuck up among the joists before putting a laconic arm round Nuala's shoulder to lead her away from the nail-hammering for a confabulation, his other hand heaving heavily upwards as if he'd stuck it in gold cement.

'Niall's the expert,' he said. 'What does he think?'

'Niall's a salesman,' she said, frowning. 'He'd sell his mother if he could get a good price. You pride yourself on your honesty, Conor, but you're as blind as a worm in the ground.'

'At least you're never complacent,' he replied, his feelings staggering under the crossfire. 'I imagine good artists are never satisfied.'

She sighed as if this was a burden she found a struggle. Then Vaun lunged through the door, interrupting them, her shirt hanging out of her jeans. 'I've put your milk in the cooler, Conor, and Mam says would you give us a hand loading later. She knew you'd forget to ask him,' she added, turning to Nuala.

'We could have managed,' said Nuala irritably. 'We make too much use of Conor.' She went back into the dye-room.

He followed Vaun outside. She waggled her gangling plumpness with what she imagined was seductiveness. 'You're just a man who can't say no.'

He blinked in the bright sunlight. The edges of the sky were beginning to accumulate tall clouds. 'You're too young to know that song.'

'What song?' she asked innocently. 'We know why you're such a willing horse and love to be borrowed. But you're wasting your time.' She danced round him. 'You're stupid like all the rest of them. All you can do is get cross and thump us.' She punched him on the arm and skipped away. 'Come on, hit me.' She leaped back, punched him again and ran off laughing, glancing back over her shoulder to invite pursuit. He stood frozen by her allusion.

'For goodness sake, Vaun,' exclaimed her mother, who had emerged unnoticed from the back door. 'You're worse than a three-year-old. Your uncle's by the hayshed, waiting for you to help fetch the cattle. Off you go now.'

'And you're blind to boot,' Vaun called unabashed as she headed for the hayshed.

Mrs Riordan's round face was varnished with a thin film of sweat. 'The sooner that girl starts her course the better, she's too little to put her mind to here. There's more than plenty to be done, but getting her to put herself to anything is like trying to stir your tea without a spoon.' She sighed. 'This heat is too much.'

Conor nodded at the bolstering clouds. 'Looks like a bit of rain coming.'

'Just showers. We could do with some good solid rain.'

Conor laughed. 'You'd like it to be pouring down daily, every gutter running, dripping off the roofs. You're the only person I know who loves bad weather.'

She laughed in turn. 'As long as the roof isn't leaking.' She turned for the door. 'Would you stop for a cup of tea?'

He shook his head. 'I've a few things to do yet. I'll be back after dinner to help load.' He was about climb into the Landrover. 'I had a letter from a friend in Darwin who says his sister is over here. As she doesn't know anyone she might look me up. He gave her your phone number, so she may ring at any time.'

He could see reactions shimmering across Mrs Riordan's ample features. 'That'll be nice for you to have a visitor from your old days.' Her voice modulated a fraction. 'Is this young lady likely to be wanting to stay?'

He shrugged. 'Could be.'

She moistened her lips. 'If she wanted to stay, it might be best if she came up here with us. Then nobody could say anything.'

'What would they say?' he asked.

She laughed, chins shaking. 'Now don't be playing the innocent with me, Conor. If you don't know what young men get up to by now, it's a bit late me telling you.'

He grinned. 'She probably won't even turn up. By the way, I've a dead lamb up the glen. Looks as though it must have fallen. Would you like some of the meat if it's OK?'

Her mouth fell open in immediate sympathy, this was something much more serious. 'That's bad luck, Conor. Just when they're near ready for the sales. And you can't afford to lose that kind of money.'

'It looked like a broken neck. I put a cut in the artery, but it must have been dead a few hours.'

'We'll put it in the freezer. Anything we use I'll pay you for.'

They both looked up at the throb in the sky above them as an army helicopter flew across. 'That's the second today,' said Conor. 'I wonder what they're at?'

'There was something on the news about a search for the people they think were responsible for that dreadful bomb in Enniskillen. All those school children in that bus. Their poor parents, such a terrible thing to happen, and the poor little mites themselves, barely sampled the world before they're taken from it. It's not right at all. These men must have souls as putrid as boils. And they say one of them was even a woman.'

Conor felt a faint unease. But there are many things one's mind refuses to turn to. 'All because the army put on one of its own buses for them as a relief.'

He drove down the old lane that wound across the floor of the valley and up to the ruined farmhouse in the glen, bumping slowly over the rough ground. Here he had to get out and shift some poles and the remains of an old iron gate to drive across the small fields to the edge of the wood. His skin prickled as he stood under the trees in the small clearing and surveyed what now seemed like the scene of a crime. The blackened remains of the fire, the mound made by the plastic sheet covering the body. He noticed she had cut two forked hazel poles to hold the rod she used as a spit, driven them well into the ground. Very resourceful, he thought. Able to adapt whatever there was at hand. And she had managed to catch and kill an agile lamb, even if it was lame. Hardly the usual attributes of someone from the sequestered cloisters of the law courts, and a woman. He felt the same unease again. But it would be no good asking what kind of woman was capable of killing a lamb without asking what kind of man would beat a woman as he had done. He pulled the plastic off, pushed the body of the lamb over with a foot. It had not yet been attacked by scavengers. He picked it up by its front legs and slung it over his shoulder, then returned to the landrover. A number of cows and calves were standing round it, cautiously curious. He heaved the dead lamb into the back and opened the cab door. The cattle backed away, sniffing, facing him with their wet noses and limpid brown eyes, smelling blood and death. He felt disinclined to act the brusque superior human who had no time for them, only concerned they should get out of his way. On the whole they were gentle creatures, and he wanted to touch them, reassure them. But his hands smelled too strongly of mortality just now. So he made a speech. They listened quietly, back-chewing the cud.

'We could say that I represent your interests and you represent mine. In the winter you couldn't survive without the hay and nuts this brings you.' And he slapped the side of the Landrover. 'And I couldn't remain an independent farmer without being able to sell you for slaughter. Sorry to bring up such a subject, but you always make me self-conscious of it. The development of the animal I am has brought about this state of affairs, where I have control over the animal you are. It's not my personal wish, you understand, just the circumstances of evolution. You like grass and we like beef. The difference between us is that we have ideas above our station. We have egos where you have stomachs. We have wild imaginations, whereas you are doggedly pragmatic. But I suspect you may be better off than us. Most of the time. However short it may be. You have the facility of reconciliation. We're just rotten with envy and insecurity. But we do our best, which isn't saying much I know, but at least you don't have to bother with that sort of affectation. So I hope you'll continue to vote for me as your representative. The alternative is the bank, who would probably prefer to fatten you in sheds. All the best now, and thanks for listening.'

When he entered the kitchen Maggie was at the sink rinsing clothes. Including some of his, he noticed. Her hair was freshly washed and dried, a tawny mass spun to amber at the tips, a cross between a mane and a halo. He dumped the dead lamb on the table. 'O Lord,' she exclaimed. 'The evidence of my crime.'

'I still can't imagine a barrister's wig sitting on all that hair,' he said.

She dried her wet arms on a towel. He could not have said what reaction he anticipated, but her vehemence surprised him. 'I don't imagine you'd understand what it's like to try and function as a woman in a man's world. And having to kowtow to all that mumbo-jumbo and prejudice. I discovered that it wasn't me or my dress that mattered, nor what I said in court. It was the old boy network. Some poor bugger who thought his fate hung on the nod from the judge had no idea it had all been sewn up long before in the judge's rooms, between the barristers, with the local constabulary.' She sighed. 'But I miss the crack all the same. I know they can manage perfectly well without me, but I enjoyed having a voice in it all.' She turned to the pile of washing. 'Anywhere to hang these out to dry that no one'll notice?'

He took a knife from the table drawer and began sharpening it on a steel. 'The line's out in the garden. It can't be seen from anywhere. And I don't suppose that chopper'll be photographing washing-lines. Mrs Riordan says there was something on the news about a search for the people involved in that busload of schoolchildren blown up last week.'

He had not actually intended that remark to put her to the test, it had come out purely conversationally, but nevertheless he watched her expression from under his eyelashes. She looked at him, blinking. 'A bus? Where?'

'Enniskillen. Didn't you hear about it? The driver of the regular schoolbus, a part-time UDR man, had been shot earlier in the week, so the army stepped in with a relief bus. But they took a wrong turning and went down a lane used by army patrols.'

'Christ.' She froze in the middle of gathering up lumps of damp washing. 'How many?'

'Eleven so far. Another fifteen badly injured.' He started to skin the lamb.

She winced. 'Trust the bloody army not to foresee that. And the provos saw a khaki bus coming and thought, great, we'll get a whole platoon in one go. It's not very Surbiton, is it?'

After she had gone out, he worked rapidly on the lamb. It was not something he enjoyed, but he knew roughly how to joint a carcase. Lucky she cut its throat, he thought. He washed out some buckets to carry the meat in, and for the entrails. Suppose she wasn't whom she said she was? What difference would it make?

Directive. The secret of good camouflage is to be self-effacing. In a civilian environment where there's risk of sniper incursion or ambush, particularly where the local population is hostile, it is essential that patrols should operate in as unpredictable a manner as possible. Never create a pattern of surveillance; the element of surprise must be in your favour, not theirs. In Belfast East there are a number of specific danger zones. . . .

'My God, that was quick,' exclaimed Maggie, coming in. 'We're you ever in the butchery trade?'

He stood washing his hands at the sink, considering the intention of her remark. 'I thought seriously of becoming a vegetarian today.'

She walked over to one of the buckets, lifted out the liver. 'Shall I make this into lunch?'

He stood looking at her, absorbing her appearance, the cream-cheese flesh, large coffee-black eyes and moth-like mouth, and whatever indescribable emotion was welling up inside, it disseminated the way an impending fart can be reabsorbed into the system. 'I never eat much in the middle of the day. A piece of ham or cheese maybe, on a slice of bread, a cup of coffee. I have to go back up to the Riordans soon, they've a man coming in to take some yearlings and need a hand.'

'Before you go, have you a needle and thread so I can mend my jeans?'

He swallowed, remembering the giving feeling of the sudden severance of her waistband, clothing pulling away like the peel off a tangerine. He went to the dresser, took out an old biscuit tin with chipped paintwork and handed it to her. 'I told them about my Australian friend's sister coming to stay.' He felt disinclined to mention Mrs Riordan's anxiety for her chastity.

Maggie smiled. 'I'm looking forward to being a bona fide visitor. Even if I am invented. We didn't decide on a name yet?'

'You'd better not let anyone see your cheque-card, then. Or is that in another name altogether?'

She tilted her head enquiringly. 'What do you mean by that?'

No, he thought frantically, this was too soon, he had no proof, he could be quite wrong. 'I just thought you might have told me a fictitious name in the beginning, when you weren't sure of me.'

She looked at him steadily. 'Don't you trust me?'

He nodded. 'Didn't I let you stay?'

'You might have done that out of misguided guilt.'

He felt the pace was hotting up. 'You killed a lamb.'

'And my arse is still sore. But . . .' she waved a hand as if to dismiss it. 'I think we both regret what we did. So doesn't there have to be more than that?'

He stared at her, his ribs packaged round an unknown excitement. When he remained silent, she gave a little laugh. 'I thought maybe this Australian girl I am to be could be doing a doctorate on alternative life-styles, the natural self-sufficiency of indigenous farming communities in the Old World, a peroration to put before the Third World that skyscrapers and discos are a hollow ambition.'

'I imagined you would see this as an ivory tower?'

'And what's wrong with that? With the world-bosses and their lunatic arms race, yours could be one of the saner solutions. What's the clear-sighted individual supposed to do, hang around while they prepare to detonate civilisation? You might as well turn your back on them.'

He took a loaf from the bread-bin, began to cut himself a hunk. 'Do I hear the barrister talking, or have we recognised each other as birds of a feather?'

'But do you see me as an equal?' She stood clutching the tin, watching him as he took goat's cheese from the fridge, sliced a piece off. 'I've never met a man who would.'

'Why would you want to be my equal?' He lifted the kettle to test if it had sufficient water, switched it on. 'I'm hardly worth emulating. I'm stunted with prejudices and disinclinations. Would you accept me as your equal?' He took a mouthful of bread and cheese.

'You know what I mean.'

The kettle boiled and he rinsed out two mugs. 'D'you want some?'

She nodded. 'Thanks. I'm conditioned to admire you as a man because you demonstrated your rage with me as an erring child. As a woman I despised you for treating me as a weaker creature you could abuse. But ultimately none of that mattered. It was like acting out some archaic tradition. You have one quality that made me stay. You listen.'

He chewed on his bread and cheese, waved at her to help herself. 'You talk. I mean you feel free to talk. Very stimulating. Very germane. She was an Aussie. That would be a good name. Or Simone. I read her too, in those existentialist days of youth. My friend's name is Benson. Greg Benson, from Port Pirie on Spencer's Gulf. So what would go with Benson?'

'When I was a kid Bernadette was great stuff. Or there's Betty Freidan or Marylin French.' She drank her coffee.

'I don't see you as a hard-line feminist?'

She laughed. 'The trouble is I like men. When you find out what their mothers did to them you can't help feeling sorry for them. I'll tell you who I really like. Dorothy Parker. I'll be

Dorothy Benson, how about that?' Her grin spread sideways like an elastic band.

He took the path behind the sheds to the Riordans. It wound through a copse of hazel and hawthorn, climbed up among limestone that half-suggested a long-since collapsed civilisation, sprouting with ferns, mountain avens and rock roses, the grass full of little sapphire-blue milkworts, and the bloody cranesbills whose pink always reminded him of the Riordans, and the occasional frothy wine goblet of an orchid. Along the crest of the ridge to the north of the valley was a strip of grass and then a loose stone wall, higher than usual, that was the ramshackle boundary between the two farms. It kept cattle back, but was generally ignored by the goats, and Belle would bound over it like a bundle of fur doing a western roll. For the convenience of humans, some nineteenth-century craftsmen had constructed a stile of cut stones and mortar, as good still as the day it was built.

Obviously the Caseys and the Riordans had long coexisted amicably. From this point he could look back and see the chimney-stack of his house rising like a conning-tower out of the lush waving trees. He could look westwards along the green gash of the valley, or turn east and look across a plain of limestone tables towards a line of hump-backed hills, or north over the wall at a great saddleback of moorland with a coil of road lashing it to the horizon.

It was a spiritual place. Implacable nature swelled round in its eternity, shrinking him to the correct puny proportion of mankind. Sometimes a great wind would drive through the trees, shaking them to their roots, making their leaves stream out sideways, suggestive of some immense power barely held in restraint. 'All right, all right,' he shouted at the sky. 'It's easy picking on me. It's the bloody governments you want to swear at. I haven't got sheds full of fertilizers and pesticides. I haven't even got a bulldozer. All right, I won't take their EEC grant. I won't clear the twenty acres beyond the glen. I prefer them as they are. If I want to get rich I should farm in Co Meath, I know, I know, you don't have to tell me. But to a starving farmer a hundred years ago you must have seemed a monstrous bony old hag. Only misbegotten pastoral idealists like me see you as the remains of the Garden of Eden. We got the blood-sucking landlords off those poor fuckers' backs. Now we've got

36

the banks instead. If I could make a wish now, it would be that you really cared.'

That was the day he'd turned to meet the gaze of Kathy, the youngest Riordan, still a schoolgirl. At first he thought she might not have heard, for she had suffered deafness since birth, always spoke as if her tongue was a membrane across her palate, and could only hear if she turned her deaf-aid towards the speaker.

'Is there somebody there?' she asked, peering in the direction he had been addressing. 'Who are you talking to?'

He crossed over to her, leaned on the wall. 'To something that rules underneath and above, Kathleen, pervades and mocks all our puny efforts, something that seems to be there and probably is not there at all.'

She stared at him, trying to comprehend what he might mean, alarmed.

He laughed. 'Your Jesus Christ is still a child against all this, an infant teacher groping for enlightenment, maybe a madman.' He could see she was frightened now, put a hand on her arm. 'But I love this world, Kathy. It stuns me constantly. It goes far beyond what our little pinprick mentalities can ever comprehend. We rush off rationalising up a thousand cul-de-sacs. Our egos swell us with false significance. We're nothing. And it doesn't matter. That's the most important thing. It doesn't matter a damn.'

'You're mocking God,' she cried. She turned to hurry away, running down through the trees, her child's body rubbery with fright.

He wished he had not alarmed her. He had always felt her impediment was like a barricade to be challenged. She seemed to be both earnestly receptive, yet still walled-in like a nun from birth. Did her approach to the world from isolation fascinate him? Or was it that she was someone he could speak to from a secret part of himself that he would allow no one else access to?

Sir, Who are these crow-black nosy-parkers who pop up in every communal activity in this country? They must be prolific spawners since all and sundry keep addressing them as father. Is it because they keep pestering women in wedlock to spawn endless numbers of children? Fathers by proxy, curb-crawling altar-men. Then they bob up in every school and bludgeon these endless numbers of children with the brutal zeal of most fathers. You must believe in what we tell you, they shout. Fathers always shout. Because we know the truth and what is right, they shout. Fathers throughout history appear to have believed that they alone are privy to what is right. Perhaps they never read the sayings of an itinerant teacher called Christ who never made it to father-dom. He pointed out that should anyone harm a hair on the head of a child it would be better for them to hang a millstone round their necks and jump into the sea. But I've always suspected it was their minds he was referring to. Yours, etc.

Damn, he thought. I've forgotten the meat. He turned and ran back down to the house. I'm getting very absent-minded these days. Like driving all the way to the creamery last Monday, and leaving the milk churns behind.

Maggie was seated at the table, pulled a pair of spectacles on to the end of her nose to look up at him. He noticed her left hand covering up whatever she had been writing. 'Forgot the meat,' he said, picking up the buckets. 'Last week I washed two pairs of socks and mislaid them. Couldn't think why there was this strange soapy smell when I opened the fridge to get out the butter.'

She laughed.

I like her laugh, he thought, heaving the buckets into the Landrover. Flows like water. Nuala never laughs. Vaun clangs like a bell. Mrs Riordan has a good laugh, though, rich as butter.

When he drove up into the Riordan yard there was no sign of the cattle-truck.

Mrs Riordan lifted joints of meat, sniffed them. 'Not too bloody. Good and fresh. Keep us going for a while.'

Vaun lounged into the kitchen, looked at the meat as if she knew all about it. 'Poor thing. I suppose she knew too much, had to go. Pushed off a cliff because she witnessed Conor's secret sex life.'

'Vaun,' exclaimed Mrs Riordan. 'You've no cause for making remarks like that. A mouthwash of carbolic'd do you no harm.'

'Spoil the taste of the lamb,' retorted Vaun, licking her lips, unrepentant. 'We should invite Father Devenney, he dotes on a good roast, his little eyes'd go red as worms.'

'Remarks like that give little credit to the juvenile mind,' said

Mrs Riordan, picking up the bucket of meat. She paused in the doorway of the dairy where she kept her freezer. 'Father Devenney's a good man. He keeps this community going, he travels miles at all hours and in all weathers to visit the sick, and if it wasn't for him the village school would have been closed years ago.'

As her mother went out, Vaun rolled her eyes resignedly. 'He only keeps it going so he can put his greasy hands up the girls' skirts.'

'Just to make sure they're wearing knickers and keeping warm,' said Conor. 'So you keep telling me. I don't believe a word of it. He'd have been run out of the place years ago, if it was true.'

'It's true enough,' she flared. 'There's too many pious mothers who believe it's just the kindness of his heart.' She wiggled her hips and leered at him. 'I wouldn't have minded if it had been you, Conor, doing it, honestly.' She scowled. 'Who's this woman you're going to shack up with Mam mentioned, some lady all the way from Australia?'

Conor sighed. 'I'm not shacking up, as you put it, with anybody. I know nothing about her, and she probably won't even turn up.'

'People'll think something's going on.'

'Why should anything go on?' he asked patiently.

'For God's sake, Vaun,' said Nuala, who had entered unnoticed. 'What concern is it of ours what Conor does with his own life, it's none of our business. Meanwhile the lorry's arrived.' She turned and went out.

'I was only worried about her not having a bathroom to wash in,' said Vaun, flinging herself out after her sister.

Conor, about to follow, caught a glimpse of a headline across the newspaper on the table. WOMAN AND THREE MEN SOUGHT. Joint operation of Gardai and RUC. He stopped to pick it up and read. There was an identikit picture of the woman and one of the men. The woman looked much harder and leaner than Maggie, and yet there was a certain resemblance. Police had information that this was the team responsible for the army coach outrage. Josephine Grant, aged twenty-eight, wanted for suspected involvement in the killing of a UVR man in Derry, and also in the south for a bank-robbery in Naas when a bank clerk was shot dead.

Conor stood turned to stone. Mrs Riordan emerged from the

dairy. 'They've come,' he said, throwing the paper down and hurrying outside.

'Conor,' she called after him.

He paused.

'Conor,' she said, walking beside him towards the haggard where the cattle were penned. 'What d'you feel about this business?'

He swallowed, staring at her, mute with alarm.

'We never used a dealer before. You know we always took the animals into the sales ourselves. Dealers never give top prices, do they now?'

He breathed easier. 'If you take into account the cost of transport, commission and the expense of a day lost at the stakes, there's not much in it. Murrough's all right.'

'You're a good man to have about the place, Conor. With no Sean, it's not easy to manage. Nuala's . . . a bit impetuous.'

The cattle were clustered in a corner of the haggard, near the Dutch barn. They were scared, brown flanks heaving, enlarged aspic eyes cupped in white china; their nostrils, pink as human flesh, were wet and flaring. There were cows, calves and yearlings. It was the latter Murrough was after. He was a small man who wore a flat cap. His long grizzled jaw had folds in it like the bellows of an old-fashioned camera. The cattle backed away from him like Jews about to be selected for the death-camps. 'I'd say you've a few there would suit me, Mrs Riordan,' he said, his deep-sunk eyes glittering like chips of glass. He wore a shapeless mackintosh that looked as though it had been hanging from his shoulders since gaberdine was invented. His driver, a young man with a pumpkin-round face, wore blue denim overalls with a brown tweed waistcoat. 'Hup there,' he shouted at the cringing cattle as if to establish at once his authority. The cattle jostled among themselves anxiously, as if looking for somewhere to hide, the smallest calves peering out from beneath other's legs. 'About eight should be ready,' said Nuala, slim in her jeans.

The prospect ahead of an hour's pandemonium, the shouting and wacking and prodding and bellowing while they sorted the cattle out, dismayed Conor. He thought it unnecessarily cruel and haphazard, but it seemed to be the traditional way, as if abuse and haranguing and confusion marked some ritual purpose long forgotten. Or else it was to hide the fact that the

40

men were themselves frightened of the cattle. He would have liked to take charge and organise it quietly.

Perhaps the participation of the two girls rendered it less violent than usual. Vaun was oblivious of her own safety to protect the small calves, and Nuala was quick with the gate to let cows and calves out. The air reeked of sweet cow-dung, everyone was splashed, the summer-hard ground ran with it, the poor beasts were smeared in their fear. 'Don't let that out,' ordered Murrough peremptorily as Nuala was about to open the gate to a big heifer. But she swung the gate nevertheless. 'She's in calf,' she explained. Conor could see Murrough was annoyed that a mere bit of a girl should defy him. 'You can put that out,' he snapped, belting a fourteen-month bullock on its flank. 'Too small.'

'That's a grand store,' said Mrs Riordan, pleased to note that Nuala did not let it out.

In the midst of the scrambling shambles, pushing a bewildered calf after its mother, Vaun slipped and fell face first into the mire. Miraculously she wasn't trodden on or kicked, but when Conor pulled her to her feet, she was caked as a chocolate statue. Nuala let out a rare shriek of laughter.

Vaun, already in tears at her predicament, scooped a handful of cowpat off herself and flung it furiously in her sister's face. 'Lady Muck,' she cried, and ran out of the yard.

Nuala stood transfixed, partially blinded. Conor pulled off his shirt, thrust it into her hands. 'Wipe your face with this.'

Calmly she cleaned the worst off. Everyone stood watching her, Murrough with an expression of impatient resignation as if this was the sort of nonsense that might be expected from young girls, the young man with his pumpkin jaw dropping down with amazement, Mrs Riordan not sure which direction to go in. 'You'd best go in and help Vaun, Mam.' Nuala looked from the begrimed shirt in her hands to Conor's bare chest, suddenly aware of the connection.

Murrough shook his head. 'Sir Walter Raleigh,' he said, as if in sudden recollection of a long forgotten piece of schoolboy history. 'Wasn't he the lad that threw his coat down in the mud for the English Queen to walk on?'

Conor recounted all this to Maggie later that evening after Mrs Riordan and Murrough had haggled a price and the dealer had peeled an amazing number of £100 notes from his roll, to make up a substantial proportion of the Riordan annual income.

Nine stores had been loaded on to the truck and it had lurched down the driveway to the road as its living burden struggled to keep their feet on this, their first venture away from the solid stone hills of their birth.

Maggie had come out to watch him milk the goats, regarded suspiciously by the patriarchs of the herd. She sat on the stone steps peeling spuds in an enamel bowl, Belle lying at her feet, nose between front paws. 'Listen, Sir Walter. Dorothy Benson's going to arrive tomorrow morning. I can't stand being stuck in here a moment longer. She arrived by train in Galway tonight, stayed in a B & B, got a lift to the village in the morning, walked from there, OK?'

Conor nodded, lifting his head from the white flank of a she-goat, hands still drawing milk into the bucket from her pendulous but depleted udder. Maggie brushed hair back from her eyes with the back of a wrist. Water from the bowl made strands wet and some stuck to her cheeks and forehead. He felt he was being drawn towards her as each hour passed. Yet he remained scared, wary. He had taken another look at the newspaper while having a mug of tea in the Riordan kitchen, sitting in a borrowed jersey, slightly alarming as it still smelled of Sean. The article said that Josephine Grant's father was believed to have been a Tyrone farmer murdered in a mystery killing in the early Sixties. He remembered Maggie saying she had been brought up on a farm. Yet as he looked at her across the back of the goat, her face had none of that hardness depicted in the identikit picture.

She nodded upwards as another helicopter flew insect-like above the hills. 'Did you know I was in Pakistan, near the Afghanistan border?' she asked. 'One of the places I visited on my way here.'

'Eh?'

'Dorothy Benson, idiot. Should be a good story to tell. How this stony landscape reminds me of their terrain, with the helicopters like the gunships hurling rockets down at the Mujaheddin. Don't you think they'll believe me?'

'I'm looking forward to hearing your accent.'

She laughed, got to her feet. 'Maybe I'll surprise you. The liver'll be ready in half an hour.' She took the bowl into the house.

She has beautiful hair, he thought. Dense as summer foliage on a copper beech. He wiped his fingers on the coarse white

42

coat of the nanny-goat and patted her. The goat moved away at once with little dismissive high-heeled steps like a woman leaving a surgery after undergoing an embarrassingly intimate examination. He carried the bucket across to the next, a tall angular goat with twin white blazes down her nose and a curly beard.

In the hazels at the back of the sheds a pair of chaffinches were noisily flitting through the leaves, showing the fans of their white-barred tails. A thrush out on the lane was singing at the top of its voice. A few drops of rain fell. The nanny-goat bleated as if urging him to be quick.

His chest felt as if bound tight with cords. Some kind of unmentionable anticipation. History decreed caution, a blind-fold to be worn at the interrogation, every acknowledgement denied despite the cockcrows. St Peter had been right. Admit to one iota of longing or belonging, and the jackasses will laugh you into the grave. That was why Nuala rejected him. Each sight of her rich, sharp colouring would impale him on the bullseye of his craving. Never let anyone see your colours, committal is dangerous. Safe enough to debate the possibility of Josephine Grant, since that was negative. This kind of cross-thought was like keeping the legs crossed rather than going to the lavatory, a masochistic delight in maintaining reminiscent aches in the groin. Of course he was afraid of delving deeper into any possibility lest it destroy what he had not yet dared consider. Too often had aspirations conjured in the mind as solid and real, in reality turned out a rotten apple. If you crossed your legs to hold in an ache, there was always the anticipation of eventual relief.

The Murray river was a huge milky torrent that sometimes made the gum trees on its verges wade trunk-deep in its flood, and sometimes would dwindle to a glutinous trickle among rocks of yellow fudge. The spray firm he had piloted for operated from Midura. A few miles outside he had rented a bungalow that stood on sandy bluff overlooking the river. The owner lived in Adelaide. One day her daughter called to collect some pictures stored in the loft. She did not leave for three weeks.

In those days he worked from dawn to dusk, tirelessly. His only pleasure was to be in the air, between his wings. However monotonous it might be to fly up and down the markers, releasing plumes of spray, switching them off at the end of

43

each run, there were moments of stimulus, the surge of power, the lift as he soared or banked round the telegraph poles. He could not have said he was unhappy.

Lyn was slim like a geometrical instrument lifted from its velvet mould in a flat leather case. She had long blond hair. That first moment had been instant conditioning as if the front-door opening had been the eggshell breaking, and the first living creature sighted was luminary to the other. He could remember feeling light-headed, weak at the knees. How was it that two ordinary people can become extraordinary to each other? There were degrees of hypnotism, trance, hallucination, fever, illness. Yet he remembered the time as serene. She did have one singular quality to perpetuate that state. She rarely spoke. As if she had no use for words where gesture, expression, a look or contemplation would suffice. She told him she even preferred to think abstractedly, in colours and shapes. He had found it extraordinarily easy to remain gazing into her oyster-green eyes for hours. Locked into each other's gaze he would feel contentment might stretch beyond eternity. Mutual hypnotherapy.

'I like you being a flyer,' she said. 'My birdman.' Did she realise how exulting those words sounded to him? 'But why spill those poisonous chemicals on to our earth? It's not only the birds and the butterflies who die. The residues of the pesticides enter our bones, corrode our systems. The manufacturers are only interested in profits. Materialistic gain before all. I don't like to see you caught up in all this.' Since she spoke so infrequently she tended to enunciate like a gardener selecting prize blooms, which added to the impact of so rare a pronouncement. Soon afterwards he gave in a month's notice. A few days before it expired, flying the firm's little airbus as a last-minute substitute, he destroyed this happiness. The irony was that the deaths of the other pilots put the company out of business.

The years passed like the pages of someone else's life. He looked back on it now amazed that it had ever happened. He looked down at the bucket three-quarters full of milk, rimmed with lacy foam, at his fingers working the wet leathery teats of the nanny-goat. Could these same fingers have handled the controls of a million quid's worth of electronic machinery operating a kerosene blast furnace impelling him round the earth's crust at 1.5 mach? Not forgetting the firepower in its belly that if armed on full-alert could send searing death to hundreds of mankind. Had that really been him? He looked up at the damp grey sky. With their swept-back wings and speed, a pair of swallows lifting over the rooftops seemed to demonstrate an ease that had no need of sound-barriers or weapons.

The liver was delicious and aromatic. 'Herbs,' he said, sniffing. 'Where did you find them?'

Maggie looked up from her plate. 'I sneaked out into your garden. Found some rosemary and wild thyme.'

'You're a good cook.'

She waved her fork in acknowledgement. 'I find it strange that someone like you should be contented with so menial a life. After what you've done. I mean you're an intelligent well-educated man. Where's the social life?'

He shrugged. 'Sometimes I get itchy feet I must admit. It may look like basic survival and subsistence level to you. But to me it's the simple life, cathartic to the soul. You learn things about yourself that have no opportunity to flourish in the rat-race of so-called civilisation.'

She got up to fetch the teapot. 'I couldn't wait to get away. It was agony to me being on a farm. So messy and crude. I went to school in Dunpatrick, and there were girls there whose fathers were solicitors, doctors, managers of all kinds of businesses, salesmen, engineers, the sorts that were all smart and had plenty of money. All we had were chickens, eggs and cabbages. Imagine bringing friends home to a sea of mud right through the back door, and an old-fashioned stone kitchen, buckets and wellies all over the place?'

'Just like this?'

She laughed. 'This is pure nostalgia now. But it's different when you're a kid. I'd go to their homes and there were neat lawns and rose bushes and shiny cars parked on crisp gravel, and inside were miles of fitted carpet and polished vinyl and the kitchens were wall-to-wall with ovens and washing-machines and deep-freezers, they were so wonderfully organised and clean. They never had half-dead lambs half-in the oven and boxes of cracked eggs on the floor, kettles being boiled for the vet, filthy great syringes lying in the sink, a bran mash for a sick cow on the draining-board, a burst bag of rape seed in the corner.' She paused for breath.

'Maybe your friends didn't mind it?'

'You're right, they loved coming out. Half of them decided they were going to become vets. Whereas all I wanted was to work in a bright, clean, unsmelly and warm office, and wear frilly blouses, high-heels and a tight black skirt.'

'So that's why you did law? Thought you'd be safe among the books?'

She nodded. 'But if my dad hadn't died when I was small I might have been brought up in the surroundings I envied. Then maybe I'd have reacted against them and longed to be a farmer.'

'How did your father die?' he asked cautiously, half-scared of her answer.

'The old cancer,' she replied. 'I was six. He was a school-teacher. The secondary C stream, all the shop-floor fodder with no prospects, forced to stay on at school, not interested in anything the system wanted to drum into them, nothing better to do than take the piss out of their teachers. My mum said he used to come home shaking. Every lesson a battle, struggling not to let them see he was near breaking-point. I remember his fingers were like rusty nails. He could smoke a fag to ash in five minutes flat. You'd think they'd want to learn something, he'd say. But they're interested in nothing but sex and pop.'

'Poor man,' murmured Conor sympathetically. 'But if he was a teacher how come you were on a farm?'

'My uncle took us in. My mother was back where she belonged, she loved the country. She could plough a field like other women could knit a sweater. Milk a cow quick as flip the cap off a bottle. She loved to wear old clothes so if she was humping a bag of spuds you couldn't tell which was carrying which. She's still at it, belting out Eleanor Rigby on the back of the old tractor. Maybe it's because of her I feel nostalgic about a place like this.'

She looked round the kitchen, grinned at him, while he waited for her to continue. 'She's a good sort. When the man who used to deliver the fertiliser and seed was blown up because he was a part-time UDR, she went to his funeral. They can shoot me, too, if they want, she said. Maybe if there were more like her, it would all go away. Though I daresay it's too late now. At least in Sicily there's only the one Mafia. Up there we've got half a dozen.'

'Were you ever involved in anything?' he asked, trying to sound casual.

'I was too scared. There must be hope in the law, I used to think. Going by the book, sticking by the rules. Justice will sort things out, I thought. More fool me. It can be cooked and twisted just like any other spaghetti. The protestant interpretation of shooting pheasants out of season is to change the season and describe pheasants as vermin. See a catholic carrying a briefcase, it's bound to be full of explosives so blow his head off. But a protestant carrying a machine-gun is only going down to the village hall for amateur theatricals.'

He wanted to ask how to tell the difference between protestant and catholic in the first place, but filled with aromatic liver and buttered potatoes he felt too relaxed to tease her. At this moment it didn't seem to matter who she was.

'People were always saying about me, the reason he wants to fly is to escape from his responsibilities, or it's some childhood anxiety, or he wants to feel superior. Nobody could accept that I simply wanted to fly like a bird. I'd always envied birds. Though I don't think I ever considered what I would do with the facility if I ever achieved it. I just felt that birds demonstrate an absolute enjoyment of life in their handling of space.'

'Your parents must have wondered what they'd hatched.'

He laughed. 'Actually my father got quite keen on my experiments at one time. We built several sets of wings together. But although I developed fantastic arm muscles, the wings were either too weak and broke, or they were too stiff to flap. My father's idea was to test-fly off bridges that were over deep water, while he waited below in a rowing-boat. But when we got a really good set of wings going, they carried me clear across into some trees. I broke two ribs and an arm.'

Maggie winced. 'The price of success.'

'It was funny really, he was sitting there on the rocks holding me up, both of us laughing and crying at the same time. But I had to go away to school in England by the time my arm was mended, so we never did any more.'

'So what happened to this great love of flying?' she said, fetching a bowl of fruit salad from the dresser. 'You seem a bit stuck on the ground here.'

He hesitated to mention his new wings hanging up beneath sheets of polythene on a wall in the barn. 'It was the crash, I suppose. Lyn dying. And the four other guys. It's a nightmare I never seem able to escape from.'

'You're stuck into guilt like the rest of us,' she exclaimed. 'Guilt is a bloody cuckoo.'

47

At that moment there was the sound of a car reversing outside in the yard.

'Quick,' he exclaimed. 'It's Nuala come to fetch the milk. Hide in the back while I throw the dishes in the sink.' Already he was collecting them up.

Maggie picked up her bag, looked wildly round for anything else that might give her away, and ran out into the passage.

It was a bare moment later, just as he placed the pile of crockery in the bottom of the sink that the back door opened and Nuala came in.

Ranging long-legged in her jeans, her gypsy nectarine colouring and the bold structure of the bones about her brilliant scowling eyes, made a flourishing impact upon him after the pale, comparatively doughy features of the hiding Maggie. 'I'm a bit late tonight . . .' she began, then paused to sniff and look round. 'I thought at first you must be entertaining.' She advanced upon the table to examine the remains of what now appeared to be just his supper. 'I never knew you do yourself so well before, Conor. I detect herbs. And a fruit salad. Was it your birthday or something?'

He knew he was blushing as he adjusted his position to block her view of the sink. 'Thought I'd try something different with a piece of liver from that lamb.'

'Full of surprises, aren't you?' she said. 'It was almost like coming into a fancy restaurant.'

'I'll fetch the churn,' he said, heading for the door.

'Mam has your shirt washed,' she said, following him. 'She threw Vaun's out, said it was beyond redemption.'

He loaded the churn into the boot of the Datsun. 'Did you make it up yet, you two?'

'Huh,' she exclaimed, starting the engine. 'She's such a child.' With a roar, she drove off, slithering over the goat-dampened cobbles.

'What a pretty girl,' said Maggie. 'I spied through a crack in the door. Is she what keeps you here?'

Conor found himself blushing again. 'I don't come into her scheme of things. She's got driving ambition and sees me as a dead duck.'

Maggie laughed. 'Maybe that's because it's how you see yourself.' She filled the kettle for hot water to wash up. 'I'm heading for bed soon, this country air flakes me out.'

48

He lay in the dark later that night, flat on his back, staring at the vague x-ray shadows of the room.

Sir, Corny to suggest that the catholic hierarchy's obsession with sex is purely the mob frustration of a gang of clerical bachelors. Now if the Good Lord had managed to produce us all into the world by immaculate conception, you could understand why the animal groping would have a bad name. Though the chances are, knowing the fickleness of our betters, if humans simply coupled for no other reason than rabid libido, lust would never have been included in the banned list of pleasures. And the orgasm might have been known as Divine Ecstasy. Yours, etc.

Of course he wanted to fuck her. The other side of the wall, cocooned in darkness, her body lay enticing and evocative. It possessed soft tactile surfaces, crevices, mammary globes, and a socket for all that electricity he pulsed and throbbed with.

Swifts mate in the heavens, small feathered bodies at forty miles an hour, seeds passed, messages coded, jerk the wings up over the diamond stones of Kilfenora church. Sally up into the cumuli, over the white moss banks, there's the silver passage to the orient. It's for later, not now. This joystick's the weapon of my violence, aimed through the arches of pursuit. It's all recoil and impact, the haunches of our mating swell into immense golden domes far above the world, there is no black space, the lies of astronauts, the heavens are endless silken plateaux right down inside us, my wings are on fire, Daedalus, is this the sun exploding in my guts . . . ?

*

He was out early the next morning, feeding the sows while Belle brought in the goats. After the milking he took the dog up to the glen to round up the sheep. There was a pen there he had constructed out of the old yard behind the ruined farmhouse. Belle would herd them into it so that he could check the lambs' weights for the market next week in Kilfenora.

Once in the glen he sent her off. Her guilt-ridden posture always irritated him, that creep on her belly. In fact her whole supplicating attitude and total obedience annoyed him. He felt like kicking her sometimes. He also despised her because she

49

was the neighbourhood whore. Every dog within ten miles could have his way with her. For some reason she never got pregnant. She would slip out in the evening, come back hours later covered in mud, and lie pleading for forgiveness at her infidelity while panting with contented satiation. Perhaps part of her problem was confusion over instinctive desire and conditioned obedience. She would creep up on sheep like a stalking wolf, fangs bared, then cringe as if imagining the eyes of her master were always on her, and hurry round apologetically to chivvy them along. Every time she looked at him he could read penitential self-reproach in her eyes for her subconscious longing to eat sheep. If ever he showed the slightest anger with her, she nearly died of shame. But though her demeanour constantly annoyed him, he could never be angry with her, she was too good at her job. What kind of little mind lurks in you? he used to ponder, looking into her anxious brown eyes. That you outwit the cunningest sheep or goat every single time?

He reckoned it would take her twenty minutes to round them up, so he went across to the other side of the valley to look at the cattle. The day was cool, overcast, a breeze shaking every wild flower like fragments of coloured tissue paper caught in the rough grass or clefts in the great boulders and half-buried rocks. A lark flew up, calling, wings whirring like a clockwork toy.

'Could rain this evening, Conor,' came the voice of old Tom Riordan, startling him with its unexpectedness from fifty feet above, as the old man nearly ruptured himself heaving a stone back into place on the boundary wall. 'Wind's gone north-west.' The old man spent his days out in all weathers mending fences, herding, doing little jobs that his feeble frame could manage, as if desperate to repay the kindness of his sister-in-law for giving him a home. As a boy he had worked in the saleyards in Dublin as a drover, then been the herd on an estate near Mullingar. He had never married. Each week he gave his pension to his sister-in-law, and she gave him back a few pound notes. That evening he would walk the five miles to the village to sit in the bar, spend every penny on whiskey. In the small hours of the night he would set off home, probably fall asleep in a ditch, whatever the season, however cold, he never took ill. The next morning he'd be out somewhere on the hills, hacking a thorn down to stuff a gap, tarring a ewe's sore foot, white stubble like flaking paint over his thin, cracked face.

He peered down at Conor from beneath an old felt hat that grew over his head like fungus. 'Saw a young woman in the glen day before yesterday.'

'Tourist was she?' asked Conor, alert. 'After the flowers maybe?'

'Carrying a big bag she was.' He heaved another stone up with a clack, hung on to the wall to get his breath back. 'Seemed interested in the sheep.'

'Did you tell anyone?' asked Conor, realising as he asked it, that the question sounded odd.

'Would I waste my breath? Tourists are common as crows.'

'Not so many this year.'

'Met a German man yesterday, wet as a sheep after the dipping. Got caught in a shower on the mountain. Had a camera as big as a television. Asked me about the butterflies.' The old man's behatted head disappeared, then bobbed up further along the wall. 'Why would I bother to tell them anything? If I tell them a calf has the scour they don't bother till it's a patch of leather on the grass.'

There was no further sign of the old hat after that. Conor saw the flock hurrying across one of the glen paddocks, helplessly intimidated by one brown fur-jacketed jailer. The way they were always hurried embarrassed him. If only the dog could have allowed them a little dignity. But they were like refugees terrified of their guard's weapon, that those sharp white fangs might be sunk in their throats. Belle had only to appear on the horizon and the widely scattered flock would rush together for mutual protection. It was all too easy. He went down to meet them.

*

As he turned in through the yard gate and passed the tailboard of the Landrover, he could not have said what exactly he was expecting.

'Hi,' said the girl standing by the door of the house. 'You must be Conor. I'm Dorothy Benson. Sorry to drop in on you out of the blue. Did my brother tell you, I might look in on you?'

Conor's skin prickled. He felt as if he had never seen this

young woman before. He stared at her, searching for something familiar. She was wearing a pink low-cut jumper with a mauve gauze scarf knotted at her throat, and a grey skirt. Her short hair was fluffed out, standing up off her forehead. She was wearing a dark lipstick, and white and rouge make-up to accentuate her cheekbones, mascara round her eyes. None of this he had ever seen before. And the accent sounded dead-pan Australian. What a disguise. And she'd cut off all her hair!

He nodded, baffled, trying to think of the right question. 'How did you get here?'

'Walked.' She grinned. 'Got a lift to Gort, then another to the village. They told me at the Post Office how to get here. That's a wonderful piece of antiquity. It's all pretty marvellous.' She waved a hand round her.

'You'd best come in,' he said. 'I expect you could do with a drink.' Perfume assailed him as he reached past her to push the door open. 'I haven't seen Greg in years. You don't look like him.'

'I take after my mother,' she said, going into the kitchen. He picked up her bag. That wasn't the same as Maggie's, was it? She pushed her lower lip up froglike and flipped her eyebrows as she gazed about her. 'It's really quaint. D'you live here on your own? Greg said he thought you did, but things can change.'

'No change,' he replied.

'Would you be able to put me up for a few days? I'd love to look around.'

He shrugged. 'It's very primitive. I've no bathroom. You might be more comfortable at my neigh . . .'

'Comfortable?' she echoed. 'I've stayed in places with nothing but giant ants and spiders for pillows. This is great. I'll kip on the sofa.'

'I've a spare room you can use,' he said, marvelling all the while at her performance. 'You should be an actress. How long are you going to keep this up?'

'Keep what up? Oh, you mean how long am I here in Ireland for? Maybe another couple of weeks. I'd better warn you, I'll be firing questions at you like a cloud of locusts. I'm doing a paper on comparative traditional agricultural systems in the Third World and the Old World.'

'But you don't have to do it all the time,' he said. 'You can relax now.'

She laughed. 'I can mix business with pleasure all right. I feel like enjoying myself here.'

Although Conor knew this young woman was Maggie, he remained baffled by the plausibility of her disguise. She seemed like someone else. Some new person who had entered his life. But since she couldn't be anyone else but Maggie, why did she insist on carrying on the pretence? There was a secondary consideration, too. Someone who could enter and maintain another character so convincingly might not even be the character she first appeared to be. He stared in admiration, feeling himself in the position of a creature fascinated by a snake. Yet he had to admit he was enjoying the unpredictability of it all, playing the game.

'Coffee?' he asked. 'Or would you rather have tea? Or a can of Guinness maybe?'

'Anything to quench my thirst,' she replied heartily. 'What do you have at this time of day?'

'You're the guest.' He wondered if she was trying to work out what Australians ought to drink.

She licked her lips thoughtfully. 'We're great tea and beer drinkers at home, swallow buckets morning, noon and night. But I fancy a can of Guinness. I'm quite taking to the stuff.'

Conor fetched a couple of cans from the dresser cupboard. She sat down at the table. 'Phew,' she exclaimed. 'My feet are like mashed potatoes tramping all the way here. At one stage I felt like Burke and Wills, would I ever make it to civilisation. That woman in the post office said it was a mile or so. Felt like a dozen to me.' She kicked off a shoe and rubbed a foot.

'It's about five actually,' said Conor, pouring the black liquid into glasses and handing her one.

'I'm not too good at foot-slogging. I was brought up in the saddle. But I can see this sort of country'd snap horses' fetlocks like caps off beerbottles. All those amazing stone slabs full of cracks and fissures sprouting with ferns and things. Still I see you've got a jeep. After what Greg told me I expected to see a plane in one of the sheds.'

Conor laughed. 'This sort of farming wouldn't rise to that. This is subsistence level stuff.'

She raised her glass. 'Down the hatch. So what's a bright guy like you doing up to his armpits in such an arsehole existence?'

'It used to belong to an uncle. And I find the place timeless and beautiful. I'll show you later on. When your feet are rested.'

'I'd like that very much. But don't you get lonely stuck out here on your own? Not a single car passed me on that road. It was like some of the desert country back home.'

By this stage he was quite unaware of how unselfconsciously he was responding to her. 'I've good neighbours. And friends about the place.'

'What about those long winter evenings?'

'Then I shall have time to finish the building of my bathroom.'

She made her frog-like grimace and flicked her eyebrows. 'None of this what-am-I-going-to-do-with-my-leisure the rest of us are stuck with. You must be the original hermit.'

He smiled, finding himself thinking of her a brash but friendly young woman from Australia before mentally checking himself, wait a minute, this is really . . . or is it? 'What about you?' he asked. 'It must take guts to set off on your own, going to places you don't know, doing your research?'

Why do I keep playing her game? he asked himself, staring at her, expecting that at any moment he would read a flicker of laughter in her eyes, the admission that this was all a charade. Was she going to keep it up all the time? But at the moment he was enjoying her, didn't want her to revert.

'I've been travelling around since I was a kid,' she said. 'I've got cousins all over New South Wales. Greg and I hitched a ride all the way to Bendigo when I was five. Did he ever tell you about that? It was on a flat-car train. He was seven and bigger than me so I took him along to help me get up on them. I only wanted to see where they went to. Anyway we both got heatstroke and ended up in the hospital in Bendigo, with police and parents convinced we'd been abducted by a child-molester. I thought the whole adventure wonderful and I've been trying to emulate it ever since. Greg, of course took to the air. Isn't that how you two met?'

Conor nodded. He glanced at the clock. 'Are you hungry? Would you like some lunch? Being a bachelor I only cook in the evenings, but there's cheese and cold lamb and bread and butter, and plenty more Guinness.'

'Great,' she said, always enthusiastic. 'I could just about eat a whole sheep. Let me help.'

He gave her a quick glance, but there wasn't a flicker. She stood waiting for him to show her where plates and cutlery were kept. She moved with quick twists of her pelvis that flung her skirt against her thighs, delineating them like a breaking wave draining from a rock. As he brought dishes of meat and cheese over to the table and she moved backwards and forwards, fetching plates, cutlery and bread, his eyes travelled about her, over the velvet carp-bellied shape of her arms, the gold-chain on a wrist, the smallness of her fingers, the damson lips on her emulsioned face and her large mascara-ed eyes, and he suddenly became conscious of her woman-ness as if suddenly drenched by a bucket of deliciously cool water on a burning hot day.

'So tell me,' she said as he cut slices of the lamb. 'How did you come to be in Midura?'

Two can play at this game, he thought. 'A bit like you coming here. Research for a book.'

'Go on,' she exclaimed. 'I didn't know you were a writer. Though I remember Greg saying you were always scribbling letters to newspapers. That must have been about my second year at college in Melbourne. Really mind-blowing days, going round the rock concerts in a cloud of hash. Loudspeakers under the stars, sleeping-bags wriggling like caterpillars as couples tried to screw in them, sausages caked in wood-ash and perching like a kookaburra over a pit of stinking turds. Meanwhile you and Greg were showering the bread fields with poison gas.'

Conor shook his head. 'Greg was the instructor. And I was only there for a couple of months to get the background for my book.'

'What's it about?'

'It's a saga about a family called Doyle. Begins at the time of Wolfe Tone. With every generation the father dies within a few hours of conceiving his heir. Always violently, except for an eighty-year old who has a heart attack. One was conceived in Co Cork and born in Botany Bay. Most of the mothers die in childbirth. So that orphan begets orphan through two centuries. But orphans are usually brought up amongst other children, so that into the genes of the Doyles is installed the instinct for a brotherhood of man. Needless to say the last but one male is a crop-sprayer pilot just after the war. He gets shot down by an irate clergyman's wife. His widow gives birth in an ambulance hurrying to hospital. It is torpedoed at some traffic lights, the only survivor is the newborn child. This child is brought back to Ireland by the clergyman whose wife had killed his father, together with his own large family. In a series of unprecedented moves this child when he becomes a young man is elected as a Messianic Secretary of the United Nations at the age of twenty-eight. And the whole Gadarene plunge of the world towards annihilation is halted, civilisation is saved. He brings about total disarmament, and the great rapprochment between the USA and Russia. He is the Kennedy Dream come true for the whole world. But he makes the inevitable Doyle mistake of conceiving a child—at the age of thirty-two.'

She shook her head in admiration. 'Have you actually written all this?'

'It'll take me a while yet.'

'So this is why you came back here, this is why you live the solitary life. I'm beginning to understand.'

Conor stood up, cleared away the plates. He felt the need for fresh air. Dorothy readily agreed. But she looked dismayed as they walked past the Landrover. 'Are we going to walk?' He didn't say anything, so she laughed. 'All right. I should have known. Just pray my feet don't go on strike. Or you'll have an invalid on your hands.'

The sky was a bright marbled grey. They crossed the emerald base of the valley towards the glen. It was very still. The dark-trunked ash trees rising up beneath the southern bluff stood like green-hued mushrooms. There was no sign of the ravens. The thick copses of hazels on the northern slopes were quilled with dead branches, the result of a dry spring. Not even the chattering song of a chaffinch came from them. But from somewhere came the faint fluting of a warbler. Then a jay shrieked and flew across to the luxuriant ash trees grouped about the ruined farm house in the glen. Then a whitear scolded them anxiously from a rock. Conor pointed out the white mountain avens, the little blue milk-worts, the rock roses and cranesbills.

'You don't need a flower garden,' she said. 'Nature does it for you. Who lived there?' she asked as they passed the ruined farmhouse.

'Doyles. The uncle said he could remember an old lady living there when he was a boy. They collected the coffin on Armistice Day in an old cart. All her family had been long gone to the States. But nobody could find any addresses to tell them she was dead. So the Land Commission took the farm. They made

56

it into one with the uncle's place. I pay them a small annuity every year.'

He found himself tingling with stimulation, as if he had suddenly come alive, unable to stop himself talking, responding to this enthusiastic young woman. Such electricity gave her the quality of reality. She moved economically, but all the time demonstrated the fecundity of her femaleness. Her reactions were practical, sensible of history, archaeology, agricultural practice. When they came to a small dell, she noted how moveable stones had been deposited at the sides to give an even green sward, even though time had obscured this to all except the most observant. She saw how walls had been built where the land was stoniest, not necessarily following contours or boundaries, and only went in straight lines across a reach of stone pavements. 'Isn't that thyme?' she asked, stooping to pluck a few leaves and crush them between her fingers to smell. Then fell on her knees to examine a purple orchid.

'I've never seen one before,' she exclaimed.

They had climbed up now on to a high grass plateau that gave long views in all directions of the countryside, distant stone hills like ocean rollers petrified in mid-surge, the hidden valley behind them, a green cleft in the grey, a vastness of space all about them. He felt stimulated to watch her stand shocked and spellbound by such an abundance of vision. Above them a sparrow-hawk stooped to catch a swallow, but failed as the smaller bird eluded it with aerobatic skill. About their knees flopped butterflies, speckled woods, meadow browns and ringlets, together with nippier blues and the occasional rapid dark-green fritillary brought out by the thin sunshine percolating through the dusty cloud. He restrained the urge to run, perform cartwheels. He waved his arms. 'This was all covered by glaciers during the ice-age. They carved the hills, then melted to cover the land with stone débris. Nobody knows for certain why people were drawn to live here. Perhaps it was once very fertile, covered in forest. But they cut the trees down and over-farmed it. Now we're the relics, hanging on, still eking out a living.'

Perhaps infected by the same urge and less inhibited than he, Dorothy began to run towards a stony knoll, startling some sheep. She spun round, skipping with the deft abandon of the child who half-wills itself to tumble. He followed her among

57

the grey rhino flanks of limestone to a stone platform pock-marked and channelled by eroding time. She stood there, panting, legs apart, bare arms like jug-handles. 'There's something about this place,' she said. She sat down cross-legged as he stood beside her. 'It makes me feel that all the decisions and choices were made long before I got here.'

She looked up at him, reached out a hand to draw him to sit down beside her. 'I can hold yesterday and tomorrow in my head. It's a rare feeling.' She turned away to gaze into the distance, her voice thickening. 'I don't know if you meant it, or if you had any idea how it would affect me.' She gripped his hand tightly. 'Thank you.'

He was disturbed by her emotion, not knowing how to respond. It seemed to demonstrate some inner part of her that he could not understand. His instinct was to take her in his arms and hold her. Yet that might be a crude intrusion into the spell. As he debated his uncertainty, she shook her head as if to free herself from some dark memory. 'Perhaps it's you, too, that makes this all seem so good an experience. You're part of this land. You've got dignity. None of this tongue-hanging-out and pawing that most men seem to indulge in.'

He looked away.

A tide of sunlight crept swiftly across the grass towards them, lit up the rocks as if lights were being switched on. She smiled at him. 'Now is the moment I feel to debate the significance of life and death. But . . .' she waved a hand round her. 'There's no need for verbal explanation. Here's the visual print-out. The map of existence.' She turned back to him, made her frog-like grimace. 'Sorry. I expect I sound like the little old lady before the Mona Lisa who has to gabble away excitedly when people just want to contemplate it in deep admiring silence.'

Conor shook his head. 'I'd have been disappointed if you hadn't reacted to . . . well, it isn't mine, but sometimes I feel as if it is.' He gestured at the landscape. 'Sometimes it makes me feel godlike. Other times it puts me in my place, just another blade of grass.'

She wrinkled her brow. 'What exactly are we talking about?'

He stiffened. 'Sorry. It probably sounds a load of rubbish.'

'No, I didn't mean that. What does it signify, that's what I meant? What does it signify that a couple of humans should feel so overwhelmed by a landscape that they sit trying to

58

explain to each other that it makes them feel good, incites them to think of life and death?'

Sir, It is said the reason the USA and the USSR treat each other as mortal enemies is not just to give employment to the unemployable in their armies or to keep their armament industries smoking, but because to have an enemy gives a sense of purpose to their people and unites the country. The different Churches cling to their Gods as unique against all the other Gods to give each religion a purpose to remain unique. But if some Lord High Creator did design this ant-packed ball dangling in space, what exactly did he have in mind as the purpose of life? If it was just to worship him and love him, it sounds more as if he was insecure and in need of a shrink. Just like any other dictator. And if that was the case, why did he let off all the other creatures from worshipping him? They just get on with eating, screwing and evolving without giving a monkey's at the prospect of being damned or whatever. What I should like to know is who invented this word 'purpose' anyway? Yours, etc.

When they got back late in the afternoon, Belle rose up from the doorstep, gave a couple of hysterical yaps as if to say, you're rotten, leaving me here alone all this time, then rolled over on her back in abject apology for her outburst.

'She's funny, isn't she?' said Dorothy, kneeling down to rub her stomach. 'Such a softie.'

When Conor sent her off to bring the goats down, Belle hurtled off, tail a wild flag, jubilant at the chance to prove her importance.

There came a squeal from the pig-sheds so he took Dorothy over to show her. 'I keep a few sows,' he explained. 'Wean the bonhams and sell them in the market.' He showed her the sheds he had converted, fitting railings made from old metal water-pipes so that the little piglets would not get crushed against the walls when their ponderous mothers lowered their bulk to let them feed. There was also a boarded-off corner as a crib where an infra-red lamp dangled to tempt the piglets to sleep away from any risk of being crushed.

'That's really considerate,' she commented.

He laughed. 'A squashed piglet is a lost profit.'

'Don't denigrate yourself,' she said, nudging him in the ribs.

'Let's say it's to your mutual benefit. They look healthy and contented. Haven't they got bright, inquisitive faces?'

'D'you notice something about them?' he asked as they leaned on the lower half-door. 'Pigs are the only other creature like ourselves with the same amount of white surrounding their irises as us. Human eyes. And they've got pink skins like us, without much hair. Probably why George Orwell chose them as the villains in *Animal Farm*.'

He wanted to show her more, to keep talking, to maintain the emotional massage of her proximity. But he could hear the approach of a goat bell. 'I must wash out the buckets,' he said.

*

When he drove up to the Riordans' farm in the evening with the churn of milk in the back and Dorothy beside him, he could not have foretold the reception her arrival would arouse. But as soon as he introduced Dorothy he was astonished to see the reactions of hostility.

'Pleased to meet you I'm sure,' said Mrs Riordan, her brief smile tightening into what verged on a knot of disapproval. 'We heard you were expected.'

'She walked all the way from the village,' explained Conor. 'Took me by surprise.'

They were all staring at her as if she was a highly infectious carrier of foot-and-mouth disease.

'It's a long diversion from Australia to visit this backwater,' said Nuala, heading for the door. 'I hope it's worth your while.'

Dorothy began to explain about her thesis.

Vaun interrupted. 'Will you be staying for long? Down there on your own with Conor?'

'This is a charming home you've got, Mrs Riordan,' said Dorothy quickly, as if deciding to take charge of a dangerous situation. 'With its lovely thatch, and its wooden ceilings and your nice pieces of old furniture. Even a settle bed. Some cousins had one at Swan Hill, and it was known as the Irish settee. That old cupboard is a real beaut. Must be hundreds of years old. I love old things. I like to feel thousands of people have used things before me. You don't feel so alone, then. Isn't that a stunning table? The amazing patterns the walnut makes.'

The acceptable currency of a flow of words lifted her out of social penury.

'My mother brought that with her,' said Mrs Riordan. 'She came from Gort. They had a few nice pieces. I didn't think you had much of the old stuff out there in Australia?'

'A few things people brought out with them. Nothing like this.'

'Come into the front room,' said Mrs Riordan, her round face softening into a smile. 'I'll show you a few more treasures.'

'Mind you don't touch any,' said Vaun. 'The woodworm has them in bits. They're only held together with the polish.'

'Don't be listening to her,' said Mrs Riordan, as they went through.

'I'll take the milk now,' said Conor, feeling that it would be safe to leave Dorothy. 'Be back soon.'

*

When he got back he found everyone in the kitchen, laughing, drinking tea, preparing a meal.

'We decided that we'd celebrate Dorothy's arrival by giving you tea here,' said Mrs Riordan. 'It'll be later than usual, but never mind. We don't need any men, so you can go and put your feet up.'

'He can help,' shouted Vaun, rushing round with an apron and looping it over his head before he could demur. 'Men have to share in domestic chores these days, isn't that right, Dorothy?'

'Spot on,' laughed Dorothy. 'Even macho men.'

'Conor's hardly macho,' said Nuala, stirring a pan on the cooker. 'He's about as aggressive as a potato. He only asserts himself to keep other people happy.'

'I've heard him shout at Belle,' said Vaun innocently. 'Here boy, take these carrots and give them hell.'

'What exactly does macho mean?' asked Mrs Riordan, laying out chops on a vast grill-pan. 'A big, tough sort of man?'

'Macho is the replacement word for Male Chauvinist Pig, Mam.' Vaun sighed exaggeratedly as if having to explain to an imbecile. 'Trying to improve their image.'

'Only to themselves,' said Nuala.

'Trying to gild the brute,' said Dorothy, cutting up apples.

'You're not saying anything, Conor?' taunted Vaun, her hands white with flour from making pastry.

Sir, As a middling piggling male averagely afflicted with sloth, greed and lust, I should like to point out to feminists that misogynists got there first. I wonder why? Yours, etc.

Kathleen had come in clutching a writing pad. 'When's tea?' She looked round surprised to find so many helping, even more so at Conor in an apron. 'What're you all laughing at?'

'We're bating Conor,' said Vaun, leaning across the table to prod him with the rolling pin.

'I'll stand up for you, Conor,' said Kathleen, coming over to him. 'What are they saying?'

'I don't think women know exactly what kind of man a man ought to be that would please them. . . .' Conor began.

'Nonsense. That's not true. We know what we want.' The girls were shouting all at once, and began to pelt him with carrot ends, potato peelings, cauliflower stalks and flour.

'Stop it,' cried Kathleen, holding out her arms protectively with all the seriousness of youth. 'Stop it.'

They ceased mainly because they had run out of ammunition. 'Thanks, Kathleen,' said Conor, dusting flour off his clothes.

'So tell us what kind of man you would like to marry when you grow up, Kathleen?' asked Dorothy.

'Conor,' she replied, going a little pink.

'At least someone knows what they want,' he said. 'Ta ra.' And he put an arm round her waist, seized her by the hand and began to swing her about in a wild dance. 'Will we elope tonight?'

She squealed and giggled, half-nervous, half-delighted.

'Put her down, Conor,' said Vaun sagely. 'She'll only wet her knickers.'

'I can't get married till I get my leaving,' said Kathleen breathlessly.

They all laughed at her. 'Anyway, marriage isn't the thing any more,' said Nuala.

'That's right,' said Dorothy. 'Independent woman shouldn't be thinking of such old-fashioned roles where she becomes tied by law to a male, and is expected to bathe his balding head when the petulant bastard's been out boozing all night.'

Mrs Riordan gave a shriek of mirth. The chops were sizzling under the grill, the pressure-cooker of potatoes was hissing, the vegetables bubbling. Nuala was stirring a saucepan, Vaun trimming the pastry on the pie-dish before putting it in the oven.

'I remember my mother telling me,' said Mrs Riordan. 'That when there was all the trouble with the suffragettes about women getting the vote, that her mother insisted it was all a lot of nonsense. Men had to be left to their games, politics or business or whatever amused them. But women didn't need the vote because they were the ones who kept everything going where it mattered, in the home. Men weren't capable of having babies, rearing children, cooking meals, running a home. Women were the practical, essential ones. The vote wasn't going to change any of that. I know that philosophy is long gone out of the window. Houses are now full of gadgets that make it easy to run them and there are nursery schools for children. But I wonder if women are any happier with this new way of things?'

'It had to change, Mam,' said Nuala. 'Men were just using women. We're never going back to that.'

'Conor's not a bad cook, you know, Dorothy,' said Vaun. 'Pity he can't have babies.'

'I like Conor because he shouts at the sky,' said Kathleen. Everyone looked from her to Conor, who gave an embarrassed laugh. 'Maybe I shouldn't have told . . .' she said, looking anxious.

'Mam shouts at the cooker,' said Vaun. Everyone laughed.

'Indeed and I shout at you,' said Mrs Riordan.

'The devil a bit of good it ever did her,' said old Tom in the doorway. 'Too sparing with the back of your hand, Sheila.' But he was grinning as he spoke, his false teeth in, ready for supper.

*

It was still light when Conor and Dorothy left at ten o'clock. He paused as he turned off the Landrover's clattering diesel in the yard. 'That's odd, isn't it? There was no mention of you staying up there, was there?'

'There was. While you were delivering the milk. I told them no man was going to lay a hand on me without risking severe damage, because us Australian girls are practised in the art of self-defence, and I smacked my fist into the palm of my hand with such force they believed me. Nearly broke it, too.'

Belle came wriggling across the yard as they got out, for a signal pat from her master, then went instantly to Dorothy and rolled on her back. 'Little sycophant,' he muttered. 'Would you like a nightcap?' he asked, once they were inside the house.

She shook her head, yawning. 'It was like being in the bosom of your family up there. I know they're not your family, but they treat you almost like a son. There was a bond between you all, like a group of people casually tossing a ball among themselves.' She yawned again. 'I'll hit the hay if you don't mind. It seems like it's been a long day. I enjoyed it.' She took a quick step forwards and kissed him on the cheek, then turned and was gone through the door.

He stood, aware of mingled pleasure and disappointment, as when a schoolboy standing on a station platform in England, somewhere like Reading, and being thrilled by the siren and roar of an express train rushing through, yet chagrined that he wasn't on it, wherever it was going. He took a can of Guinness from the dresser cupboard, then pulled out the cutlery drawer to find a box in the back. There were about five Giuliettas left. He lit one, poured out the Guinness and carried the glass to the door. Belle opened an eye. He waved her to remain. He walked through the garden, took the path up to the boundary wall. The wind had fallen, the air was still. Birdcalls were occasional and indistinct like someone trying to speak with their mouths full of toothbrush. The sky above was one great grey fishnet stocking pulled up over a pink leg. Over in the west was the glowing flesh of an uncovered thigh, going white as a hip over the long mountain. He loved this protracted dusk, sat on a rock and inhaled his cigar, aware already in the lowering light of the red glow of its tip.

A silent bird flew past, soft-edged like a white handkerchief, dropping down beside the hazels. An owl. He could not help himself following it, like a Giotto angel, his primary feathers fanning to lift him up, vanes closing on the down-stroke, just that wobble of muscle control as he levered himself up through the air. Already he was tilting forwards, increasing speed, till the air was hissing past. He could see both his own kitchen window glowing and a light down at the Riordans'. Now he was high enough to catch sunrays on his covert feathers and see the bright watermelon slice floating beyond the Arran islands. Below him the valley gleamed like angelica, the cattle studding it like cloves. And then he was beyond it, soaring above the stony hills, corkscrew roads, the dull orange glow from lights in isolated farms, the dark fur of forestry plantations and the hieroglyphics of the limestone pavements. He hung in the air and sucked his cigar so that it glowed like a navigation light should anyone look up to see. Sometimes when he reached the coast at Fanore, high above the wrinkled sea, he would travel down as far as the cliffs of Moher. But tonight he turned back, reluctant to go too far away from home. It was darker now, farmlights were twinkling, car headlamps bright as stars. The valley was a deep sleeping lake. He descended in a long glide, finally spreading his allula feathers to slow him as his feet reached for the ground. With a flourish of primaries he folded his wings, stood swaying for a while, his body a humming gyroscope from its momentum.

For a second his eyelashes and nose gleamed as he inhaled the cigar, then all was dark, except for a few sparks in the smoky steel dome above, the early planets and brighter stars. He picked up his glass and drank deeply, sat on the rock, contented.

*

It became an oddly self-conscious act to walk to his own bedroom, close the door, get undressed and climb into bed, knowing there was a young woman in the next room, and they were alone.

He dreamed of being in a train, wearing his dark-blue suit, his collar and tie tight and uncomfortable, carrying a brief-case on his lap, cradling it protectively as if it contained something that the slightest jolt might spill or damage in some way. He only knew that he must take great care. Two elderly women sat opposite, wearing pink felt hats like those sagging shapes of blancmange he used to gag on at school dinners. They were chatting away non-stop about the doings of their grandchildren. He gazed out of the window. The telegraph wires rose and fell like a stiff skipping rope. Cattle stood about knee-deep in the rushy fields like abandoned prams. Suddenly he realised the brief-case was no longer on his lap, and he started in a panic. But there it was, between his feet where it must have slipped down. The two women paused in their conversation to stare at him. Then as they looked down, he saw that something was oozing from the brief-case, something dark and sticky. . . .

After the milking he spent the next morning with the pigs, weaning one plump litter of bonhams, then castrating the males of a younger litter. Then the monthly delivery of pigmeal arrived by truck. Dorothy watched everything, taking notes on a clip-board. 'Time and motion, is she?' asked the driver. 'Going to make you more efficient?'

'The opposite,' replied Conor. 'She's from the EEC. They want all production slowed down. They're giving grants to farmers who produce less. So they can cut the size of the food mountains.'

'Is that a fact?' exclaimed the man. 'Would you credit the things they think of?'

All through their midday meal Dorothy questioned Conor about the way he farmed, making notes. 'The net productivity per acre is quite similar to Third World countries, relative to the average price in the market. Are the prices fairly stable?'

He shook his head. 'They talk about guaranteed prices. But if nobody wants the beasts because trade's taken a down-turn, what do you do? Take them home and keep them longer, hoping demand'll come back? That might work with cattle for a while, but not with the lamb trade. And I couldn't afford to fatten pigs at the price I'm charged for delivering meal this distance. So we take a loss.'

'At least you don't suffer from drought.'

'Are you joking? Two years back the stream dried, and I was fetching churns of mud from a pool in a dried-up lake near the village. Water can be a problem here. Most houses have big cisterns built to store the rain, but there's a limit to how big you can make them. We were just starting the goats then and the yield went right down. We nearly had to give up.'

'For God's sake, Conor, you've got a tap with running water most of the time, you drive a vehicle, you drink Guinness with your dinner. I've been with people who have nothing but the rags they stand up in, whose children are unlikely to ever reach their tenth birthday.'

'We've had our famines here, too,' he retorted, wondering why he was getting so heated. 'This country once held eight million souls. Just over a hundred years ago they were dying in thousands in these parts as if their catholic God of Grace was grinding them like ants under his heel, together with their landlords from across the water till there were just three million left.'

'But you're not poor like them, Conor. It's poverty that creates famine. People with no reserves, people with only a few sticks and half an acre of stones that's had no rain at all for two years. Why, there are plenty of farmers back home that have gone bust in a drought, corn merchants made bankrupt, and many of them would have looked at this place when their herds were fat, and laughed and called you a smallholder. But they were big-time gamblers, they took risks. This is an old traditional safe-system you're working. It's not going to make you rich, but you're not going to starve.'

He banged his hand on the table. 'I won't deny I'm better off than millions in the Third World. But it's a matter of scale. Most of this place is owned by the bank. I'm just their lackey. Every night I get out the accounts and sweat a little, wondering if I'll still be able to manage by the end of the month.'

'You seem to me to be managing pretty well.'

'I'd like to see you try it.'

'I've a few ideas.'

'You try them out on stones.' He was breathing heavily, annoyed at his defensiveness.

Dorothy got up and walked over to the open door, stood looking out. She turned her head. 'Maybe when your book's finished you'll become a millionaire.' Then she stepped outside into the sunlight. 'Coming?'

*

They stood at the bottom of the valley, looking up at the bluff, the line of limestone crags jutting above the ash trees. 'There's one of the ravens. It's said they've lived up there a thousand years. It's not as steep as it looks. D'you think you can make it?'

He knew he was still flailing her with his resentment. Her attack had been unsettling, yet he knew the fault was his own for being so defensive.

'It looks mysterious up there,' she replied. 'Like the Hanging Rock. It just has to be investigated.'

Halfway up, under the ash trees, he paused, pointed through the trunks to a heap of soil. 'Badgers. There's a network of tunnels under here that has the ground like Gruyère cheese.'

'I've never seen a badger,' she said, lowering her voice and peering at the mounds of clay.

'They only come out in the evening. We'll have to come out near dusk.'

They climbed up a narrow sheep path that took them above the tops of the ash trees. The bluff was not as steep as it appeared from below. The ravens had flown away down the valley, resentful at their intrusion. The farmhouse and buildings below them seemed small as models.

Once over the crags they reached a grassy, rock-strewn plateau that descended in a series of stone pavements and hazel copses all the way to the distant village with the short bell-tower of its modern granite church showing above the cluster of roofs.

'Is that a castle?' she asked, staring at a low and massive circular structure of stones about a hundred yards away.

'Ring-fort,' he replied. 'History is laid out for anyone to see in this part of the world. Not much has changed in a thousand years.' As they crossed the pavements, stepping over the fern-filled cracks, he explained the purpose of the ring-forts, fortified ramparts that surrounded the wattle and thatched dwellings of the early farmers. 'They must have been dangerous times, not being able to trust anyone, bands of marauders always trying to make off with your cattle or your wives.'

'Yet it all seems so serene now,' she said, stopping to gaze around. 'I can see why you live here, Conor. The rest of the world doesn't seem to exist.'

'My ivory tower, you mean?'

She went on towards the fort. 'Shangrila.'

Circling the massive walls, they came to an entrance, the lintel stone still intact. Inside there was nothing but a rich sward of long grasses, banks of nettles and marguerites. The walls were uneven, having fallen in places to only a few feet in height. In the centre, Dorothy sank to her knees, brushing her hands through the grass.

He sat down beside her. 'My ancestors lived here.'

She lay back, cradling her head on her arms and closing her eyes. She smiled. 'I love the thought of that.'

Over a distant stone hill small white clouds puffed like a flock of balloons. Bees and hover-flies hummed, butterflies with false eyes on their wings fluttered among the clover and marguerites. Above them sang an invisible lark. He looked down on Dorothy stretched out beside him, and the evocative delineation of her body, the sun on the skin of her throat and arms, made desire arouse in him like lifting hackles.

'One of my favourite puddings,' he said absently. 'Caramel custard.'

She opened one eye.

'Your skin,' he continued. 'It's smooth like caramel custard.'

She closed the eye again. 'Make-up, that's all it is.'

'You're very attractive.'

She opened her other eye. 'Up here I'm the only woman in the world.' She closed the eye. 'What are we going to do about it?'

He leaned close, let his mouth alight upon hers. Instantly she undid her arms and wrapped them round him, and they were clasping each other, kissing hungrily.

Later when he undid the button on her waistband, she grasped his hand. 'Not here. I'd rather be on your bed.'

'But this is where the family bed stood, a palliasse of straw. Now is the moment, under the sun.'

'All right,' she agreed, and without further ado kicked off her jeans and pants, lying back with her knees up and thighs apart for him to crawl between.

What is this doing out here, put it away, it's not very nice, good little boys keep it inside their clothes and only bring it out to do tinkles, they never play with it because it's not very clean, so put it away quickly before I get cross, then go and wash your hands. Crikey, look at de Burgh's horrible great prick, it's like a piece of revolting meat, a dead conger eel, all rotting and suppurating, covered in worm-holes and oozing pus, run quick before we get infected. Put it away, put it away, make it go down, it's not nice, it shouldn't be seen, it's obscene, the sight of it makes me feel sick, put it away, aaaaagh!

'Fuck me slowly,' she said as he sank into her soft wet interior and her legs met over his back. 'Try too hard and you flood the carburettor, as my old dad used to say of his flivver.'

Hug me, hug me, hug me, hug me, hug me, hug me, hug me, hug me, hug me. I want to hold you, hold you, hold you, hold you, hold you, hold you, hold. I want you, want you, want you, WANT YOU.

Silken threads of cloud trailed like an unravelling silk shawl far up in the jade blue heavens. Tiny swallows arced across.

The leaves of a group of alder trees outside the walls rustled. The ructions of space obscured the voice of a German woman tourist pausing in the entrance, as she peered in as if uncomprehending at what she saw, exposed human flesh half-obscured in the long grass. Then she turned to block her husband's view, pushed him away.

A man lay sprawled on the beaten clay in the shape of an X, each wrist and ankle strapped by thongs to stakes driven into the ground. A few scraps of filthy cloth clung about his lean body. A dark pig snuffled the ground nearby. From the stone chimney of one of the nearby huts rose a thin column of grey smoke. The man licked his dry lips. High above him tiny swallows darted with illiberal freedom. There were voices coming from the hut, loud, argumentative. He rolled his head sideways to look in its direction. Just beyond it he could see two small naked children standing in the doorway of another hut, watching him. Beyond them, by the wall of the fort were tethered two cows. A woman with long lank auburn hair was squatting down milking one into a clay pot. The coarse-woven gown she wore was caught by her posture to reveal the shape of her body beneath. He licked his lips again, at the thought of the woman, and the thought of the milk she had in her pot. Suddenly a number of men emerged from the hut, came towards him. They had long curly moustaches, clean-shaven chins, wild hair chopped about six inches long, and carried staves. They stood round, shouting at him. Even though he was tied, they were afraid of him. In their fear and to disprove their fear, they began to beat him. They struck him about the head and body with their heavy sticks till he was senseless. When they were satisfied he was rendered harmless, one of them cut the thongs with a knife, then they lifted the unconscious man up and bore him to the massive door, unbarred it and carried him outside. They were laughing and confident now. There were many trees about, alders, ash, hawthorn and hazel. They came to the rocks of the bluff where there was a drop of at least fifty feet on to more rocks on the slopes below. As they flung him, the rush of air revived him, brought back consciousness. He stretched out his battered arms, tried to fly. . . .

Conor jerked away, sat up, choking back a cry, stared round at the swaying grasses, the nodding pink heads of the knapweed among the marguerites.

'What is it?' asked Dorothy, raising herself on to an elbow. 'Did something bite you?'

'A dream,' he replied slowly.

'Tell me,' she said, stroking his arm.

He told her, too disturbed to relax. 'Maybe you've got second sight or something,' she mused. 'I can never make up my mind about dreams. Sometimes when you're asleep it's like your mind's a TV studio shut up for the night. All that equipment lying idle. Then somebody breaks in and switches it on. They bring in a strange crowd of actors, people you've never seen before to play characters you seem to know. And they use strange locations that seem familiar. People love to read meanings into it all, but it seems to me they're like art critics inventing interpretations for paintings to sell their own viewpoint.'

Conor laughed. 'We've things in common, you and I,' he said, enjoying the tender solicitousness of her fingers.

*

That evening they had nearly finished milking the goats when Vaun came clattering into the yard on an old bicycle, alarming the herd. She stopped astride it, her pink cheeks pinker from the ride. 'Sure that isn't a billy you're milking, Dorothy?'

'If it is,' replied Dorothy. 'He's going to have problems carrying out his duties.'

Vaun laughed. 'Could be the new multipurpose male, fixes two at a time.'

'They only seem to teach you one thing at that school,' complained Conor.

'It's not true,' Vaun replied. 'When they tried a bit of sex education, they used the diagram of a ewe. So I asked if she'd been dipped first for the maggot. Leave the class this instant, Siobhan Riordan, shouted Sister Joseph. So you see, I missed it.' Dorothy laughed. 'By the way,' added Vaun. 'Mam asked would you take the milk this evening? The car won't start. We tried pulling it with the tractor, but it felt like we should have given it the last rites. See you later.' She turned the bike and wobbled away with a wave over her shoulder.

'Right,' said Dorothy, after they'd filled the churn and cleaned the buckets. 'While you're delivering the milk I'll cook you a real Strine bonza beano.'

He laughed and kissed her, relishing the access to her face as if it was a new dimension in his life. But when he drove up to Riordans and saw Nuala emerging from the dairy, he felt his temples suffuse with an onrush of guilt again.

'Bloody car,' she said crossly. 'It's like a corpse. I was supposed to go down to Lisdoonvarna tonight.'

'You can take the Landrover if you want,' he offered.

'It's all right. I rang Niall.'

McCarthy's mandarin Mercedes, he thought enviously, then checked himself. How could he be green after his own unfaithfulness?

'I hear you've got Dorothy slaving for you already,' she said, bringing one of the churns out.

'It's all good experience,' said Conor, heaving the churn up into the Landrover. I wonder if Nuala's the least bit jealous herself? he thought.

Driving down the lane to the village, he found there were hints of elation in his mood. But some cautious inner voice bade him be wary. Admitting to optimism was tantamount to risking its destruction. Sow seeds, watch the delicate first leaves unfurl, throw open their tender throats, and the next morning find them stripped to a few bony fibres and no sign of the slimy black vandal who'd committed murder in the night.

He'd mortgaged all his emotions before.

The lead weight of that plane with its airscrews like assegais impaled through its shoulders. How rapidly did microscopic scenery become all too solid ground, and tiny peas of green expand into barricades of cannon-trunked gum trees. The shriek remained in his mind, the ache in his bursting tendons trying to make the plane respond, steer, pull out. He had hardly been aware of Lyn beside him, her mouth wide, one hand catching at her hair, the other gripping her seat, a whole, live person, seconds away from . . .

'Why do you insist on taking all the blame on yourself?' the therapist had asked him. 'Because I can see quite clearly,' he replied. 'If I had acted differently, she would still be alive.' The therapist was plump as a Buddha and wore large spectacles that gave her the appearance of tearfulness. 'We know the enquiry exonerated you. We know that the proper pilot failed to report the faulty fuel gauge. But still you blame yourself. Naturally you were angry at such a terrible loss. Do you remember as a child, when you were angry because you were so powerless when adults took things away from you?' He did not find it easy to talk with this woman, her manner veered from being coy to being authoritative, and she never seemed completely at ease, kept trying not to appear to be glancing at her watch. 'You mean I was a spoiled brat?' he asked. She shook her head. 'A child doesn't know the rights and wrongs of possessions, it has to learn them. Parents often treat their possessions as more important than their children.' 'My mother was scatter-brained,' he said. 'She was always losing things. Car-keys, handbags, tickets, letters, rings. It used to worry me, so I was always trying to find things before she lost them, putting them ready for her to find. I hated to see her flap, it seemed to threaten my security. What I liked about Lyn was her unflappability. She had this inner serenity. Things weren't important to her. If there were more people around like her, the world would be a far less crazy, neurotic madhouse. Then I go and kill her. I can't stand my own stupidity.' The therapist had curiously translucent teeth, like grains of rice that have been soaked in olive-oil. She smiled at him encouragingly. 'So you find this world crazy and threatening, do you?' she asked, glancing at her watch again. He had to repress the temptation to laugh hysterically.

The cheese-making plant was operated in an old cottage behind an amazing modern house, with a canted wooden roof suggestive of the sails of an Arab dow. It was hidden in a grove of beech and hornbeam at the end of a long lane that twisted among hazel groves and hump-backed limestone boulders. So that coming upon this startling house in an area where even modern buildings tended to echo centuries of conservatism, came as a shock. As Conor swung round to pass round the back of the house, he noted a garda car reverse from the front-door and drive off. As he was unloading the churns Neve Cullen came out. She was a heavy, florid woman of thirty, always in jeans, with wavy hair that descended like the roof of a pagoda. She already had four children. She was the cheese-maker; her husband, Eamonn, a repressed Corbusier, was the salesman and deliveryman.

'Did you see Sergeant Conolly?' she asked, helping with the churns.

'That was his car?'

'He was with some detective from Galway. They were enquiring about strangers. Trouble-makers from across the border.'

Conor felt his blood chill by degrees. 'Is it about that bus that was blown up last week?'

'I think so.' Before she could vouchsafe further information, the children came galloping upon them, leaping and clinging to Conor as if he was their favourite rocking-horse.

'Hup there, Rosaleen, Diarmaid,' he cried, lifting them up. There was always horseplay when he came delivering milk. He swung them about, tickled them, chased them round the Landrover, while they squealed with delight. It was a ritual they expected and he was happy to indulge, though had anyone asked him if he was fond of children he would have been mystified, never having considered the matter. Sometimes they kept him half-an-hour till their mother rescued him. So that it wasn't till he was halfway down the drive that he remembered Neve's remarks, and accelerated in anxiety to return.

All was quiet when he swung into his yard. He ran to the door, pushed it open. Dorothy, swathed in an apron, was at the cooker, pans were bubbling. 'Another fifteen minutes,' she said, brushing a forearm across her flushed cheeks. 'Sit down and I'll bring you a drink.'

The Australian accent was like sweet music. He grinned with relief. 'I'll just take the empty churns back up to Riordans.'

There before the Riordans' front-door stood McCarthy's fat Mercedes, a sight that normally made him seethe. But tonight it was almost a symbol of reassurance, not being a garda car.

'Would you ever take a look at our car?' pleaded Mrs Riordan, meeting him as he brought the empty churns into their dairy. 'It's sitting there like a dead hen, and I've dozens of messages to do in the morning.'

He nodded. 'Neve had the Gardai round. They didn't call up here, then?'

Mrs Riordan shook her rotund face. 'What did they want?'

'Some enquiry about those bombings in the north.'

He lifted the bonnet of the red Datsun just as Nuala came out of the front door of the house, wearing an olive-green dress. She was ushered by the dandily-suited Niall McCarthy into the passenger seat of the Mercedes. McCarthy gave him a salute of the hand before getting into the driver's seat. 'Keep up the good work, Conor.'

Only half able to see, such was his annoyance at what he felt were condescending words, Conor peered uncomprehendingly at the murky engine, the maze of grimy pipes and wires. With unerring instinct or amazing intuition his groping hand accidentally dislodged the main cable off the battery terminal. Its looseness could be the problem. As he went to collect the toolkit from the Landrover, the Mercedes slid opulently away, its exhaust purring like a contented cat.

After cleaning the terminal, hammering the clip down and tightening it with a spanner, he went round to turn the key. Gratifyingly, the engine burst into life.

'You're a marvel, Conor,' exclaimed Mrs Riordan. 'What would we do without you?'

'Don't forget your usual remark now,' called Vaun, passing. 'That we need a man about the place.'

'He might keep you in a bit of order,' shouted her mother.

'He might make an honest woman out of me,' said Vaun over her shoulder as she went into the house.

'You'd soon get your ears boxed for your impertinence,' her mother shouted after her. She turned to Conor, breathless with irritation. 'Vaun is the only one of my children to cause me bother. The others were always obliging and considerate.' Conor forebore from reminding her of Sean and her despair at his drinking. 'I just don't understand where she gets her lip from. There are times when she's like the warbles under my skin.'

'Maybe she finds it difficult to keep up with all these bright sisters before her, Mary a doctor, Eileen a teacher, Nuala a weaver.'

'You'd make excuses for anyone, Conor.'

He was becoming anxious to return home, still gnawed by a faint anxiety about the gardai. He put the toolkit back into the Landrover. 'What were you thinking of when you were her age, Mrs Riordan?'

'Getting married and raising a family, I suppose.'

'Then I suspect Vaun is like you.'

'Get away with you, Conor,' she exclaimed as he started up the engine. 'You'd try and argue me into a pair of shoes half my size.'

You're not here to argue, de Burgh, you horrible Irish turd, you're here to get off your festering arse and shift wherever I tell you. Her Right Honourable Majesty the Queen, God bless her soul, does not run a creche for twelve-stone jellybabies, she has honoured you with her uniform to protect her realm from the likes of Gadafy, Amin and Brezhnev, and when they turn up with their screaming hordes there won't be time to cock a leg or open your bleeding mouth to argue, it'll be the first fucking fully-fit fighting man into action and blast them off this sceptred isle and chase them all the way back to Benghazi, understand, you miserable worm-faced, sister-screwing tit-sucker?

Pay attention, men. The IRA are the only preserved terrorists in the world. And Ireland is their nature reserve, all of it. Ulster is the part where there is a shooting-season. Now being shooting men you probably know you're not supposed to bag hens. Only cocks. Something to do with the hens being sacred to carry on the breed for the next season. Though it beats me why anyone should want to perpetuate this species. But we don't want to get into anything political, do we? We're just the scum of the British Army, doing our duty as cannon-fodder. The great British public, god bless them, get very upset when any of our boys cops one. That's if they happen to register the information on the news between the Scargills and the tits and bums. And our political masters don't like it when the voters start cribbing. So they've issued strict instructions about not getting in the way of IRA bullets or bombs. This means ambushes are out of bounds to all ranks between the hours of 6 a.m. to 6 a.m. Another problem we have is that there is an alternative terrorist breed inhabiting the same reserve. And they are out of season at all times. Whatever they do to us. This is because they worship the same God as our Noble Queen, God bless her. How do you tell them apart? you ask. They both speak the same incomprehensible bungle of the English language. They both wear the same blue anoraks. So you shout out, Fuck the Pope. If they cheer, don't fire. If they loose off at you, those are the McCoys. Let them have it and pray they're not a bunch of women and kids. If you lay a hand on anyone under ten, even if he's cuddling a Kalashnikov-40, nobody'll want to be in your shoes. At this point you may ask, how does one tell them apart from the indigenous population? If you see someone running doubled-up carrying a Sam missile, no problem, bang, bang. Except that he could be one of ours. If you meet a parson with his dog-collar and carrying an umbrella, and think of saying good morning, reverend, don't, get down fast, that umbrella's probably recoilless, the man's probably a commandant of one of their top cells. You see a squat over-weight granny borne-down with shopping bags, and you think to offer her a hand. Call the back-up quick, she's probably laden with TNT. I hope you're beginning to see the problems now. Any questions?

'Smells good,' said Conor, entering the kitchen, instantly admiring her subconscious dissemination of femaleness, the turned wrists, cocked hips, unflung throat, and her eyes and lips rich as fruitcake. He folded her close, kissed her. It felt so electrifying to have a woman in his arms, bodies pressed willingly together, vibrant as jets of water, firm as a sheaf of corn.

'Don't undo me before supper,' she whispered, pushing him away. 'Come on, it's all ready.' She led him to his chair, then brought the casserole from the stove, followed by a dish of potatoes, took the lids off and sat down. 'I had to make do with what I could find.' She ladled several spoonfuls on to his plate, then anxiously watched his expression as he tasted it.

He put a hand across to rest it on hers. 'You're full of hidden delights today.'

She pulled her hand away, covered her face and unexpectedly, began to cry. 'Don't say so many nice things to me, I can't take it.' Her voice rose to a little-girl wail. She got up and ran to the sink, dabbed her eyes with water, looked at herself in the little shaving mirror hung above the tap. 'Talk about something else before I become a mess.'

Disturbed at her emotionalism, he was uncertain how to react. 'When I was down at the cheese-factory, a squad-car from Ennis was just leaving. Neve said they were looking for those people from the north who blew up the bus full of school-kids.'

'Strewth,' she exclaimed, returning to the table, blinking. 'You don't half change the subject.' She began to busy herself eating.

'You people must find our troubles pretty strange?' he said.

She shrugged. 'We have our guilt too, you know. The civil rights of the Abos.' She frowned, considering a mouthful.

77

'Could do with some garlic.' She waved her empty fork in the air. 'We've got great backsides for sitting on the fence. Look at the situation in Poland. What else can you expect from the commies, they say. But the old country? That's a bad business, they shake their heads. You'd think they could sort that one out. What do you feel about it?

'This is really tasty,' he said, helping himself to another spoonful.

'Don't prevaricate. D'you think the British should get out?'

'The protestants think of Ulster as British.'

'Come on, what's your gut response?'

'Suppose there existed a great cluster of old ramshackle buildings that over the centuries had risen up, one on top of the other, leaning against each other, holding each other up, and now the whole structure is in a dangerous condition. But there's nowhere else for the residents to go. If an architect was called in, what would be the first thing he'd suggest?'

'Pull the whole thing down and start afresh?'

'But there'd be fierce resistance from the residents. Some would refuse to accept the structure was dangerous, others would protest their particular section was of historical merit. And even if they could be persuaded that it was so dangerous it must be dismantled, do you imagine they'd ever agree on the form of the new building?'

'There's always hope.'

'There's always genocide.'

'Tinned peaches for pud. And creamed goat's cheese.' She dished him out a portion. 'Here we are feasting like plutocrats, far from the crazy crowds and their lunacy, alone in a beautiful landscape not unlike the Garden of Eden. What can we do to put the world to rights? We're as powerless as fleas.'

Conor was halfway through his second glass of Guinness, his head felt rich and herbaceous, dense with verdant words and lily-tongued. He wanted to draw them close with talk. 'Will you mind if I say a few more nice things about you? Like the way you move, the way you use your body, that sort of casual, confident control that is a pleasure to watch, like the swallows effortlessly. . . .'

She held up a hand. 'It was just chance that guided me to you.'

'No,' his fat therapist had said. 'Chance is an excuse used by those who don't want to take responsibility for their lives. Your life is your own, nobody else's. You have the freedom to choose if only you will take it.' He sighed. 'But my depression was caused by a terrible mistake.' She shook her many chins. 'You are not to blame. It was simply a combination of circumstances.' 'I would have called a combination of circumstances, chance,' he muttered. She avoided reacting by staring fixedly at her watch. 'Don't you think you must take risks in order to live a full life? Would you never drive out into the country for a picnic for fear of having an accident?' It was his turn to avoid reacting: 'I learned the perversity of chance in childhood. I was in the garden once when a stone flew past my face. I didn't see where it came from. But it smashed a glass cloche to bits. There was nobody else but me in sight. The evidence to my parents was irrefutable. When I denied it, they said how despicable to add to my crime by lying. Their disapproval of me over the next few days almost made me capitulate, admit to it just to get forgiven.' The therapist waved a finger. 'Have you ever considered that could be an example of where you deliberately obscured the truth to yourself? For reasons you did not like to admit to? Perhaps you were suffering feelings of resentment towards your parents at the time?' He laughed. 'You're one of them, aren't you?'

Conor ate a portion of peaches. 'I suppose there must be somebody back there? You're bound to have a fellow, an attractive girl like you.'

She licked a dollop of cream cheese off her lower lip and nodded. 'I'm engaged, would you believe it?' She grinned, made her frog-like grimace. 'He's my insurance policy. No, you needn't look at me like that. It was his idea. He spent years talking me into it.'

Conor nodded, thinking of Nuala. Wouldn't he have accepted her on those sort of terms if she'd given into him? 'What does he do?'

'He's a barrister. He's bright and handsome.' She shrugged. 'It's unbalancing to have someone want you too much. They topple over, put themselves out so much they demean themselves. I've done it, too. You become somebody else, no longer the person who was fanciable in the first place.'

'Would you like to be married?'

'It's men who like the idea of marriage. They've been tricking women into it for centuries. And mothers, damn their blinkered eyes. What do they think they're up to? There they are, trapped in their own stale worn-out rabbit-hutch frustrations, and what do they do but try and pitch their daughters into the same misery.'

'It's this problem of forming an alliance, because each sex appears to like each other's company. Isn't it possible to share a life on equal terms?'

She laughed. 'If you were proposing to a girl, would you expect them to come and share this isolated place with a bunch of goats and no bath?'

'Yes.'

'But what about the girl's life? Why wouldn't you go off and share hers?'

'Aren't you an agrarian economist?' he asked, waving his arms round. 'Isn't there land enough here?'

'But we're not talking about me . . .' Her voice trailed away. 'Are we?'

He stood up, his chair scraping the flagstones. A passionate declaration rang in his mind, but all he said was: 'I want to go to bed with you.'

'Supposing I don't want to go to bed with you?'

'We could play racing demon or watch the late news,' he replied.

But she stood up and kissed him. 'I must go to the lavatory first.'

When she entered the bedroom, she was wearing only her blouse and carried the rest of her clothes. He was lying stretched out on the bed. As she turned to put the clothes on a chair, he noticed a number of marks across her buttocks. A flicker of disquiet crossed his mind. He had forgotten.

As she knelt on the bed and began to crawl up on him, her breasts hung over him like two giant incisors, her white teeth gleamed as if some unimaginable retribution was about to be exacted upon his totally exposed body. Then her breasts melted on to his chest and her lips closed softly over his mouth. 'I like your smell,' she murmured. 'It's like vanilla pods.'

'What would you like me to do?' he whispered.

'Eat me,' she replied, turning round. As her striped behind lowered her crotch close to his mouth, it seemed like some symbolic stigmata of centuries of man's brutality to woman swollen witih the intention of engulfing him. Then all extraneous thought was whisked away to his centre and sucked up in a pillar of sensation.

*

The night was short and warm. Conor was woken by a gold bar of sunlight glowing on the wall. Dorothy lay as flat as a fillet of plaice, deeply asleep. In the sharp early-morning light he could see pale outlines delineated on her skin as if labels had been removed. He covered her with a sheet. Crossing the room his left foot kicked a small notebook that he could see must have fallen from her jeans as they hung over the chair. As he picked it up, the chafed black cover fell open. He could not help reading the name on the flyleaf. And rereading it. Josephine Grant.

He felt as if his heart had stopped. Without turning his head, he let his eyes swivel to check she was still asleep. Quickly he knelt to replace the notebook on the floor beside the chair-leg. Then, still keeping an eye on her, he collected his clothes and took them into the kitchen. Belle wagged her tail and yawned. He filled the kettle for hot water to wash and shave with. His heart still seemed barely to move, all his reactions numbed with shock. He shivered. He did not know what to do, what to think. It seemed important to keep going, functioning at least.

While he fed the pigs and cleaned out the suckling cows, he found that he was continually looking over his shoulder, as if expecting her to creep up on him. However ridiculous the likelihood he could not rid his mind of the threat. He kept finding himself peering in the direction of the house, checking to see if the door was still closed, expecting to glimpse a face at the windows, listening in case he heard footsteps.

Sir, To whom should we impute the blame for childhood terrors, for things that go bump in the night and bogeymen stalking in the woods? As the stew burns on the cooker, the baby sits screaming in his high-chair, and husband shouts from in front of the TV for his tea, what does mother do as she spies little daughter opening the backdoor and about to toddle out into the night? Don't go out there, she shouts, or the monster'll get you. Then at bedtime Dad reads her a fairytale to lull her to sleep. Little Red Riding-Hood? Hansel and Gretel? The Three Little Pigs? Heavens alive, people say, children love to be frightened. And others add, but we must teach them to be on their guard. There are indeed strange people out there. The trouble is that the child-molester is not usually a fierce vulpine creature with dripping fangs, he's likely to be some friendly uncle figure full of jokes and carrying a bag of sweets. Yours, etc.

Conor jumped at the sudden clatter in the yard. It was the arrival of the goats herded in by the indefatigable Belle. When he entered the kitchen cautiously, to fetch the buckets, all was quiet. There was only the tick of the clock on the wall. He did all the milking that morning facing the house. Despite the unconcern of thirty goats wandering about, a sky like a glowing sapphire, swallows cartwheeling overhead, choirs of blackbirds and chaffinches in the trees.

He was washing out the buckets in the sink after filling the churn. 'You should have called me and I'd have come and helped.' He jumped so violently at the sound of her voice that he dropped the bucket with a clatter in the sink, spinning round, not knowing what to expect. She was standing before him, yawning, and still as naked as when he had last seen her.

'You gave me a fright,' he exclaimed. The vulnerability of someone naked was totally disarming. Tension drained from him so fast he almost collapsed, and had to hold on to the sink.

'I must have slept like last year's Christmas pudding,' she said. His eyes darted from nipple to navel. 'I'll make you some breakfast while you're taking the milk up to Riordans.' She turned back, silent-skinned, in the doorway. 'By the way, why do you always take the milk up there?'

'I haven't a cooler. Theirs is big enough for all we produce between us.'

She nodded. 'I approve of cooperation.' And soundlessly was gone.

He turned the buckets up to drain and carried the churn out to the Landrover, his thoughts whirling in turmoil. It said in the papers that there were extradition papers out for Josephine Grant by the CID in London in connection with bombings there as well. How could she be that sort of person, a cold-blooded, ruthless killer?

Riordans seemed unusually deserted as he humped the churns into the dairy. He looked into the kitchen, called out, but there was no response. Both the car and the tractor were parked outside the sheds. He walked into the haggard. A cow and her newly born calf were lying peacefully by the Dutch barn. He was about to turn back when he caught a glimpse through the far gate of goats clustered in the paddock beyond. When he reached the gate he saw Vaun, Mrs Riordan and old Tom amongst them, milking. He knew Mrs Riordan and Tom found it difficult to manage, so he hurried across to see if he could help.

'Conor,' groaned Mrs Riordan as she tried to ease her bulk down to the level of a goat's udder.

'Let me,' he said, helping her to stand up.

She rested a hand on his shoulder. 'That's the best suggestion there's been today. I'd appreciate it, Conor.'

'The cavalry to the rescue,' cheered Vaun, just her head showing above the back of a nanny-goat. 'Why don't you and Uncle Tom get your breakfast, Mam? I know you hate milking, Uncle Tom.'

'It's not me that hates milking,' said old Tom, creaking to his feet. 'It's the back that hates it. And the fingers that hates it. And the knees that hates it. Going to Mass once a week is enough for my old knees. I'll bring the full buckets with me.'

'Nuala not well this morning?' Conor asked, busying himself with the milking. He was glad of a diversion from the prospect of Josephine Grant.

'None of us knows how well she is this morning. She didn't come home yet.'

Conor looked across at Vaun, imagining she must be joking.

'I expect she was deflowered in forty different artistic fashions in the bridal suite at the Spa Hotel,' she said. 'Or in the back of McCarthy's Mercedes.'

'No wonder your mother was acting strange. She must be worried out of her mind.'

'Aren't you green with jealousy?'

Conor moved on to another goat. 'I'd be worried in case there's been an accident. Did anyone ring the hospitals?'

'Mam nearly died this morning when the squad-car passed by, thinking it was going to pull in and tell us bad news. I told her the gardai don't usually call out specially to inform mothers their daughters have lost their virginity.'

'You didn't really say that, did you, Vaun, you're dreadful,' groaned Conor.

'Anyway, I don't suppose you're bothered now you've got Dorothy down there.'

Conor tried to steady his reactions with a deep breath.

'If I'd been you,' said Vaun archly. 'I'd have had her knickers off quicker than the ring off a beercan.' She got up to empty her pail into a larger bucket. 'I don't know how Nuala resisted McCarthy for so long. She told me he was always trying to get her up to the flat above the gallery for a bit of you know what. I asked her if she fancied him at all. He's just a good businessman, she said. So maybe he's made her an offer she couldn't refuse.'

'I don't believe any of it,' said Conor emphatically. 'It doesn't sound like her.'

'Still hoping she's keeping it for you?' Vaun asked sweetly.

He would have liked to empty a bucket of milk over her head, but forebore.

'They probably had a breakdown. She could have stayed with your aunt in Kilfenora.'

As they spoke the goats had begun to turn and face the road and flow towards it in one coordinated movement, even those being milked pulled away. 'Come back, you pinheads,' shouted Vaun, futilely.

The goats fanned out along the wall that bounded the road, many of them standing on their hindlegs and placing their front hooves on top to peer over, others jumping and standing on the wall, till there was a long line of horned heads all gazing with wrapt attention in the same direction, at something that was passing along the road.

Leaving their buckets, Vaun and Conor hurried down to discover the cause of this extraordinary behaviour.

Walking along the road, not a little alarmed at the formidable array of horned creatures so intently interested in it, was a large but young fawn Great Dane dog. Following it came Nuala and Niall McCarthy, hand in hand, she still in the green dress she had set off in the evening before, and he in his shirt-sleeves, his jacket draped over a forearm, apparently out for a morning stroll. Behind them the sleeping stone hills were like pewter in the early morning sun.

'Isn't he beautiful?' cried Nuala, pointing at the great dog, who was casting anxious glances at the goats, and dropping back to be near her. 'Niall bought him for me. He's an engagement present. Niall'll keep him in Galway for now.'

'That's a grand parade to welcome us,' laughed Niall, waving a hand at the goats. He had a pale pudgy face freckled like nougat, and wispy red hair.

Conor could willingly have shot him.

All right men, settle down, take it easy. I've called this parade because all of us are bloody angry. Come on, settle down. I share your anger absolutely. In my book it's completely justified. Three members of our battalion dead, five severely injured. By a dastardly and cowardly act. But we are not the same as the ruthless murderers who carried out the killing. I repeat that. We are not the same. We will not stoop to such a level of human behaviour. Do I make myself clear? I know exactly what you feel. You want revenge. Those who died were our mates, they were a part of us. But revenge is not the answer. It's too good for murderers, too quick. What we want is justice. It's only when killers are brought into court and their crimes paraded and proved for all to see, that people will understand what they are, cruel, mindless thugs. That is not a description I want applied to us. We are British soldiers, honourable men, loyal to our Queen and all that she stands for. We are not sodding brutes who don't give a fig for human life. You can rest assured that with the snappy undercover work of our intelligence section, we'll catch up with these criminals in no time at all. And hand them over for burial. Is that clear? Right. Dismiss.

*

It was unbelievable, thought Conor as he took the Landrover back. All in the space of a couple of hours, Nuala engaged to that creep McCarthy and Dorothy deformed into a dangerous terrorist. He felt close to despair, a black pit of emptiness opening at the sense of loss. However unobtainable Nuala had been, at least she had always been there, and hope was rekindled at every sunrise. He sat in the yard, the engine switched off, hands still gripping the steering-wheel. And all the time, Maggie or Dorothy or whatever her name was, had really been Josephine Grant, murderer of innocent children. He closed his eyes, sweating. He had begun to feel something for that woman, damn her. What was fate playing at? He could remember his feeling of relief as the plane levelled out, at last, thank God, you're beautiful, you glass pig . . . but what were those stupid trees doing there, standing in the way like reactionless drunks?

He slammed the door of the Landrover and crossed the cobbles. The kitchen was rich with the aromas of fried eggs and bacon and coffee. Dorothy, swathed in an apron, wiped her brow. 'That was well-timed. I was afraid you'd be back long before I was ready. I was running my legs off for ages to get washed and clean up after last night.' She placed a plate of succulent breakfast before him.

He sat down, forestalled by such domesticity and his own hunger. 'Dramas up there,' he began. 'That's why I was so long . . .' and he began to explain.

Dorothy ate her own breakfast as she listened. 'Must have been quite a kick in the guts for you. I know you fancied her.'

His anger suddenly returned. 'Not half such a kick in the guts as . . .' he hesitated, as if caught up in a last minute debate about the wisdom of such confrontation.

'As what?' she asked, puzzled.

'Finding out that you haven't been telling me the truth.'

She put her knife and fork down. 'About what?'

'About who you are.'

'Who do you think I am?'

'Josephine Grant.'

Her expressionless reaction was disconcerting. 'Josephine Grant?' she echoed. And for a moment he thought he had made a terrible mistake.

'It's not the person that matters to you then?' The Australian accent had vanished beneath sharp Belfast inflexions. 'It's how they're labelled?'

He continued eating as if trying to ignore the dangerous ground they were entering. 'I thought we were getting to know each other. But there seem to be a few things you didn't tell me.'

'Tell you what?' she demanded. He felt a pang of regret for the loss of that ready affection that had been in her eyes before breakfast.

'The killings. That busload of kids.'

Her eyes narrowed. 'What do you know about these things except what's been on the news?'

'No sane person could condone the murder of innocent

children.' He wondered if she carried a gun, whether it was wise to confront her. She was growing angrier by the second.

'You sit down here safe in your ivory tower and pontificate with all the self-righteousness of a priest telling women with six kids and a drunken husband on the dole how to run her marriage. You don't live in a country occupied by foreign troops. You don't live in a country ruled by a foreign power so that you have no voice in anything. So how the hell can you understand anything of what goes on?'

'But nothing was ever achieved by murdering children.'

'Do you imagine anyone would deliberately set out to blow up a busload of schoolkids? It's the insane press had to make a show of it, use the chance to paint us black and obscure the true facts.'

'What true facts?' The conversation was making his skin prickle.

'Why did the army take that bus down a road that had been mined many times before?'

'But couldn't you see it was full of kids?'

She got up to fetch a leather bag he had never seen before from the sofa, pull the zip and take out . . . for a moment his heart stopped. But it was only a packet of cigarettes. She lit one, her hands shaking a little, exhaled. He had never seen her smoke before.

'It was remote-controlled. That was never mentioned by the press.' Muscles in her jaw flickered, tautening and loosening, altering the shape of her face like fingers behind the skin of a glove puppet. 'Will you turn me in?'

He could not take his eyes off her, this woman who was radically changed, yet remained the same in outward appearance. He continually searched her face for signs of the monstrous and pitiless person within her, yet she seemed more nervous than he would have expected, unsure of herself and agitated. He shook his head. 'If you've been on the run how do you know what the press has been saying?'

'I wasn't on my own, you know. That lamb was meant for four of us.'

Conor was alarmed. 'Where are they?'

She laughed tersely, clouded with exhaled cigarette smoke. 'Don't worry your little bourgeois soul, they'll be many miles further south by now. You scared them off.' Just for a moment a flicker of feeling loosened her expression, then it hardened again. 'That little wood in the glen, so secret and far from anywhere, happened to be remembered by one of us. He'd done a botany degree at Galway. We're not all mindless cretins, you know. Some of us happen to be educated idealists.'

'Not too many I should imagine.'

'You know nothing about us. You're like the whole sub-island and the fat leech lying off to the east, packed with prejudices like a tin of frankfurters is full of preservatives.'

'But why were you on foot, hiding out in the wild? Why didn't you use cars, get to safe houses?'

'You demonstrate the reason. You've got the same pedantic chip of logic stuck between your eyes as every police inspector from Malin Head to Skibbereen. That's what we were expected to do.' She stubbed her cigarette out on the edge of her plate. 'We've been training to live rough for just such a contingency. Imagine the hysteria from across the water if that bus had been packed with the military. A dozen of their lovely boys in bits. The south would have been bludgeoned into finding us.'

'I don't understand how you can delight in killing.'

'Don't be wet. This is war. There's ten thousand of them parading round our little corner of Ireland, each one like a miniature arsenal. They're not there for decoration. When are people like you and a few million others going to appreciate there is no democratic process available in the north?'

'But how can you ever win? The prods are four to one.'

'So what are we supposed to do? Just sit around in ghettoes till Adolf Paisley remembers the Final Solution did wonders for the Jews? You're afraid of reality, Conor. Reality is a dirty business. It's like the jungle, eat or be eaten. That's why you cling to this place, the nearest you can get to the Garden of Eden.'

'Have you . . . ever actually killed anyone?'

She picked up the aluminium teapot, filled her cup. 'Is it important?'

He was silent for a moment. 'I'm damned glad I thrashed you.'

'That's great. Listen to the big man.' Then she laughed. 'That's the first bit of genuine feeling I've heard from you. I'd have been ten times angrier if I'd been you.'

Her words stung him. Like a pianist incarcerated in darkness reaching out and feeling an imaginary keyboard, the skin of her body was reshaped under his fingers and he remembered all the words he had been unable to speak, all the emotions that he wrung out mute as he fucked her.

He poured himself more tea, action to hide the disturbance within, as she took another cigarette from the packet, struck a match. 'I'd better be going. It was a mistake to have stayed.'

His voice shook. 'I want to understand.'

'No leopard changes his spots,' she exclaimed. 'Trying to talk to you would be like arguing existentialism with a faith-to-God catholic.'

'Why d'you say that?' he retorted, shocked that anyone could think him so illiberal.

'You've been hiding your true colours, Conor. From what I've found out.'

'What do you mean?'

'You were in the Brit military, stationed near Enniskillen. you were fighting us. You're an enemy, Conor.'

He could not prevent his colour rising. 'You've been nosing in my files,' he shouted angrily.

'It's on our check-list, always confirm your host's credentials. There are more grasses to the square mile of Ireland than blades growing in your paddocks. So what have you to say now, Conor?'

'It was a long time ago,' he protested.

She looked at him, an elbow on the table, cigarette stuck between two fingers, licking a fragment of tobacco off her lower lip, waiting. He felt himself go cold, sweating, as if this was the hour of accounting he had always half-expected. Since his military service was something he had regretted the more his political awareness grew, he could not help feeling on the wrong foot, even before this . . . terrorist. 'What about the last few days?' he asked, searching her face for signs of the response he desired.

'I could have killed you any time,' she said. He thought the cigarette in her hand shook like his own tremor of fear.

'I could do the same now,' he retorted. 'Self-defence against a dangerous criminal.'

She shook her head. 'You wouldn't kill me, Conor. It's not in you to kill a woman. But we're different, and we don't like traitors.'

'Why talk like this? You know I'm not a traitor.'

'Grovel, Conor, go on, plead for mercy. Now it's my turn.'

'Doesn't it mean anything that I've changed?' He swallowed

angrily. It seemed ridiculous that he had no control over this situation, could not rationalise it. It should be her trying to justify her actions, not he his. 'I was only eighteen, then. What were your politics when you were eighteen. I bet you didn't have any clear ideas.'

'When I was fourteen, three UVFs burst into our lounge one evening. They shot my dad in front of us. He'd never held a gun in his life. He was a school-teacher, he loved kids. But he happened to be local secretary of the SDLP. Those bastards should have shot me, too, because that night nailed me to the cause. My brother Dominic was seventeen, he spent most of his time listening to records or going fishing. He joined the provos the next night. Within six months he was caught in an SAS road-block. My mother's hair went white.' She went over to the window, stood with her back to him, looking out into the yard. 'She doesn't speak much now.'

'Perhaps I was like your brother,' said Conor. 'All I wanted to do was fly. I didn't even know what politics were. The airforce here had only a few antiquated jets they couldn't afford to fly. Being at school in England it was natural to try for the RAF. But I ended up flying choppers for the army.'

She turned round slowly. 'Killing your countrymen didn't concern you?'

He stood up. 'Why do you think I got out as soon as my term of service was up? Going there was my political awakening. I was sickened by what I saw.' He was suddenly conscious of how much larger he was than she.

'So you ran away to Australia?'

'D'you think I wanted to become part of a murderous crew like yours? Just what the hell good does it do, killing people? D'you imagine it makes everyone afraid of you? All it does is revolt people against you.'

'You've as much political wit as a hedgehog has road-sense. We want them to despise us. We're the bogeymen. They respect us.'

'You're mad,' he exclaimed. 'Nobody respects you.'

'Not in feelings or words. By deeds. Fifteen thousand of their best troops tied down. Millions of quid of taxpayer's money spent keeping them there. England hobbled with security checks. And half the world saying, tut, tut, how come the British, the great mother of democracy, can't keep her house in order. When someone has a knife at your throat, you respect them, however much you hate them, boy, do you respect them.'

'And you imagine that eventually they're going to say to hell with it, it's all yours?'

'Come on, Conor, don't insult us. There's still more than a million bone-headed Prods to be dealt with.'

'What are you going to do with them, butcher them, one by one?'

She stubbed out her cigarette. 'I knew it would be a waste of time talking to you. You're all the same, you want your little lives to continue without interruption. If injustice is out of sight, it doesn't exist. I think I'll be going.'

'Where'll you go in broad daylight?'

He half-wanted her to go, half-wanted her to stay. He wanted the spiky, rabid terrier person to go, the hard-line ideologist it was impossible to argue with. But he was attracted to the small defiant woman. He thought he detected beneath the harsh bluster a desperate uncertainty. There seemed to be a constant internal battle indicated by the muscles in her jaw, the restlessness of her large brown eyes that seemed to be trying to escape from beneath her crushing brows, and her hands gripping and clutching at the air, herself, her cigarette or the table like those of a blind person trying to establish their whereabouts. There was something alarming about her as well, suggestive of an unstable volatility that might suddenly erupt. He did not expect her to shoot at him all of a sudden, even if she had a weapon, but all this snap-arguing made him extremely tense.

'What do you care?' she cried. 'You needn't bother your head about me.'

He moved closer, within reach of touching her. 'I do care. You know I do.'

She seemed to shrink inside herself, like a retracting tortoise. 'I know no such thing. We've nothing in common.'

He stood still. 'Have it your own way. If that's the way you want it.'

'You're like all men.' She spat out the words, her head low but tilted up at him, eyes dark. 'You say things to a woman to make her feel wanted, when all you want is to screw her body.'

He found himself unaffected by her venom this time.

'The historical obligation,' she continued, more as if to herself. 'Buy her a couple of vodkas and expect to pump your seed into her. Why wouldn't you, they say. Where's the harm? It's

91

as natural as shelling peas. I shouldn't have come into your house. I should have known you'd be no different.'

'I've known women act insulted if the man they're out with doesn't make a pass,' said Conor, going over to the kettle to make more tea. 'But I don't see you as a woman in particular. I just see you as a . . . terrorist.'

But she did not seem to hear, and ranted on. 'Even when we'd be sitting in a car, watching a target, they'd start. My wife hates me, Josephine. I haven't had it in ages, I get this terrible pain. You've got a lovely body, Josephine. They resent it when you refuse, take it as a personal insult and get stroppy, make life a bloody misery.'

'Is that how you came to . . . ?' he began, realising as he spoke that it was an error.

'God,' she exclaimed. 'Is that all you think of women? How typical, how bloody typical. We couldn't possibly have the same ideals, the same understanding as men, could we? We're only second-class, aren't we? We're only useful as cooks and camp-followers?'

Conor brought a fresh pot of tea over to the table. 'As a means to an end a fuck is a bit less terminal than a bomb. So why does it bother you if you're an idealist?'

'You know as well as I do,' she exclaimed. 'It wouldn't matter if men saw women as equals. But they treat us like apples. Once they've taken a bite, we're reduced to apple-cores.'

He refilled her cup. 'I don't want any favours.'

'O yes?' she asked mockingly, lighting another cigarette. 'So what do you want?'

'We could try to understand each other better.'

'What's the point?' she exclaimed tersely. 'You'll try and persuade me that human life is sacred and all that crap. And I'll try and persuade you that democracy is fine for those who already have it, but doesn't work for those who haven't. . . .'

'And all that crap,' he interjected.

Her first smile flickered, albeit briefly. 'And you'll try and persuade me that the north is none of your business, that you really love living up to your arsehole in shit. And I'll try and persuade you that we are dedicated to a Socialist United Ireland and that death is the only tactic we have like the cigarette-end to burn off the fat leeches on our backs. And so on, bombarding each other with clichés, world without end. We should get married.'

92

He laughed. 'Have you thought how alike we are?'

She crushed out her cigarette, still sprawled in her chair. 'I'd best be moving on.'

'Suppose I say I don't want you to go?'

The words vanished into invisibility, left them seated round the table like two people approaching each other across a vast empty expanse, and as they come near, their as yet unspoken greeting poises in infinite variety, its unknown form begins to swell to bursting.

'I see it all now,' she said. 'What's behind this is because Nuala is no longer available.'

Conor rose in his anger, banged a fist on the table. 'You're vicious, through and through.' He almost threw himself from the room, down the steps, tripping over the startled Belle. He hammered his boots across the cobbles and out on to the lane, clenched fists before him. He stormed down the grass-and-stone rutted lane along the valley bottom, his eyes unregarding, his mind like an incoherent tape-recorder winding back with shrieks of rage, playing forward brief garbled scenes that he cut-off instantly with furious shakes of the head.

Belle followed him about fifty yards behind in a series of hesitant dashes, wondering if she might be wanted. Cattle lifted their glistening noses from grazing, watched him stamp by with the same lowered heads they might present to a passing fox.

Sir, How can a country that calls itself civilised tolerate barbarians in its midst? Perhaps civilisation is too effete a concept. We are but decorative butterflies whose caterpillars ravage lilies. The mystery of the Mona Lisa relies on none of us putting a hammer through it. A darling child can be crushed from life by a passing car. So where should the sacredness of life begin and end? Upon the precept of trust. This mere animal achievement that allows us to walk the streets and mingle freely, knowing that we respect each other's persons. There are many who say that those who break this trust only demean themselves, and are poor, pitiable, pathetic creatures. But I say they have made their choice, and now their lives in turn should be forfeit. And thus we preserve the sacredness of life. Yours, etc.

He was well past the ruined farmhouse and high up at the end of the glen before he stopped his ranting pace. He flung himself down on to a boulder and sat looking back down the valley, his body still shaking.

How could he have sat and talked with such a creature? Drinking tea with a public enemy, a bus-bombing bitch from hell who couldn't give a fingernail clipping for the bereavement and misery she caused children, parents, wives, husbands. . . .

Darling it's very important not to give offence. You don't say, isn't that man fat, in a voice so loud that he can hear you. He might be very upset. Besides, he's not really all that fat. Imposing, perhaps. . . .

But that was only one of the many turbulences introduced by his mother, and thus, by association, all women. She, the cardiganed and tweed-skirted womb of his security, was always putting it at risk. She would go out and leave him. As simple as that. There was no resentment later against his father on that count, he expected him to be absent because he was consistently going out to work. He hated it most when she went out with the Duhallow Hunt. She would dress in a quasi-military uniform, crested buttons on her jacket, a velvet Norman helmet over the sausage-roll hairnet, her legs cased in black leather boots. Then she would ride off on a huge muscle-bound monster with iron feet. He knew that people were always being flung off them, having their limbs broken, even being killed. Perhaps that was one of the reasons he aspired to fly, admiring the confidence of birds that had no fear of falling because they never fell.

But she had always returned, brought back that aura of warm reassurance. Only when he reached the age of nine and she despatched him to boarding-school in England, did he cease to long for that enticing aura. At school it was rapidly brought home to him that not only was he alone, one among hundreds, but that mothers were soppy.

Attention was turned to a new form of female, though access was generally limited to paper versions. But conjecture was rife. General opinion had it that girls were large pink dolls into which you inserted part of yourself and then jumped up and down. They did not appear to have any other purpose. But they were an extraordinarily popular subject.

Some boys seemed quite unable to talk about anything else. There was much measuring of erected organs to establish record precedents for size. Some would stick their members up the bottoms of other boys to practise. Others had set up as dealers in a thriving second-hand business, in magazines that by the time they were finally shredded into illegibility, must have changed hands for twenty times their original cost. He had found that some of the women portrayed in them had been able to stir the dust from a faint memory that lingered from his childhood, a memory that still suggested enchantment. It sometimes rose from a particular conjunction of a smile and the texture and shadows between the breasts.

That bloody woman Josephine Grant had been right. He had looked at her with different emphasis since learning of Nuala's engagement. Trying to discern the woman underneath. Nobody could really be the odious monster the Press made out—despite the ratification bulleted out by her pitiless attitudes. It was possible to make excuses for her bitterness. Seeing their father killed before their eyes would twist the minds of most people. To some, vengeance might be the only expiation. But anyone could see her aggressive exterior was only a mask devised to hide behind, he thought. He sighed. At least she would be gone by the time he returned. That would be a relief. In one sense.

The valley lay scooped out before him, tranquil and green. The cattle were dotted about the glen, heads down. An Indian file of goats was emerging above the crests of the ash trees, climbing up the bluff. The sheep were all over the north hill, among the limestone boulders and outcrops. He had often thought of them as a mobile crop sprouting from the grass, woollen bushes full of meat. Only when close enough to look him in the eye, did they become individuals and stir him with guilt. Belle was lying about ten feet away, snout between forepaws, trying to be unobtrusive. While he got to his feet, she leaped up, watching him for instructions, quivering with excitement. Her obsequious enthusiasm annoyed him at once. 'Heel,' he growled, setting off for the house.

He turned into the yard and went behind the Landrover to enter the barn. He used the barn partly as a store for meal and tools, and partly as a workshop. The interior was well-lit, for he had taken off some of the old sheets of corrugated iron and replaced them with clear fibreglass sheets. Along the entire length of the back wall, some thirty feet long, hung huge folds of dusty plastic. He rested a hand on the big vice set up on the workbench beneath, and looked up. On closer examination there could be discerned the outline of a construction suspended inside, something familiar about its outline: a giant pair of wings.

He got up on the bench and began to pull the plastic sheeting off, folding it up. Based on the reconstruction of a pterodactyl, the wings were thirty feet long. He had been encouraged to consider the flying dinosaur because palaeontologists had calculated that the average pterodatcyl's body weighed about twelve stone, and some fossil bones discovered had made up a wingspan of thirty-six feet. However many experts disputed that the creatures could ever fly, reckoning the most they could manage was to glide; developing the wings as a system for catching prey by running and gliding, or swooping down from high points. So he had modified the design to follow the shape of a Horse-Shoe bat's wing. It seemed more logical to follow bats rather than birds. The body-weight ratio of a bat allowed its limited muscle power to flap its 'arms' enough to propel the thin membrane-covered wings up and down. But in experiments conducted with his father long ago, he had discovered that human arms were not strong enough to flap the necessary wingspan. So the principal problem that had constantly taxed his ingenuity ever since, was how either to augment the human arm, or substitute some other means of physically flapping the wings. He had read endlessly what others thwarted by the same limitations had attempted, waving their fists at the heavy heavens that kept them grounded. Everything he had tried so far was too clumsy, too heavy or too feeble. His arms remained like matchsticks trying to wave a marquee. But over the last few years he had been putting together a system that used powerful, lightweight springs.

'What on earth's that?'

Even as the voice spoke behind him he was caught in a conflict of dismay and excitement. He half-expected her to be different, and was surprised to find her unchanged, still with the belligerent stance, still wearing the furry scowl. As he explained about the wings and his plans, he was aware of his reactions like hot and cold water refusing to mingle in the shower head, struggling for supremacy, chill anxiety at her continued presence, yet warmth to see her again.

'So one day you'll be jumping off the bluff up there, to test them? But you won't try till you're sure. You'll experiment on the ground first?'

He couldn't tell whether she was mocking him, or really cared. 'So you didn't go yet?'

She had her arms locked across her body. 'You don't have to shit in your pants, I'll be gone soon. Don't want the local gestapo to find you've been harbouring one of the enemy.'

'I don't mind if you want to stay.'

'That's your politeness they taught you in the English schools. But you don't want the heavies to arrive and do you over, you don't want your peace disturbed.' She sighed. 'I'd probably feel the same if I were you. If you haven't got the stomach for the real world, people like me must make you scream inside.'

This time her words did not get under his skin. 'Is it safe for you to skip in broad daylight?'

'That's why I hung around,' she replied. She turned and pointed to a bicycle half-obscured by a wheelbarrow and some paper sacks of pigmeal. 'Can I buy that off you? And you've a lightweight blue hold-all in your room . . . ?'

'Take them.' He went across to pull the bike out, leaned down to check its tyre pressures. 'I don't use them.'

'I appreciate it, Conor.' She took the bicycle from him, wheeled it to the door. 'You carry on contemplating the metamorphosis of man to bird while I get ready. I'll give you a shout before I go.'

Conor sat on the workbench. He felt sad that she was going. Women always leave, he thought.

Sir, Whatever feminists may scream about the shortcomings of the male, the fact remains they begat us. For nine months they trotted about tossing us inside them like a maggot in a windy apple. They gave up smoking so we wouldn't be stunted. They were sick as cats, sweaty as navvies humping boulders. But were they doing it in the hope of a little girl? Did they put the boy babies out on the mountainside? Not a bit of it, they leaped up in the small hours, rammed their bulging breasts down the little sods' throats, changed their stinking nappies, dusted their little willies and crooned idiotic love songs over them. Then they spent years loving us, washing our smelly clothes, cooking us nourishing dishes, taught us to read. They never stopped looking after us. So what did they do? They made us utterly dependent on them. Yours, etc.

'Hallo,' came a hesitant voice from the yard. 'Is there anyone?' That doesn't sound like Josephine, he thought, puzzled. He went outside.

A girl in a light-blue track-suit stood astride a cycle in the gateway, as if she had just ridden up the lane. She wore dark glasses, and on the carrier behind her was strapped a blue zipper-bag. 'Excuse me, please,' she said in an accent he thought sounded Dutch. 'I look for a ruined . . . I think it is a fort, a round one.' She whirled a bangled wrist in the air to demonstrate.

Her hair was short, pressed against her skull like damp cress, perhaps sweaty from cycling. She wore a necklace of white beads round the base of her throat, set in the blouse-like opening of her track-suit, and matching white earrings. He did not recognise her at all.

'Very good,' he said. 'I wouldn't have known you.'

'Excuse me?' She wrinkled her nose. 'I do not understand?'

'Where'd you get all the gear from?' He waved a hand at her.

She put her head on one side. 'The gear?' she echoed, looking down at herself, bewildered. Then she twisted round and pointed at the back wheel of the bicycle as if suddenly enlightened. 'The gear, yes, yes, I have the gear.'

He laughed. But he began to feel uneasy, glancing at the house, wondering if Josephine might still be inside. The change of clothes had been rather speedy, the transformation quite amazing. He had a feeling his bicycle had been a woman's, too, but one bike looked much like another. Belle was walking round her, wagging her tail, but then she behaved like that with all women. And blue bags like the one on the carrier were commonplace as coca-cola cans. But of course it must be Josephine, how could he be taken in? 'All right, I'm convinced. The disguise would fool your mother. You're a tourist, cycling round Ireland. Holland, is it?'

She gave him a broad smile. 'Ja. I am from Holland, yes. From Amsterdam.' She held out her hand. 'Inika Van Winken.'

He took her hand, noting the white stone ring on her second finger, all the bracelets on her wrist. 'Inika . . . that's pretty.' Her hand was small, her fingers soft and lingering.

'And you?' she asked, her head on one side again. 'You are . . . ?'

'Conor de Burgh.' It felt stupid telling her his name.

'Conor,' she repeated. 'It sounds like a bird. But de Burgh? Is it Irish?'

As he explained the Norman origins of his name, she nodded and smiled, wet-lipped, with an ingenuous amiability he found attractive. 'You are with friends?' he asked, finding himself adopting the simplicity of her method of speaking English.

She nodded. 'I have been with them staying in Doolin.' As she spoke she got off the bicycle, leaned it against the yard gate. 'They are very liking the music. I like it, too, but there are too many peoples there, it is a very big crowd. I prefer a little time to be with myself. I like to see old places very much. So off I go and . . .' She waved a bangled wrist about, pointing at the countryside. 'I have never been where it is so empty and so beautiful. At home in the Netherlands we have half the land and four as much people, and it is all flat.'

'But you're so much richer than we are.'

'Of course, what do you expect? If it a boring land there is nothing to do but work and have money. If you have beautiful land, you do not need money in bank, big houses full of pictures, jewels, you already have richness round you.' She put her head on one side. 'You do not think so?'

He nodded. 'I think so. But most people who live in these parts would not agree.'

'Then I'm glad I have met with you.' She paused, looking round her. 'Am I correct, there is a round fort near here?'

'I'll show you if you like. But first may I offer you some refreshment?'

She looked baffled. 'Refreshment? What is that?'

'A drink perhaps. A cup of coffee or a glass of beer?'

She laughed. 'I am thinking you mean a bath. Thank you, that would be good after all the work with the bicycle.' But she seemed dubious, and glanced at the house, then back down the lane. 'You have . . . a wife?'

He shook his head. 'Why do you ask?'

'A woman on a bicycle pass me.' She nodded her head at the lane. 'I stop to ask her about the fort, but she is going like a train.'

The sunlight gleamed with polarised intensity on the roof slates of the house, on the cobblestones, on the metal frame of her sunglasses, on the bicycle, the gate, the Landrover, as if permanently etching that moment of time, stopping it in order to superimpose another image. Conor could feel his senses struggling to adjust and recognise it, aware of the switch between past and future hesitating for a fraction of a second, as if it might flick either way, his consciousness honed to such razor-sharpness that the slightest shiver might sever everything, even his sanity.

He blinked, shook his head. 'I don't have a wife. That was another visitor.'

He looked round the yard, at his house, the buckets at the back door, the wheel-barrow and four-grain fork by the pig-sheds, the Landrover beside the barn, the ring of roofs rising to the hazel and ash trees behind, and the distant hills beyond, and it all exuded unconcerned practicality as if shaped like a pair of gloves ready for wearing, a view ready for using daily, fitting the eyes with the same surety that an awakening myopic puts on their spectacles and knows the blur before them will instantly become clear. But in the midst of all this absoluteness there had materialised someone of questionable substance. A young supposed Dutch girl imposed upon the scene like a transfer upon the backscreen of a car, a passing fashion, a whim of the owner's, Nuclear War No Thanks this week, vote Fine Gael next week. If she was pretending to be someone else, then she would say she had just passed the person she really was, as a decoy. But on the other hand, if she really was whom she said she was, she would have passed the person she wasn't, anyway. Which left nothing clearer.

'First,' she said, following him into the kitchen as he crossed over to switch on the kettle. 'I need the toilet.'

He showed her the way, then quickly looked into the spare room. The big shoulder-bag was lying on the bed, and a few clothes. But he would have expected that. Travelling light on the bike. The blue zipper-bag wouldn't have held so much. He looked quickly through the clothes. Nothing with a name-tag. He tiptoed back into the kitchen, turned off the kettle. He wondered if he had caught this habit from Mrs Riordan, who, hospitable to the last, offered all and sundry cups of tea, and therefore was generally to be found heading to or from the kettle.

'You have not the basin?' Inika stood in the doorway. 'I look everywhere. It is in another room?'

He pointed to the sink. 'The bathroom's not finished yet.'

Now I'll catch her out, he thought, as she ran the tap to wash her hands. 'What brought you all the way to see this particular ring-fort? There are hundreds in these parts.'

She dried her hands on the towel he produced. 'It is called Caherconnacht?'

That surprised him. Not being one of the well-known ones, it was not on any map he knew. 'How did you hear of it?'

'I have a book. It is in my bag, I will show it. The writing is in Dutch, of course. Earlier I was come to Cahercommaun, with the cliffs. But in my book Caherconnacht is special. It is the only fort with a carving.'

'A carving?' he echoed. 'I've never seen it.'

'This is a picture. It is like a bird, or perhaps an angel.'

He shook his head as he made the coffee.

She pouted with disappointment. 'I have made a mistake? The book is old, maybe thirty years ago. I fetch it and you will see.'

He watched her unzipping the blue bag on the bicycle carrier. The notion of freedom of choice at each given moment of life, he thought, presupposes that others will not thwart these possible decisions. Does it assume that it will not upset other's choices? It must hope most will willingly contract an accord with it, either sacrificing their own, or accepting it as their choice. Thus the most influential such as the law, exert determinism on the rest. How could it be otherwise? Billions of lunatic humans wielding their individualities would rapidly terminate the species. He watched her tuck a book under her arm as she wrestled to rezip the bag, and observed relevant to his thoughts, how the crutch of her track-suit was so drawn up into the cleft between her buttocks that the fabric must be rubbing tightly against both privy orifices.

Sir, I must complain about the provocativeness of women's dresses. I can hardly believe it's an accident of fashion that their hindquarters are so explicitly depicted. In previous centuries the accentuation was on bosoms. Though even then there was much emphasis upon the cleavage, which will be noted by those with any anatomical experience, was duplicating the only other area of the human body that possesses such a juncture. However, at least then the reminders of this erotic zone were kept controllably beneath the male gaze while he could be distracted by the lady's wit, the sparkle of her eyes, the rose of her lips. Meanwhile the rest of her was so well-encased in petticoats and skirts that it took considerable unravelling should she wish to find some inner part of herself such as in the simple expedient of wishing to evacuate her bowels or shell out a child. Indeed a lady of fashion could have required the assistance of several persons well-versed in the intricacies of unlacing before she could present to her lover what Eve had only needed one bite of an apple to lay before Adam. What we have now is tantamount to provocation or the rape of the male as Judge Arvald made clear in *The Caucasian Chalk Circle*. Or else, whatever you ardent feminists may clamour, it must indicate loud and clear women's availability, and their everlasting emotional dependence. Yours, etc.

Inika spread the book out on the table, then paused. 'Last night I stay in Lisdoonvarna. At a Breakfast and Bed House. Do you know if there is one near to here?'

Conor waved a hand. 'This is a Guest House. It is not of very high standard. But allow me to offer you hospitality. Many farmhouses do the same.'

'You are recommended?' she asked. 'You are on the list provided by Bord Failte?' She pronounced the last words with the elaborate care of one who has recently been introduced to them.

He shrugged. 'My rates are very reasonable.'

She put her head on one side, musing. 'It would be convenient. What about the meals?'

'Of course. As you wish.'

She nodded and sipped her coffee, then returned to the book. He stood beside her as she turned the pages, watching her small slender fingers stroke them apart, admiring the slim conduit of her neck, the delicate flesh-shells of her ears, the pale-blue packaging over her salient body. The book was full of rather bad photographs interspersed with interesting pen-and-ink drawings. It seemed to be entirely about Ireland, but the text was Dutch. She spread it flat and pointed to an illustration. It was recognisably a ring-fort seen from the inside. The lintel stone over the doorway had a strange figure carved upon it, half-bird, half-man.

He shrugged, frowning. 'I think that stone is missing. The answer is for us to go and have a look.'

Halfway across a paddock on the floor of the valley, she stopped, rolling her dark-glassed gaze around. 'It is . . .' she searched for words. 'Prim . . . not primitive, but. . . .'

'Primeval?'

'I think so. My English is not good.' She waved a bangled wrist. 'Is it all yours?'

'The bank's.'

She laughed and shook her head. 'What can a bank know of this? You are a fortunate man.' She rested a hand on his arm. 'To live here like a king.'

He enjoyed the way she kept touching him. 'Unfortunately most of my subjects are stones.'

'I like places that are old,' she said as they continued on their way. 'My father he buys and sells old furniture. He has a business in Amsterdam. He comes to England many times with a big truck. I come with him sometimes. We go in the car and the truck comes afterwards. When it is full we go home. That is how I learn a little English.'

'Don't you have old furniture in Holland?'

'I think so, but the Americans they come and buy it all. So we have to come to England to fill up again. Restock, my father calls it.'

'So you're here in Ireland to buy antiques?'

'No, not at all. I am here with a holiday. I come with friends. We have a minibus with our bicycles on top. We are camping sometimes. If the weather is kind.'

By this time they had reached the slopes at the bottom of the grove of ash trees that rose up towards the bluff.

'I work at home with my father. I look after what is like a hospital where everything is made to be better. Often the furniture we buy has many legs missing, or maybe is full of cracks. And everything is always dirty. Afterwards we put on the polish. But we do not make them like new. My father he say we only give them back their dignity.' She put her head on one side. 'There are some who do not make the recovery. We have a little crematorium.'

Conor smiled at her, urging her on. He could not have admitted to himself that he was enraptured by her accent and peculiar manner of expressing the language.

'When I leave school six years ago, my father bring me to the office. He make me sit in a big *fin-de-siècle* chair. Now, he say, the business live for one hundred fifty year. Six generations of Van Winkens. How you like to be generation number seven? Of course I will be generation number seven I tell him. But first I will go to college and learn economics. Under his desk there is hiding a small refrigerator. He takes from it a bottle of champagne. I have not realise it mean a lot seven generations for my father. He calls to Claus Torpmeyer, foreman for the workshop, and Hendrik van der Maas, the manager, and then my uncle Carl he come, and later it feel very good to be the next Van Winken in the business. The first woman, say my uncle Carl. We have woman as queen, it is natural. I am two years now, working. I am getting the experience. I was to be a teacher, but this is better.'

Several times he had been tempted to point out some feature, a raven's nest just visible on a crag jutting out from the bluff, the badger earths, a red squirrel, but her quaint discourse dissuaded him. Now, as they emerged above the slope of ash trees and were climbing among the great piled slabs of lime-stone that constituted the bluff, Inika turned to look back, down into the valley behind them and across the views extending in all directions, and became silent, her mouth slack, her face going pale and shiny as lard, her hands reaching anxiously to grasp at every handhold of rock. A solitary raven, sentinel on a tall ash tree, regarding them suspiciously, gave a loud croak. Inika's legs gave way and she crumpled down. Conor grabbed her before she could fall, wedged her into a sitting position, her sunglasses falling off.

'I need to go down,' she murmured, saliva dribbling over her chin. As she tilted forward, Conor thought she was trying to throw herself down, and held on, while he heard the rasp in her throat and saw with surprise the creamy vomit spill out. He kept a hand firmly on each shoulder and when she had finished, pulled her back, fished a handkerchief from his pocket and passed it to her. She leaned against him, limp, her eyes closed, grey-faced. 'Please excuse me,' she murmured. 'I should not come. I get the vertigo.'

'I'll take you down,' he said. 'As soon as you feel you can manage.' She must only be used to flat land, he thought. No heights in Holland. But wait a minute . . . a thought came rising upwards like a bubble, then burst and was gone as it

104

reached the surface. All her limbs had gone slack, she had passed out cold.

For a while he sat supporting her dead weight, not knowing what to do for the best. Should he wait or slap her face to bring her round? Or just carry her down? He was startled when the huge black shape of a raven flew close overhead. But the raven was equally surprised, soaring upwards, its deep croaks like a string of imprecations. That decided him to bring her down. Perhaps the exertion might revive her. It was not easy to manipulate her inert body on the narrow path. First he had to haul her backwards till he reached the trees, then he was able to pick her up. Cradling her against his stomach, one arm under her knees, the other round her shoulders, her face close to his, he was aware of the dichotomy of his pleasure in holding her in a virtual embrace, of her palpable physical proximity and at the same time the strain of having to lean backwards to keep his balance, the difficulty of seeing where he was going, the fear of tripping over a root or rock. Once on the level he put her down on the grass. As he knelt beside her, he found he was soaked with sweat, trembling and panting from the effort of carrying her. To his relief she opened her eyes. 'Thank God it is the ground,' she said, closing her eyes again, stretched out on the grass.

He lay down himself, stared up at the sky. Titanium-blue space full of small black shooting-stars. Occasionally a sparrow-hawk would come hurtling on an intercepting strike among the carefree swallows, almost catch one when the little bird would flick aside like a fighterplane in a dogfight, and the hawk go straight on, empty-taloned. In the reverse of such a situation he had often seen the swallows mob the hawk when it was patrolling by with insufficient acceleration to match their manoeuvrability.

'You understand your desire to fly?' his therapist had asked him, squat as a Buddha in a barrister's wig. 'It's because I'm so insecure,' he replied, 'that I'm going way beyond the womb, I'm trying to be a sperm flying all the way back to return to my father's penis.' The therapist's face remained passive. 'Actually,' he said. 'I imagined it as taking responsibility for myself, trying to be independent, escaping from the restrictions of being a child.' The therapist nodded thoughtfully. 'So you didn't mind leaving your mother down on the ground?' 'Of course not,' he retorted. 'I was showing her what I could do, look Mum, I was shouting, look at me, aren't I clever? The therapist rolled her wrist as if testing its flexibility rather than examining her watch. 'You wanted an exceptional power,' she said. 'Something that would impress your parents, make them appreciate you, make you superior to your fellows.' He sighed, as one who is never understood. 'I used to play scrum-half in rugby at school because it gave me the chance to fly through the air. There used to be a photograph of me in the dining-hall. I was stretched flat in the air, flying over the entire scrum. I often did it, but a boy had a camera there that day. I used to pin the opposing scrum-half before he could get the ball away. But what I enjoyed was the exhilaration, the power of using my body.' The therapist nodded. 'The power that made you superior. We all try to find some way of being superior to each other.'

Inika sat up. A little colour had returned to her face. 'You must think me very stupid,' she said. 'That I am so weak.'

He shook his head. 'If it wasn't for women there'd be nothing to live for.'

She was too weak to laugh, it came out in a gasp. 'You would not wish to have my body. It is like a chair that break when you sit down. Many time I wish I was a man.'

'I'm glad you're a woman.'

She put her head on one side. 'You should be careful about women. They wish to put you in their hearts. Then they are always disappointed.'

'Don't women want to be possessed, too?'

'To be possessed, as you say it, it is like money you put in the bank for the day when rain comes down and the dykes are breaking. But perhaps, too, the banks will be drowned.' She rolled on to her knees to get up, swayed. 'My head,' she groaned.

He rose to help her. 'Shall I fetch the Landrover?'

'You think I am old woman?' She stood, breathing deeply, holding on to his arm. 'I will walk.' She let go and started out for the house. She seemed better by the time they reached the kitchen. But once inside she pressed a hand to her brow. 'I think I should like to rest on the bed. Is it all right?'

'I'll show you,' he said. 'Then I have some jobs to do. I will make dinner for you about seven o'clock.'

She smiled, put a hand on his arm. 'I think I will like this guest house.'

While Belle went to collect the goats, he cleaned out the sows and fed them and the weaners, thinking as he worked that he was getting behind, he hadn't walked the farm recently, herded the stock, checked the walls, done any maintenance, the garden was a wilderness, and wasn't Inika comical with her head on one side like a bird, and the bare way she had of speaking English, but that vertigo was a strange affliction. Down at the cliffs of Moher, six hundred feet sheer into the boiling Atlantic, there among all the tourists and sightseers he had felt a strange magnetic pull trying to draw him over the edge and down among the milling seabirds. He had had to crawl away on hands and knees, get behind a wall, avert his eyes, the drag had such an insidious power. But that wasn't vertigo. He had not known it could make someone so ill they would faint. And it didn't seem like play-acting. Why should she, anyway? Why should he even have such a suspicion?

After milking the goats and bringing the buckets into the kitchen, he went in sock-silent feet to see if Inika was all right. The door was ajar. She lay on her back, still in the blue track-suit, mouth fractionally ajar, her breasts rising and falling. All these women passing through his life, he thought, returning to the kitchen to put his boots back on. He filled the churn and took it up to Riordans.

All was quiet. He found Mrs Riordan in the kitchen, sitting at the table, staring at an empty teacup. When she saw Conor, she reached out to feel the teapot. 'I'll make a fresh pot,' she said. 'Sit down and take the weight off your feet. I feel I'm going out of my mind, Conor.'

He sat down, aware that for the last eight hours he had completely forgotten about events up here, he hadn't given a thought to the consequences and reactions of Nuala's night away and her unexpected announcement.

'I don't know what's to become of us,' said Mrs Riordan, lifting a lid on the cooker and pushing the big kettle on to a ring. 'There've been Riordans here for hundreds of years. Like there've been Caseys down at yours.' She fetched him a cup off the dresser. 'She calmly tells me this morning that she's going to Galway as soon as they're married, all within a month. She has it all planned out.' Mrs Riordan became flushed and angry. 'Never a thought about us any more. It's all too isolated, she says. Too far for people to come and see her weaving. I said but with Sean gone, wasn't she supposed to run the farm, ready to take over when I'm gone? Vaun is just itching to have the place, she says.' The kettle boiled and she made the tea. 'Huh,' she exclaimed. 'That Vaun hasn't the sense to keep a pet rabbit, let alone a farm of this size.' He knew this was a calumny, but let it pass. 'I always wanted you and Nuala to join up. Why did you never persuade her, Conor? You were too slow. Now somebody else's got her, plucking her like a fox in the night.' She shook her head at him. 'I said to her this morning, will there be a mortal sin to answer at your next confession, and she didn't answer me.' She slumped down in her chair again. 'How am I supposed to manage with poor Tom as much use as a broken pitchfork and Kathy still at school when Vaun goes off to college in September?'

'You could take on a lad,' suggested Conor. 'We'll manage somehow.' He was aware that under normal circumstances he would have been as depressed as she at the prospect of Nuala going, but just at the moment. . . .

'It's not the same as your own family,' she said. 'And I'd have to find the money to pay him, labour's very dear these days. I never thought she'd fall for a showy kind of man like that Niall McCarthy. O Lord,' she exclaimed. 'She's arranged that he'll come tomorrow and drive us all to Galway for Sean's Requiem Mass. And I'd as soon ride with Paisley. You will be coming with us, Conor?' There were tears in her eyes.

He reached out a reassuring hand. 'Of course I'm coming.' Although in fact, he had quite forgotten.

She nodded gratefully, unable to speak as sobs began to permeate her heavy body. He slid his chair close so that he could put an arm round her, surprised to find himself acting as comforter, surprised to discover as he clasped her seal-like form how much he loved her. She hugged him, her fleshy arms as big as legs, and he pulled her head of shaggy grey curls on to his shoulder, stroking her, while she cried till his shirt was soaked.

'We'll manage,' he said. 'You and I between us, to keep things going.' He tried to think of subjects that might soothe her anxiety. 'Maybe you should be proud of producing all these young women with such strong characters. I don't care overmuch for McCarthy either, but then I'm prejudiced. Perhaps with him Nuala'll have a better chance of selling her rugs and becoming famous.'

Mrs Riordan sat up, dabbing at her eyes with her apron. 'I'm disappointed in you, Conor. The least I thought you'd want to do was to break his fat neck. Weren't you soft on Nuala?'

'You can't make a prisoner of someone's affections,' he said, defensively. 'I'm contented to live in this place, but she's got ambition.'

'She's been the backbone of this place,' she said, red-eyed. 'It's been a long struggle keeping it going since my man died. Then when Sean went it was nearly too much for me. If it hadn't been for Nuala, with the energy of ten men, I'd have let it go. But for her to leave now, I keep asking myself why, why is it happening all the time? What have I done wrong?'

'It's never you that's to blame, Mrs Riordan. There's no blame on anyone. It'll be all right.'

Mrs Riordan was tearful again. 'It's just that I've put so much store by this place, put so much of my life into it, d'you see, reared my children here, and it was this farm that gave them their start. Now one by one they leave it, like the swallows before the winter. Or maybe the rats leaving a rotten ship.'

'You shouldn't overlook Vaun. She's the only one wanted to study agriculture.'

Mrs Riordan patted his arm. 'Conor, you're as good at moonshining as your uncle, God rest his soul. When all's said and done, there's not much else for us to do. Have your tea now before it's cold.'

He could see that she had regained some of her old composure, and was probably about to launch on some criticism of Vaun when the door banged open and Vaun herself barged in, hair awry, sleeves flapping.

'Do I smell fresh tea?' she exclaimed, falling over a chair. 'I'm parched. If it isn't the great lover himself. Where's Dorothy? What have you done with the answer to every bachelor's prayer? Flattened her with your passion?'

'Vaun,' cried Mrs Riordan, twisting round in her chair. 'I don't want to hear that kind of talk.'

Vaun, only then aware of the distress visible in her mother's complexion, leaned over. 'Are you still upsetting yourself, Mam?' Conor had never heard such concern in her voice, Vaun mothering her mother. 'You'll do yourself no good. You knew it would happen sooner or later.'

Conor looked at her in surprise. 'Did you know about it, Vaun?'

'For heaven's sake,' she exclaimed, filling up a mug with tea. 'They've been flushing red as traffic-lights at the sight of each other since lambing.'

'If that's so then I must be blind,' he said.

'You see what you want to see,' said Vaun, sitting down again. 'I told Mam weeks back that I knew Niall was trying to talk Nuala into moving to Galway. That way she might get more commissions, she'd get labour to work the looms so she'd have leave to research designs.'

Mrs Riordan sat slumped over the table, shaking her head. 'When Sean was taken from us, she said, it's up to me now, I'll have to run the farm. That's what she said to me.'

There was silence while they drank their tea, as if in each of them rankled resentments released by these revelations. But if Mrs Riordan was depressed at every turn by them, Conor noticed that Vaun seemed wound up and excited, the Riordan rose-pink cheeks pinker, her eyes like clicking marbles, shooting them from him to her mother and round the room. And he knew then she was dying to say something she could not bring herself to mention. So he decided to say it for her. 'You'll have to run the place now, Vaun.'

She caught her lower lip in her teeth, held her breath as her mother threw a look of irritation at Conor. 'I think we'd better see how you manage on your course before we make any plans.'

The outer door rasped, and Nuala poked her head round, a lock of dark hair fallen across her forehead. Conor felt his chest contract as if emptied by a vacuum-pump. He could see it was no surprise to Vaun or her mother, but he had somehow imagined she had already left. Never had she seemed so attractive.

'Hullo, Conor.' She smiled at him, unaccustomedly friendly. 'I'm just going to take the milk.'

'I'll give you a hand loading,' he said getting up.

'Don't you want a cup of tea?' asked her mother.

'No time,' she replied, and her mother looked dismayed as if the refusal was further evidence of family rejection. 'I'll be back in half-an-hour.'

Lifting the churns into the open boot of the car with her, Conor felt his tongue like the shorn-off stump of a sapling. Ideas for statements were there, but they would not sprout into words.

110

'D'you think I'm doing the right thing?' she asked him.

'It's not for me to say,' he replied, taken aback by her question.

'D'you not have any opinions, then?'

'Your mother's been in bits because she sees it as another blow against the family, Vaun's all excited because she sees it as a chance she never thought she'd have, but looking at it from your point of view, I can see it could make sense.'

She looked pleased as she went round to open the driver's door. 'And from your point of view?' Then she laughed. 'No, it's not fair to ask you that.'

As she turned to get into the car he had a strong desire to respond to her remark by grabbing her, maybe tickle her, make some physical gesture.

But though he could have done so with ease to Vaun, because of her natural playfulness, he had always been constrained from touching Nuala, nervous of offending her. Perhaps this sudden inclination was brought about by her newly-acquired air of liberation. Even though she now belonged to somebody else.

'D'you know, Conor,' she said, as she sat in and closed the door. 'A few weeks ago I would have thought Niall the last man I'd marry. But then it came, like a conversion, the blinding light on the road to Tarsus. I felt, what have I been doing all these years, bottling it up inside myself? This is the life and this is the man. Do you know what I mean?'

He nodded. 'I'm happy for you, Nuala,' he said, somewhat astounded at her confidence and not at all sure how to respond. 'As long as you're sure you'll feel the same tomorrow, and the next day.'

She started up the engine, transfixing him with a wry smile. 'Why wouldn't I be sure?'

He watched her drive away, the milk-churns standing in the boot like a row of Kremlin generals. How was it that he had failed to see what she needed? A woman doesn't require paralysing respect. He'd acted as if all designers of aeroplanes had been convinced the only way to propel them was to flap their wings.

He remembered with guilty unease that lying in his own house was another young woman he desired. How could he justify, let alone balance, feelings for two different young women? Lust? That damned driving pain between the legs that threw aside all judgement, as if his pants were on fire and could only be expunged by jumping into a vat of woman. Choosing a partner, in the words of old Tom Riordan, who had carefully avoided doing so all his life, should be like selecting a gilt for sending to the boar. Did she have the temperament of a saint, was her mother as fertile as a sycamore, did she gladden the eye, did she have enough tits? But selectivity was a cold-blooded constraint. Those patterns were already conditioned in the genes that makes one willow-warbler prefer another rather than try its luck with a pretty chaffinch, and there was passion waiting to rise up like a great sunflower where before there had only been dandelions.

He was walking towards the Landrover when Vaun came rushing up, arms and legs whirling in that disconnected gaucheness of one who doesn't care as long as they get them there. She practically knocked him down, grabbed him unselfconsciously with both hands. 'Conor,' she exclaimed breathlessly. 'Thanks a million, Conor.' She stepped back as if to express her feeling clearer. 'You can have me any time.' She waved her arms about to demonstrate her intention. 'Any time you can spare from Dorothy. I don't want to become a frustrated spinster like Nuala, I want it now.'

'Vaun,' he said, moving quickly to get into the Landrover. 'You're shameless. I'll see you tomorrow. What time is Niall coming to collect us?'

'The great Galway lover,' she enounced, 'will be arriving at 9.30 precisely. Now there's a man who knows how to get what he wants. No bloody pussyfooting about like you.'

As he started up the engine, she came up close to the window. 'Tell us, does Dorothy use the pill?'

He reached out and tweaked her nose, then drove away, laughing. You had to laugh at Vaun, he thought. It was the only thing to do. He wondered if he should have pointed out that Dorothy had . . . left, and explained about his Dutch guest.

All was quiet in the yard. The bicycle was still leaning against the wall of the house where Inika had left it. He could hear the rhythmic grunting of a sow as she suckled her litter. Two pigeons perched on the ridge-tiles were cooing. The sun still high over the glen shone like a newly-minted coin.

Belle rose up from her portion of flattened earth beside the back-doorstep, wagged her tail and looked at him with the expectation of a beggar who knows the chances are limited, but the meanest token of approval will make her day. Conor was perfectly well aware of this and paused briefly to press his hand over her furry skull like a priest giving benediction, sufficient to satisfy the believer.

The house was so quiet that he could easily have assumed it was its normal empty self. But just to make sure he took off his boots and crept sock-footed to the door of the spare bedroom. Even though it was reasonable to expect her to be there, it still came as a shock to find her curled on her side, one arm hanging down over the edge of the bed, fast asleep. How trusting people were in their repose, he thought. There was something intrinsic in her vulnerability that made him want to weep with the pleasure of beholding it. Trust was a difficult constituent to assimilate. It was all right to begin with, as a child. . . .

He remembered his grandmother used to walk as a chair might walk, stiff-legged and square-hipped, and she would come to a halt and assume instant rigidity, inclining very slightly in his direction, the better to hear. Conor, don't you ever wash your face? His reply, often quoted back to him in later years, was typical of most small boys. But it only gets dirty again if I wash it, Gran. Although irascible in manner, his grandmother tended to dote on him. If you go and wash now, we'll go up to my room and see what's in my chocolate box. Cleanliness was achieved in a trice, three fingerfuls of water smeared over mouth and cheeks, then a good rub on the towel. His grandmother had an ornate sitting-room on the first floor, opposite the upstairs drawing-room. They went up the great staircase together. He remembered the hall as vast as a railway station, with its high glass roof and the balustraded bridges created by the stairs dividing halfway up. He would visualise rumbling engines and lines of carriages gliding in beneath the gallery that circled the upper half of the hall and led to the upstairs rooms.

Her marquetry bureau was near the window, so that she could sit and look out across the park. He climbed up on the window-seat over the fat central-heating pipes, his cheeks bulging with chocolate, and saw the boy Oliver working in the flower beds in the centre of the circular drive. The boy Oliver had a long neck and walked with a stoop like a guinea-fowl. Beyond the ha-ha cattle were grouped beneath the beeches, some lifting their heads to nibble at the branches they kept

113

trimmed to a horizontal exactitude. Do you think you should take a chocolate to your mother? she asked after he had been given a second one. He shook his head, mouth full again. She's busy, he said later. Busy? queried his grandmother. Kissing, he replied, watching the boy Oliver pushing the laden wheelbarrow across the grass, his narrow shoulders hunched like a tent. She told me not to interrupt, he added. I looked through the window and saw they were kissing. That was naughty of you to watch, said his grandmother. That's being nosy. Did they do anything else? This question puzzled him. Just kissing, he replied.

The therapist had been interested when he told her the story. 'What was your feeling at the time?' she asked. 'Did you feel resentful towards your mother? Were you jealous of the man?' 'I thought what they were doing looked very enjoyable,' he replied. 'I liked the way my mother reacted when she was kissed. I wanted to try the same thing. So that night when she came to say goodnight, I knelt up beside her, cupped my hands round her face and tried to kiss her on the mouth as I had seen the man do. But it made her angry, she pushed me away and slapped me. So of course I lay down and cried. That made her sorry for hitting me, so she cuddled me and I liked that very much. I was a primitive little beast. I knew how to get my mother to make me happy.' The therapist nodded thoughtfully. 'Is that what you seek in your relationships? A woman who knows how to make you happy, who makes you feel safe?'

Conor had taken out of the fridge the last piece of the lamb that he had kept back from Mrs Riordan's freezer. Now it was roasting in the oven, pierced with small cloves of wild garlic. He had brought carrots, broccoli, courgettes and new potatoes in from the garden, together with a bowl of raspberries. He had the potatoes in a saucepan of water with sprigs of mint, and all the other vegetables cleaned and chopped, when he decided it was time to wake her.

He tapped on the door. 'Dinner in twenty minutes.'

She rolled over, yawning. 'I like the bath first.'

'Unfortunately this humble guest house does not rise to the dizzy heights of a bathroom. By next year, I hope.'

She sat up. 'So what is it that you do when you must clean yourself?'

'Either I use my neighbour's bath, or I put a large bowl before the sink in the kitchen and wash myself there.'

She reflected for a moment. 'I don't know if I can manage this. Is it included that the director help to wash his guests?'

'The service is free. But first I must boil a kettle of water.'

'You are putting boiling water on me?'

By the time she appeared, just wrapped in a towel and clutching a washbag, he had the saucepans of vegetables heating on the cooker, the sink full of warm water and the bowl ready on the floor before it. He had not been certain that she meant to go through with it. But she calmly draped the towel over the back of a chair, handed him a bar of soap from her washbag and as if it was the most natural act in the world, stepped into the bowl. 'Ready?' He filled a jug from the sink and poured water all over her, then began to soap her.

She lifted her arms, then nodded at the saucepans on the cooker. 'You have washed the potatoes and . . .' she peered into the pans. 'I see carrots and courgettes. Now you wash me. You make me ready to eat, you are cooking me next?'

He laughed as his hands slid about her slippery body, turning to adjust the flames on the cooker as the vegetables began to boil, then continuing to wash her, under her arms, over her shoulders, her softly ample breasts, down her back. It was as he soaped her well-rounded buttocks that he noticed curious linear marks across them. Birthmarks perhaps, he thought. But a shadow had already crossed his mind, a qualm increased by the significance of the aroma of roasting lamb. It was as if he was a child suddenly aware that the voice of reality was about to call him back from the illusions he had built to play with.

He shook his head to dispel such interference, and turned to take a spoon to baste the meat in the oven. Nothing was going to disturb his pleasure. He returned to washing Inika. As he soaped her hips, her belly, her bush and her thighs, he was surprised and distracted by the pressure of his erection, as if it might burst through his trousers. As he continued to soap certain places she began to moan with pleasure. 'The cooking it smell so delicious. I feel it is me who make the smell of cooking. I feel like I am full of flavours.'

He felt the need for urgency, and poured jugfuls of water over her to rinse her, but she kept grabbing his hands to continue washing. 'My breasts and here . . .' she touched her genitals. 'They are not clean yet.'

115

'It's beautiful, your body,' he said, feeling it tremble beneath his fingers.

She parted her knees and projected her pelvis. 'Don't stop,' she moaned. As he reached for her towel, she grabbed his arm. 'No, please, do it now. Do it.'

As he thrust his trousers down, and his organ fell out like a third arm, she seized hold of it to guide it in, moaning, her hips gulping hungrily. In their efforts to unite, they trod on the edge of the bowl, now full of water, spilling it over the floor, soaking his trousers. Almost instantly, beating his back with her fists, she came. Then she clung to him as he came, and they stood locked together amid the scents of roasting meat and aromatic vegetables.

'They'll be overcooked,' he said, after a while, detaching himself, picking her up and putting her on a chair, draping her towel over her shoulders. He used his sodden trousers to mop up some of the water, then tipped the vegetables into the cullender, prodded potatoes, fetched bowls to serve them in, laid the table, able to act swiftly and coordinately despite the pithy sensation in his thighs. He dished up the lamb, made some gravy, fetched glasses and cans of Guinness. And all the while Inika sat glassy-eyed, draped under the towel. 'A very good guest-house,' she murmured as he began to carve the meat. 'I tell all my friends.'

When her plate was put before her she sat up, took the towel off her shoulders and wrapped it under her arms sarong-style. 'Delicious,' she said after several mouthfuls. 'You are good cook.'

'Thanks,' he replied, caught in the anomalous position of those who are complimented, when they know what they have done is nothing special, yet appreciating that to reject the compliment is to belittle the giver's judgement.

'You are good at giving the wash, too.'

He laughed. 'You were very nice to wash.'

'I think if I stay here I am dirty a lot.'

When he served the bowl of raspberries set in goat's cheese between the two black glasses of Guinness she clapped her hands like a child. 'I never forget this evening.'

He took the bone from the serving-dish and tossed it to Belle, who seized it apologetically, as if desperately ashamed of the greed she imagined she must appear to be displaying.

'My friends did not want me to go away by myself. They

imagined a girl alone is in danger.' She licked goat's cheese off her lip. 'Perhaps now they say, we tell you true, see what happen, see how you have suffered.'

They both laughed. 'Are these friends from Amsterdam too?' he asked.

'We have been at school together. Erika, she is working in wine business. Like me, she work for her father. Jan, he is with computers. He is very tall, like a pole for the light in the street. Margrethe is teacher in school. She has face like moon and always make joke. They are all mad for the music, the pipes, the violins, the accordions, the old music of Ireland. I am liking it also, but not all the day and all the night, and no time to see the beautiful country.'

As she talked, regarding him with her brown eyes darkening to jet, with her flat, bemused smile, often tilting her head to one side, he felt the endearment of familiarity growing. They were in some kind of second or third stage, as if he had known her before, her appeal already further up his temperature scale than the normal position for someone only met that day, as if she had arrived with credits in long-established intimacy.

'At home there is fiancée for each,' she continued. 'But we make this journey because we are old friend, to have a sort of relaxation.'

'You Dutch are very civilised,' he said.

'I think we are like you, too. A small country. For many years ruled by a foreign people. But you have roots with times much more old, with the bones of civilisations that you live beside, even today.'

He was moved that she should feel as he did. When it grew dark he took her to bed, as all good hosts should do. 'Your body is like the ripest of fruit and the holiest of lands,' he said, and he used his tongue to lick her mind and tickle her body, till her desire to have him fuck her was the urgency to obviate torture.

Later, as they lay beside each other, flat and close-fitting as a set of crayons, she turned to look at him. 'At this moment my fiancée, he does not exist. My life in Amsterdam is nothing. I have not the wish to return. I have only the wish to be here. With you.'

'And tomorrow?'

'Tomorrow I wish to be the same, like today. Tomorrow I will be strong, I will climb up to see the fort.'

'Tomorrow I have to go to Galway with the Riordans for a Requiem Mass for their son who died last year. But I'll be back in the afternoon and we can climb and see the fort then. There are more gentle routes. Will you be all right on your own for a bit?'

'I can go for a walk,' she murmured. 'So that I may need a wash when you come back.' She sighed, nestling closer, if that were possible. 'You make me think of my life, about my work, about that I am promise to a business, to live inside a city of poisonous gas, about marrying a man I know him already like a Gouda cheese, good for the appetite perhaps, but not very interesting. You make me wish for a different thing.'

'How d'you know I'm not as dull as cheese?'

'You think I am stupid?' She pounded his chest punitively. 'It is because you have made the chosen to put yourself in this beautiful wild place. You could have put yourself like most peoples, into the middle of civilisations, find big job, have big money. But no. You want to walk out from your house and there is the old world of nature all round you. All the birds healthy and free. All the wild flowers making the country a garden. It brings to my mind the beginnings, before there is history.' Her voice began to slur with sleepiness. 'Maybe I should try this sort of living. Maybe you . . .' her voice became a blur, faded into steady breathing.

*

Next morning he slipped from bed early, left her sleeping. He had fed the pigs and cleaned them out and milked the goats before eight o'clock. Then he came in and made himself some breakfast, washed and went into the bedroom to put on his suit. Although he tried to make as little noise as possible so as not to disturb her, she woke and lay watching the transformation.

'Who is this different man?' she asked sleepily. 'I never see him before.'

Conor eased a finger round his collar, trying to make it more comfortable. 'I hate these things,' he said. 'They choke me.'

She closed her eyes. 'I don't see this man. Go away, and come back the man I remember.'

He bent over her, put one hand over her eyes, kissed her. 'Help yourself to whatever you want to eat.'

He put the milk-churns into the Landrover and drove up to Riordans. It was an unusual sight to Conor, all the Riordan women in sober cotton dresses and wearing hats. For them it was no different from dressing every Sunday for Mass, but they were usually home and out of their finery before the pagan Conor arrived with the milk churns. But for them today the vision of Conor in a suit was also extraordinary. The suit was no longer a good fit, although being too small at least it stretched out some of the crumples. 'No sign of Niall?' he asked, entering the kitchen in expectation of a cup of tea as they waited, only to find everyone, gloves and bags in their hands, heading for the door.

'Lover-boy's fancy motor's broke,' said Vaun. 'He's just rung to tell us we've got to bounce all the way in the old red hen-coop.'

'He did offer to hire a car to come and fetch us,' said Nuala crisply as they went out.

'I was looking forward to travelling in style,' said Kathy, who was carrying her prayer-book and wearing a straw school-hat.

Old Tom stood in the doorway, hunched like a rheumatic heron, watching them as Nuala got into the driving-seat, her mother beside her, and Conor and Kathy got into the back, with Vaun in the middle. Tom waved a stiff, cramped arm, grinned his few surviving teeth at them as they left, but none of them noticed.

Vaun pressed against Conor. 'This is as good as a cuddle. Would you not be more comfortable if you put an arm round me, Conor?'

'Vaun,' snapped her mother sharply, turning her head and glaring at her. 'I don't want any of your nonsense this day.'

'I was only joking, Mam,' she pouted. 'Conor doesn't mind, do you, Conor?'

'I can't imagine what you'll be like when you really fancy someone, Vaun,' he laughed.

'She'll be like a female spider,' said Kathy with her thick, clogged words. 'She'll eat her husbands.'

'I might as well,' sighed Vaun. 'Men are so weedy.'

The heavily laden car ground its way laboriously up the long gradient that lead over the hills.

'I wouldn't say much for the reliability of this fellow of yours, Nuala,' said Vaun. 'Wouldn't you worry that on your wedding day, he'd send word that he had the toothache?'

119

'Having an accident is not a sign of unreliability,' said Nuala tersely, concentrating on the narrow road.

Conor closed his eyes.

Sir, Any observer in the jungle is usually impressed by the intensity of the nutrition industry. Without consideration of the beauty and intrinsicality of a creature smaller than itself, another one, larger and equally amazingly devised, will munch it up in a matter of seconds. Eat somebody daily is not so much their creed as their need. And if their luck's out, it's them that gets eaten instead. Humans, of course, have as good a set of teeth as anyone. Able to munch up prawns and chickens and lambs with gusto. But who eats humans, bar the odd crocodile, bunch of piranhas, shark or berserk lion? Humans eat humans. Eat a child, friend, parent, brother, sister, partner is our need. Our voracious appetites are disguised by other names, like jealousy, anger, love, politics. Our egos are our stomachs. They must be rewarded daily. They must feel superior. Behind all our ingenious physiological machinery, there's a rather basic beast. With the most ridiculous conceit. Yours, etc.

'What was it that really happened?' asked Mrs Riordan.

'He was out celebrating the engagement with some friends,' said Nuala with a wry smile. 'They hit a bollard. Nobody was hurt or anything.'

Vaun laughed. 'Pissed out of his arty mind.'

'You know nothing about it,' snapped Nuala.

'I can see why you want to get away from us,' cried Vaun. 'So's you can have a riot of a good time in the city.'

'I'd hate to live in a city,' said Kathy before anyone else could boil over. 'It's all bricks and concrete, it's all hard.'

'I could never abide it either,' agreed her mother. 'No air to breathe, and all the crowds of people. I never thought that Nuala would go. I thought the land was in her blood.'

'The land, as you put it, is in all our blood, Mam,' said Nuala, as they began to descend towards Kinvara, the car's brakes groaning at a tight bend. 'But out there in the rain and the wind, I've often thought it the ugliest place in the world. If there are better opportunities somewhere else what's the point of martyring yourself to hardship and poverty for the sake of tradition?'

'If it hadn't been for Sean going,' sighed Mrs Riordan. 'None of this would have been important. I would have expected all you girls to be off sooner or later, after husbands or careers, like Mary and Eileen.'

As the car groaned at another bend, Conor prayed nothing would break, thinking that it was rarely if ever serviced, only visiting a garage when something needed repairing.

'So what do you think made Sean take to drink and turned him ill?' asked Nuala. 'It was because he dreaded what was expected of him after Da went. Underneath he hated the farm, he longed to get away, do something different, but he tried to suppress it because he didn't want to let you down.'

'That's never true,' exclaimed Mrs Riordan. 'How can you say such things on the anniversary of his going? How can you run down his good name, the unfortunate boy. In all conscience, I'm surprised at you, Nuala.'

'But I'm not blaming him,' retorted Nuala. 'It wasn't his fault that he was born here. What killed him was loyalty to you fighting ambition to move out and live his own life. Why else was he so bitter? If you want the truth, ask Conor.'

Conor, feeling relief that at last they were down off the hills and on relative level land and a straight road was now in dread that Mrs Riordan would ask him.

'And why wouldn't I ask Conor?' exclaimed Mrs Riordan. 'Isn't he proof there's a living to be made on the land? Didn't he turn his back on the fine livings to be made in the cities?' She turned to him over the back of the seat. 'You've told me, Conor, that the continuity of your family having lived there meant a great deal to you. Isn't that so?'

He nodded. 'But don't forget I'm older than Sean or Nuala. I've had time to try out different lives.'

'Tell her what Sean said to you,' urged Vaun.

He frowned, undecided whether her incitement was malicious or merely compulsive, the two alternatives to her nature he could never quite settle.

'I remember Sean saying he wished he were dead . . .' said Kathy earnestly.

'People say things like that when they're ill,' interrupted her mother dismissively.

'Sean used to tell me I was mad to want to be a farmer,' said Conor. 'In his view it was like being a convict on a penal settlement and having to work with mud and stones. Who'd

121

want to be slave to a bunch of half-witted sheep day in and day out? he'd say to me. Don't you remember he called me Conor de Backwards?'

'But what did he want to do instead?' asked Nuala. 'I don't remember him ever saying.'

'Maybe he never had a chance to find out,' replied Conor.

They had passed through Kinvara and rounded the tall stone castle that marks the innermost point of Galway Bay, the sea like a great silver dance-floor all the way to America.

'Did he tell you that he wanted to get away from the farm?' demanded Mrs Riordan flatly.

Conor nodded.

Mrs Riordan shook her head sadly. 'If it's true then isn't it a shame his own mother didn't know what was in his mind? If only he could have talked to me. Sure I know young people are leaving the land all over the country. But we're hardly dressed in rags, even though there were times so bad we thought there was no saving us.'

The road they were now on was thronged with traffic, delivery trucks, coaches, tourists in their travel-stained new-model cars from Japan and Germany. The busy commercial activity the empty lanes in the hills were free from.

'It's a grand day for disinterring Sean,' said Vaun brightly. 'Will we send word it's all been a mistake and he can come back now?'

'Maybe it would have helped if all of you were more honest,' complained Mrs Riordan.

'Maybe we didn't want to disappoint you,' murmured Nuala.

'There's been Riordans on our land for hundreds of years,' said Mrs Riordan. 'Despite the Penal Laws, despite the famines, despite the British, despite De Valera. It's a sad day when they all want to give up of their own accord. It's like everyone is afflicted with itchy feet. . . .'

'I haven't got itchy feet, Mam,' said Kathy plaintively. 'I don't want to leave. . . .'

But they were all laughing at her.

In Galway city the traffic-lights winked like dancing-masters, and formations of cars and buses halted and turned and filed obediently past the silent stores and closed offices of the Sunday-observing metropolis, dispersing to locate places of worship or hostelries more generous in their dispensing of equivalents to the blood of Christ.

122

The church where the Requiem for Sean was to be included in the Mass was a huge and popular edifice of stone, whose architect might well have been a pastry-cook who half-baked the gothic. They parked among hundreds of other church-goers and joined the throngs surging towards the entrance steps, everyone neat as pieces of Wedgwood china. Special seats had been reserved for them as if they had been going to the theatre. Conor realised with a start that the red-haired man in the navy-blue suit who appeared among them, taking Nuala's arm, whispering in her ear, was Niall McCarthy. The church had a fine organ that rose across the transept in a stockade of giant gilt whistles, and some virtuoso was performing gentle trills that could just be heard over the scuffling footfalls that echoed down the aisle and the rustle of skirts and whispering as people took their seats.

As the procession of choristers, acolytes and celebrants entered, Conor decided that he would devote the service to remembering Sean, as a conscious act, not so much a mark of respect or duty, or even as a contemplation of mortality, affect who it may, but as an opportunity to revisit an old friendship.

His eyes lifted over the fields of hats all around him, reached the plaster saints in their niches, and the pastel-shaded murals of the stations of the cross, and he swallowed, his collar like an iron necklet.

Sir, If God existed would he tolerate being caricatured as the sickly milksop the Church sentimentalises over? Icing-sugar seems such a curious medium for expressing so powerful a person as someone supposed to have hewn out the universe, and the effeminately bearded weed with watering eyes who droops about in the chocolate-box murals seems hardly the sort of person who would have had the intellect and inspiration to invent the fantastically intricate marvels of living matter. Or has the whole institution been taken over by Walt Disney? Yours, etc.

Conor's roving eyes settled for a moment on Nuala and Niall McCarthy, seated in the row in front. Niall's head was tilted as he whispered something to her, and as she lifted her face, smiling back, there was a tenderness in her expression that Conor recognised, the exclusiveness of lovers. It came as a delayed shock, the moment of realisation that he had really lost her, as if before he had pretended to himself that she was doing all this in single-minded furtherance of her ambitions, and that she was not completely lost to him, could still be available. Breathless with the pain of his discovery, unable to take his eyes off them, he felt his eyes prickle with tears. He turned away, stared relentlessly up at the pink pseudo-gothic vaulting with its wedding cake decoration. If anyone saw his tears, he thought, they'd think he was moved by thoughts of Sean.

Sean had known of his feelings for Nuala. He had approved. That'd be a grand thing, you two wed, my little sister'd put feathers on your arse, my old Conor the Bird. Then his face had darkened, an ability all the high-coloured Riordans could achieve with one snap of their black brows. I wish I had her guts, I reckon we got mixed up, she should have been me, and I her. And if I was her I'd fancy you, you've a fine figure for a Batman, when I caught you washing like a peeled spud at the sink, I thought, it should have been Nuala caught you, she'd have been transfixed as a gosling breaking out of its shell. The trouble is you're the only one who ever said to me, get out, leave, and if I'd been her, I'd have gone, and if she'd been me, you wouldn't have fancied her. Would you?

When Conor's eyes were clear again and the service was in full throng, several hundred husky throats responding to the high-pitched calls of the celebrant, choirboys sending their robin voices soaring in the rafters, he let his glance fall back on Nuala as she stood beside Niall McCarthy, urbane in his blue-black suit. He felt calm now, even found her quiet radiance touching. There was no point in dwelling on her rejection of him, her preference for someone like Niall. He had considered him a poseur, an opportunist, one who would exploit people and situations to his own advantage without consideration, in other words a shit. But then his attitude to any rival was steeped in acid from the start. The man must have some qualities to appeal to Nuala's standards; he had to admit some of her tart perceptions of himself had found their target with alarming accuracy, yet he'd long suspected women were susceptible to blandishments and ideals rather than reality. How benign he was feeling. Was it the memory of Sean permeating him with magnanimity? Of course not, it was because of Inika waiting at home, like a warm glow of hope. How basic.

Mrs Riordan was in front of him, solid as an oil-drum in her voluminous black suit. Kathy was beside him, Vaun the other side of her. His collar grated round his throat like rope.

A little more than a year ago Sean had been alive. If he closed his eyes, it could have been yesterday. Or ten years ago. Like Lyn. Mortality was a delicate matter. In a ten-million pound complexity of machinery and electronics like a jet fighter-plane, one small connection could fail, let alone a major component, and the whole expensive structure become useless. Fall out of the sky. The human body alone would have cost millions to create on a work-bench. As for the human brain, that jewel of a cauliflower, a world within a knuckle, how could it ever be valued? There were times when it was hard to credit that anything so complex could have evolved from a few cells squirming in the liquid turmoil of the early bubbling planet. Yet the alternative, a Creator such as these ardent Catholics devoutly kneeling all around him believed in, would have to have been an inconceivably brilliant engineer with access to vast experience and labyrinths of information. Sometimes he suspected the truth was a third alternative that no one had ever considered.

He felt irritated that the words of the Mass, with its inclusion of direct references to the Requiem, were so ethereally fanciful. The fairy-tale concept of a paradise jingled like the brain-wash of advertising. It was as if reality, as it appeared, was too unpalatable, and had to be disguised in strawberry syrup. Mortality could not be stomached. A pretend future had to be invented to pacify the qualms of those who feared to die and return to the nurturing soil.

Sir, I must protest at the lack of information available about the next world. The Catholic Paradise Travel Agency may paint rosy pictures of their permanent Holidays in Heaven, but they don't specify where it is, and they give no guarantee of accommodation, or even if the hotels have been built yet. Yet each day half a million depart. We can only assume there are sufficient check-in terminals to deal with the queues. And the organisation to cater for all these accumulating souls must be colossal—presumably an ever-expanding job market there. There could be conditions of appalling overcrowding for all we know. The imagination quails at the prospect of crowded transit lounges and eternal refugee camps. Of course, Outer Space is pretty large by anyone's standards.

125

But by all accounts it appears to be mostly hollow. And the expenses of getting a couple of astronauts as far as the moon suggest accommodation on the stars is out of the question. Quite apart from the light-years it would take to get there. And the fact that they could be full up with souls from other galaxies. So where are we going? Yours, etc.

There was an inadvertent sniff beside him, and glancing down he saw that tears were trickling down Kathy's cheeks. She was staring between her mother and Nuala, listening with every nerve to the Mass. He put an arm round her shoulder to comfort her, and she nestled close to him, clutching his other hand tightly. He looked over her hat at Vaun, who smiled at him, small dimples in her cheeks, an unusually mature, womanly smile, and he found to his surprise that it was he, if anyone, who was feeling a sense of reassurance.

*

When the service was over he waited outside while the Riordans spoke with the chief celebrant, Father Carroll, a tall, military-looking man. To his embarrassment he found himself in the company of Niall McCarthy. Both were constrained to awkward silence at first. The sky was roofed in with grey that allowed a dancing wind freedom to chill. Conor raced through his head all the questions he might put: have you the honeymoon planned? Was the car badly smashed up? What was Nuala like to fuck?

'D'you think it'll rain?' asked Niall.

'Maybe this evening.'

'I suppose you knew Sean well?'

Conor nodded. 'We worked together.'

'Nuala thought a lot of him, didn't she? She told me he had a drink problem. Was it that killed him, d'you think?'

Conor suddenly felt a great sense of relief. He could at least still dislike him. That square, podgy freckled face was sly, he was seeking information to ingratiate himself with his fiancée. 'No doubt it didn't help,' he replied. 'Cancer was the main cause.'

'Shame to take away someone so young. I felt bad that Nuala's going to leave the farm, especially after Sean going. But she insisted it was her decision.'

When the Riordans joined them, Nuala slipped her arm into her fiancé's. 'Niall'll bring me back later,' she said. 'I'm sure Sean'll drive you home if you're tired, Mam. What am I saying? I mean Conor.'

'I thought your car was off the road?' queried Mrs Riordan, none too happy at this change of arrangements.

'I've borrowed an old yoke that belongs to my mother,' said Niall agreeably.

Nuala tossed the keys to Conor. 'See you tomorrow,' she waved as they walked away.

'I was hoping Niall would invite us to lunch,' complained Vaun.

'He did,' snapped Mrs Riordan, dark-browed as they walked back to the car. 'But I told him we had to be back.'

'Mam,' exclaimed Vaun in loud disappointment. 'Why in the name of Moses did you do that?'

'D'you not like him at all, Mam?' asked Kathy. 'I think he's all right.'

Kathy's innocent acceptance made Conor feel guilty of his dislike.

Mrs Riordan snorted as she stood waiting for Conor to unlock the car. 'Come on, now, we'll go and have something to eat on our own.'

Under pressure from Vaun and Kathy they went to an amazing Beefburger Bar that was in style somewhere between a disco and a giant American Wild West shack. It was brash and colourful, every table had a cluster of macaw-bright sauce, a juke-box lit flashing lights up on the beams, and waitresses skipped about in gingham pinafores and wearing paper hats. The food was fat burgers and piles of chips, fresh salads, and what the girls had really come for, exotic milk-shakes and ice-creams. 'We'll have a bottle of wine, too,' said Mrs Riordan grimly. 'This is our own little party.'

'I thought they'd mention Sean more in the service, Mam,' said Kathy.

'It's all we could afford,' said Vaun.

'D'you have to pay?' asked Kathy, scandalised.

'Grow up, Kathy dear,' said Vaun. 'There's nothing free.'

They sawed their way through their juicy beefburgers, covered them with red and yellow sauces, munched crisp pieces of lettuce and onion.

'It was a beautiful Mass all the same,' said Kathy in her thick,

127

impeded voice. 'Father Carroll's sermon was so sad. You'd wonder why God would let young people die. Why wouldn't he give them a chance?'

'Wouldn't you think,' mused Vaun, after a long draw on the straws had emptied half her milk-shake. 'Bad things should only happen to people who commit a deadly sin? So it would be natural justice if Nuala broke a leg.'

'Is that why Sean died?' asked Kathy, wide-eyed. 'Because of his drinking?'

'Hold on,' said Conor. 'He wasn't bad. What about the really wicked people?'

'Of course,' exclaimed Vaun. 'Conor the arch-heretic and sinner. And never a rash of boils or a cold in the head to afflict him.'

Even Mrs Riordan joined in the laughter.

'What I meant,' he said, 'was that according to your logic, Vaun, corrupt leaders of countries who deny human rights, ought to suffer retribution now if there was any justice.'

'Won't they go to hell when they die?' asked Kathy.

'Hell's been abolished,' said Vaun. 'It'll be Heaven's turn to go next. Like the old cinemas. Pre-marital sex is a mortal sin, but there was Nuala going off and having carnal knowledge, and there was nothing Mam could do about it. Times are changing.'

Mrs Riordan sipped her wine, for once not reacting to Vaun's mockery. 'Times are changing is right. I was very disappointed by Nuala. There were several things I could have done, but I decided that it was better to preserve what little there is left of our family. At least there's going to be a wedding.'

'Times are indeed changing,' said Vaun irreverently.

Conor felt a resurgence of ¦is affection for Mrs Riordan. What a battering all this had been for her.

The journey back was uneventful. They discussed Conor's idea for a milking-parlour for the goats, a cooperative venture between both farms, that he had suggested before. 'I've been thinking of giving the herd up, Conor,' sighed Mrs Riordan.

She took his arm when they got back. 'Thanks for driving us back. I was glad to have you there.' She gave his arm a little squeeze.

He climbed up into the Landrover and drove down to his own farm. He felt a lift of excitement, as if a gust of air had blown in through an open window on a hot day. He wondered what Inika had been doing all morning, and imagined her walking the land, perhaps enjoying the solitariness from people, and the company of birds, insects and flowers, as he often did. He parked the Landrover, and though desirous of bounding towards the open front door, restrained his eager arms and legs, modulated the smile swelling his cheeks, checked the words rising in his throat.

*

As he stepped into the house, it was as if all his reactions were upon that instant decapitated. He had to close his eyes and re-open them, to make sure he wasn't dreaming. He stood there rigid as an icicle, searching the scene before him for meaning.

The kitchen was a shambles. Chairs strewn about on their backs, the table knocked over, broken china all over the floor, cutlery and food scattered, the fridge and the cooker overturned, the sofa ripped, pictures torn from the walls.

He stood listening, the skin all over his body as pimpled as wild cucumber, the hair on his head standing on end. But all was silent.

Could Inika have done this? Had she gone mad?

A faint squeak from behind made him jump. There was Belle, rolling over in anguished abasement on the floor, as if convinced she must be personally responsible for the devastation. With rare feeling he knelt down and picked her up, held her close, stroked her. 'What happened, Belle? What happened?' But all she could do was lick his face in frantic excitement at his forgiveness.

Alarm continued to run through him like waves of cold sea water. There could be worse to come. He put Belle down, still stroking her, stood up and went to the door, stiff with apprehension, dreading what he might find.

Every room had been ransacked, drawers pulled out, clothes scattered, mattresses and beds ripped, their stuffing spilled. If he had thought this might be the handiwork of Inika, the sight of her clothes strewn everywhere, her bag slashed to ribbons, make-up strewn over the floor, brought a terrible fear. Would he find her mutilated body? The violence suggested frantic search, desperate men. Even the lid of the lavatory cistern had been wrenched off. What could they have been looking for? And where was she?

Galvanised with anxiety, he rushed out of the house, ran from building to building, searching each one, the barn, the pig sheds, the garden, the pig-paddocks, the copses, the lane, calling Belle to help, as if her nose might locate what he dreaded to find. She hastened after him, sniffing eagerly, as if imagining he had something to show her.

He went everywhere a second time, slower, more thoroughly. The sows stared at him amiably, grunting, tilting their glossy snouts, expecting their feed, their piglets squealing as they scurried to and fro. He was crossing the yard from their sheds when he saw fresh tyre tracks in a patch of mud. He recognised the tread of a Michelin tyre. There were more by the gate. There his own tracks, the heavy-duty coarse-ply of the Landrover obliterated them as they went out on to the lane. At last it began to dawn on him that she must have been abducted.

He looked at her bicycle leaning against the wall of the house. She might already be dead.

Slowly the questions began to consolidate through the random fever of his thoughts. What should he do? What could he do? Of one thing he felt sure: this was not the way the Gardai operated. This violation of his privacy was the handiwork of somebody else. So should he not first contact the upholders of law and order?

He backed the Landrover out on to the lane. He would not involve the Riordans, he thought. Neither would he use the village call-box. Conversations on that could be listened in to. So he drove all the way to Kilfenora. A recorded message at the Ennis station informed him he would have to call Limerick. Of course, it was Sunday. A bored voice came on the line.

'Is it an emergency?'

'My house was ransacked this afternoon.'

'A burglary?'

'There was a girl staying in the house. I think she's been abducted.'

'Was it a family quarrel?'

'I don't know who she was.'

'Are you calling from your home?'

'From a call-box.'

'Give me your number and I'll call you back.'

He was standing waiting when a girl with short blond hair came up. 'I'm waiting for a call,' he said.

'I won't be a minute,' she replied, slipping inside. He could see her hair was dyed, the roots beginning to show. Her blouse was open so that he could see the tops of her ample breasts, and his eyes were drawn to a small gold crucifix that hung there on the end of a chain round her neck. This chain was gathered between the forefinger and thumb of her free hand, and as she talked, she would swing the chain so that the crucifix swung like a pendulum. Then at some agitated moment of response she would plunge it down between her breasts as a fisherman lowers his bait, then jigs it up and down to lure a passing fish. When she came out and departed without a word, ten minutes had passed. Another ten minutes passed. He was aware of a sharp sense of isolation, of being totally remote from reality. A number of tourist cars passed by. The phone rang.

The voice was different, sharp and authoritative. 'What exactly is your complaint?'

He paused. 'I think some harm could have come to a girl who was staying. There are signs of a violent struggle.'

'Give me your name and address.'

Conor gave the man directions. 'I'll leave my Landrover parked out on the road,' he added. 'It's the pick-up type.'

Driving back through the great empty landscape, the evening sun blotched by smoky clouds that belched across the sky as if from some incandescent furnace, the spent dust of billions of incinerated beings, he wondered if he might have dreamed it all, if he might not arrive back and find all was normal.

When he got back, the chaos in his kitchen seemed as if it had been fixed in time like a photograph taken fifty years before. The overturned furniture, the broken china and mess all over the floor seemed to have been there for an age. He felt alienated from it. Such ravaging intrusion into his own home and space cut him off from it.

Practicality returned, Belle on her own initiative had brought the goats in, they were bleating in the yard. Feverish and agitated, he made a clumsy job of the milking. It was considerably less milk than usual that he took up to the Riordans. He half-expected them to need a hand to finish their own milking, without Nuala. But between them, Kathy included, they had finished by the time he drove up. He was anxious not to remain, not to get engaged in any talk, afraid of questions, or that they might notice his agitation. He would have liked to ask old Tom if he had heard anything while they were away in Galway, but didn't get the opportunity.

Back in the yard, he fed the sows and the hens, then went into the house to assuage his own hunger. He crunched across bits of broken china, cut a hunk of bread, rummaged in the chaos in the bottom of the overturned fridge for some cheese, picked up a can of Guinness from the floor, and left, repelled by the carnage of his own home.

He went out through the garden at the back, took the path up through the hazel groves to the boundary wall and sat on the stone that gave him view to the west up his own valley, and also looked back down the main vale the road ran through. Dusk was beginning to leach the luminescence, tint the land with tweeded grey. A few swallows still paddled the sky with their effortless ease among bats flitting with trembling wings. Thrushes and blackbirds still made medley among the hazels.

He munched the bread and cheese, washed them down with swills from the hole in the Guinness can. The peaceful evening world around him was a restorative. It was something he could hold on to. If only he had foreseen the inevitable. Once again fate had inserted its hand, leaped in before him and cheated him of the unobtainable. He had failed to take precautions, assumed too glibly that nothing would disturb the unfolding pattern. He should never have left her alone.

The abductors must have been waiting for him to leave, watching from some hidden viewpoint before descending. But even had he remained, would desperate men have given him second thought? What resistance could he have offered if taken by surprise against probably armed thugs? He might this minute be lying among the wreckage in his kitchen, staring sightless at the ceiling, his blood congealing among the spilled coffee and cheese on the flagstones. He shivered. Who could they have been? Why did they want her so badly? He fell to remembering her face, to hearing her voice. As they had lain locked together, he had whispered love-tokens in her ears, filled her body with the plasmic milk of his genes, listened to her cries of engulfment, felt her hold him with roots of longing. He crumpled the empty can in his hand. Rage boiled up in him at his loss, fury at the cheating. Once again he had lost all at the moment it seemed sweetest.

The only light left now was the sky, leaving the hills and valleys dark as coffee-grounds in the bottom of a glass jug. He was overcome by a sense of desolation.

In the distance, like a sunbeam in a dark forest, came a car's headlamps probing across limestone pavements, illuminating ragged thorn trees. They rounded a headland and a pair of white eyes turned towards him. He got up and walked back to the yard. He came round the house just as the car swung into the yard, igniting the buildings. It sat there, engine throbbing, lights blazing, like some primeval mechanical monster. A door extended outwards like a stubby wing. 'Mr de Burgh?'

For a moment Conor froze, his assent checked a second away from the consequences of its pronouncement. Were they really Gardai? Suppose . . .

'This is the place.'

The engine was switched off, and in the ensuing quiet, all the car doors yawned open and five shadowy men emerged, three in uniform. Conor went across to turn on the lights in the house. He was surprised at so many turning out on a Sunday.

'Detective-Sergeant Flynn,' said the tallest, following him in. He wore a lightweight sportsjacket and flannel trousers. 'You didn't touch anything?' He had a chevron moustache and cold eyes. 'Good man,' he added, as Conor shook his head. He stepped carefully across the scattered débris.

The kitchen seemed to darken and grow small with the ingress of so many large men. The other man in plain clothes carried a camera and flash. One of the uniformed men was armed. At first it was a relief to have them in the house to share his disaster. 'I'll show you the other rooms,' he said. 'I've searched everywhere for her. I can't imagine what they were looking for.'

'I wonder did they find it?' mused the sergeant. 'Right,' he said, after they had viewed the lavatory and the wrenched-off cistern lid. 'Let's get on with it.' And he began to detail each of the men, while Conor leaned against a wall, feeling insignificant against their purpose, and suddenly resenting their authoritative intrusion.

It reminded him of the way doctors in hospital assume seigneural rights over patients' bodies, impose regimes of tablets and injections, carry out examinations, operations, pour in x-rays, with only the barest if any acknowledgement of the patient's private existence. Except that doctors wore bland coats. Dark uniforms were intrinsically alarming.

'Better get a few details,' said the sergeant, opening a notebook. 'Who was she?'

Who was she? His head reeled for a moment, a rush of blood and panic. 'She . . . she was just a visitor. I didn't know her.'

'Name?'

Name? Which name? 'She said her name was Inika Van Winken.'

'Was she anything like this?' The sergeant took a picture from his pocket, just as the photographer's flash went off for the third time. It was the identikit likeness of Josephine Grant that he had seen in the newspaper up at Riordans.

So that was why they were here in such numbers, he thought. 'Her hair was very short, not like that. She had a Dutch accent. I suppose it's a bit like her.'

'I wouldn't have said it likely that a normal Dutch visitor would have caused somebody to come and do this to a house they were staying in,' mused the sergeant. 'Would you, now?'

'That's why I can't understand it,' said Conor.

'Unless, that is,' continued the sergeant, 'you yourself had something that somebody else wanted very badly? They could have taken her because she was here.'

Conor laughed derisively. 'Unless it was the bank to see if there was anything more they could screw out of me.'

After more than an hour had passed, after the entire house had been closely examined and photographed, and the yard outside had been searched with powerful lamps, the five gardai righted chairs and the table and sat down as if exhausted by the inconclusiveness of their efforts. Conor filled the kettle to make a pot of tea.

'Damn all,' said the sergeant, methodically stuffing a pipe with tobacco. 'Big batch of Josephine Grant alarms this week. Been like the doctor has to answer every call though he knows well most of them are hypochondria. But this is the most interesting.'

'Could it be Orangemen took her?' asked the youngest Gardai.

'If anyone took her.' The sergeant waved a hand dismissively. 'If it was the one we're looking for, I'd be interested why she would choose this place as her safe house if she didn't know Mr de Burgh from Adam.'

'But why ransack the place?' asked Conor, as he handed round mugs of tea, put out a half-bottle of Jamieson that had survived the devastation.

'You could have done it,' suggested the photographer, who

had been unwinding the film in his camera, taking out the spool. 'You could have fallen out with her.' He turned to the others. 'D'you remember that woman with the dogs who rang up one night and said, you'll find an intruder inside 19 O'Connell drive, he's up to no good. We picked the man up and he wouldn't give an account of himself, so we put him in the cells. Turns out the lady was his lover getting her own back because he'd kicked one of her dogs.'

The largest policeman leaned back after dolloping whiskey into his mug. 'He couldn't say anything for fear his wife'd find out. Didn't he get two months for breaking and entering?'

'I was thinking more of the McKilroy business,' said the sergeant, burning his fingers as he puffed to get his pipe alight. 'Much worse than here. Half the walls were knocked out, the house was near collapsing. He'd used a JCB to smash up his home all because his wife had run off with a carpet salesman from Co Meath. He was taking another run at the place when the bucket caught on the ESB wires. He was in hospital for two months. The nuns had to take his children in.'

The photographer was reloading his camera with a fresh spool. 'What about Mrs Delaney? That was more like this. Half the furniture smashed, sofas and beds cut to ribbons, the carpets torn, the backs ripped off books, every drawer emptied, even the fridge and the cooker had been attacked, and there were piles of soot where the fireplaces had been raked out. It looked as though a dozen CIA men had spent a week in the place. And my husband only dead a week, she said. When they hear of a woman left defenceless, in they come like vultures. It'll be a big bill for the insurance, she says. It used to be put about that he had money hidden in the place. Turned out that it was she herself that turned the place over, looking for it.'

'An unfortunate woman,' said the sergeant, exuding dense clouds from his pipe. 'She need never have gone to all the trouble. The money was rolled up and kept in old treacle tins in a storeroom full of pots of paint and boxes of nails. She cleared them all out and gave them to a tinker called Clancy. We found him near drowned with drink and his wife screaming and tearing off her clothes crying she was being attacked by rats. They must have been at it for days. Clancy never recovered. We found some of the old treacle tins. Mrs Clancy told us they'd been stuffed full. They couldn't believe their luck. Blew most of it at the races. Thousands of pounds.'

'You'd never believe a tinker'd be that bad a judge of a horse,' said the big policeman.

'You remember the body found in the woods near Sixmile-bridge?' said the policeman who had not so far spoken, a swarthy man with heavy black eyebrows. 'A woman dead a couple of months in a shallow grave, some lads with their dog discovered bones sticking out of the ground. Nothing to identify her except a stain on a finger where a ring had been cut off, so tight it left the imprint of the initials Y. D. Mr Jimmy Daly had called us in one night, frightened out of his boots, shaking like the train to Dublin, he'd got back from the pub in the middle of the night to find the front door wide as a field, the lights on like it was the middle of the day, and blood and bits of clothing everywhere, and furniture scattered like a tornado had gone through the place, and no sign whatever of his lovely wife, Yvonne, and she was something, the photographs'd tell that, the sort of woman you wouldn't be able to sleep nights thinking of.'

'And it was my pictures that put him away,' said the photographer. 'The bunch of hairs they found clenched in the corpse's fingers, and the bald patch the size of a ten-pence piece on Jimmy Daly's head in a picture. Of course they matched.'

'Then out came the confessions,' said the sergeant, his small cold eyes dwelling on Conor. 'First of all it was an accident. They were fooling about, and she fell downstairs and hit her head. Then it was a quarrel and he pushed her. Then she attacked him and he was forced to defend himself. Then there was this man's watch he found in their bed, and he belted her just a bit too hard. . . .' He sucked on his pipe to keep it alight. 'Each time, of course, he panicked, made it look as though she'd been abducted, put her in the boot of the car, fetched a shovel from the toolshed. Maybe he never knew exactly what happened. But it's rare you need to look further than family or lovers in a murder . . . or a disappearance.'

Conor had made more tea, sat back on the sofa as they talked. He was exhausted, his eyelids drooped.

He woke with a shock, cold and unnerved by the glare of his surroundings, by the silence. He looked at his watch. Two a.m. His gaze travelled slowly round the empty room, trying to recollect all that had happened. The table was completely cleared except for an empty whiskey bottle. There was a cluster of mugs upside down on the draining-board. He stood up, stiff, walked across to the door. The yard was empty. He turned back. There were still bits of china and mess all over the floor, but the torn pictures had been picked up and leant against the walls, the fridge lifted up and pushed back into place, the television replaced on the dresser. Belle on her rug by the fireplace yawned, watching him. Then he noticed there was a note pinned beneath the empty Jamieson bottle. It was a receipt, signed James Flynn, sergeant. It was for a list of women's clothing together with items of make-up, washing-materials, a bag, bracelets, earrings and necklace. He looked round again. He would deal with it all tomorrow. He staggered into his bedroom, shoved the ripped mattress back on to the bed, gathered bedclothes into a heap and lay down among them.

*

The next day was grey and wet. It was always a messy business milking the goats in the rain, squatting under a cape. He trudged across the dripping land, water matting his eyelashes, to look at his sodden livestock beneath the squeezing sponge of a sky. Even the bluff was hidden in mist. But wherever he went, he walked a bit further, looked behind banks, walls, inside the ruined farmhouse in the glen, in among the build-ings, just in case. . . . He spent the rest of the morning methodically restoring and cleaning up the house to as near normal as he could. In his bedroom he collected up all his scattered papers, replaced the typewriter on the desk.

Sir, All judges should be burgled. Then they'd know what it feels to suffer the disgust, the outrage, the violation . . . and have a little less mercy on the villains.

But he was too upset to finish it. At least the typewriter still worked.

He was about to shut the cover when he found it was reluctant to fit properly. Something was preventing the catch from reaching the base. He took it off and looked inside. There was a pocket inside the lid, and it was sticking out for some reason. He felt inside and drew out a thick wad of papers. He stared at them, puzzled. They were unfamiliar. How had they come to be tucked away out of sight?

He opened the papers out and flipped through them. There were letters, photocopies, typed statements, photographs, a mass of notes and a wallet. He opened it. Bank cards and business cards, all with the name Nel Farrell on them. It seemed she worked for the Irish Press. There were also three hundred pound notes. And a few receipts for meals and petrol.

When he turned back to the wad of papers he saw to his surprise the top letter was addressed to him.

Conor, I hope it won't ever come to you reading this. But if it does, would you do me a last favour? Take the papers to a man called Stephen Monaghan at Dublin Castle. Don't let anyone know you have them, not even the Gardai. If you read them, you'll get some idea of what I was doing. Unfortunately I had to stop before I could finish the job. There are some powerful citizens in high places who would do anything to suppress this information. And they're on to me. I didn't lie to you in that respect, as if you're now reading this, you'll no doubt appreciate. I used to do a few small parts on the stage and for RTE before getting the job on the Press. I thought it best you didn't know who I really was. These people don't have a very friendly record. Use the money. It's the least I owe you. I should have liked to stay longer. Take care. Love, Nel.

A cold prickling sensation encased his skin. He looked out of the window, then got up and went quickly into the kitchen, stood frozen observing the yard. But there was nobody about, nothing moving. Those papers were dynamite, he thought. Since they hadn't found them, they could be back. Suppose they tortured her till she confessed? He returned to reread the letter, fingering her cards from the wallet, searching it for any more evidence. In another pocket he found an Equity card and a small photograph. She was like Maggie in it, masses of hair. His heart was thumping. It was as if these small pieces of paper, plastic cards with her name on, brought her close to him. One moment he felt elated as he looked at them, read her words, hearing her voice speak them. Then cold chill returned to shiver his skin as he realised the real implications. They sounded the sort of people who would kill. He must read the papers and find out more. This evening, when he'd finished work. Postponing examining them gave him a little hope to sustain him.

At this moment they might just be holding her. Rather than have already . . . disposed of her in a bog somewhere. He replaced everything in the wallet except the photograph. Then he folded the papers round it again and stuffed them back into the lid of the typewriter. It wasn't the perfect hiding-place, he thought. The searchers might be more thorough the next time.

Nuala was back when he took the churns up to Riordans in the morning. The rain had reduced to a fine mist. 'What have you done with Dorothy?' she asked. 'Haven't seen her in days.' Despite the day, her soaked hair and dripping anorak, she seemed more cheerful and outgoing than he had ever known her.

'Dorothy?' he echoed, momentarily caught out, and having to make a deliberate effort to adjust to whom she could be referring to. 'Didn't I tell you? She's gone to stay with some people near Killorglin. She sent her goodbyes.'

'That's a pity,' she said. 'She might have suited you. Couldn't stick your discomforts, I daresay. Maybe you'd better lift your finger, Conor, after the lambs are sold. You'll never get yourself a good woman without a decent bathroom.' And she laughed. 'Which reminds me, Mam says will you stop in for tea?'

For a moment he hesitated, thinking of the hidden papers. But he'd rather not be there if searchers came. 'Thanks. Will I take the milk?'

'It's O.K. I've to give Vaun a driving-lesson. Must check the old roan, she's produced her eleventh calf, late as usual.'

He watched her march across the haggard, her legs swinging with the long stride that reminded him of the thoroughbred mares in his father's stableyard. Perhaps this was a watershed in their relationship, he thought. As if before, his yearning, bristling with unmentionable longing, had been a barrier between them, made them both self-conscious. Now that sex had been assigned elsewhere they were free to be friends.

But as he turned towards the house, the warm feeling was chilled by his underlying anxiety. He had not yet emerged from a state of suspended shock. Waves of unease and horror kept coming back and washing away equanimity. What could he do about Nel Farrell's disappearance? How was he to get her papers to Dublin? Was it for the best not to inform the Gardai? And over all was the ache of her loss.

'Where's Dorothy?' asked Mrs Riordan. 'Will you go back and fetch her?'

He explained again about her leaving. Vaun, who was desultorily mashing potatoes, brushing hair out of her eyes with her elbow, suddenly became frenziedly active, fist pumping up and down the masher.

'Conor,' said Kathy, coming in from the front room. 'Can you help with my homework after tea?'

As he agreed, Mrs Riordan, face crimson from the heat of cooking, lifted a casserole on to the table. 'We had a visit from the gardai this morning. Did they call on you, Conor?'

He shook his head, feigning disinterest, ears on stalks. 'What did they want?'

She pushed out a bowl of steaming peas. 'It's still this same business, they're looking for those people who bombed the bus in the north. Had we seen anyone, you know the sort of thing.' She turned to Kathy. 'Call your uncle, tea's on the table.'

Conor sighed inwardly with relief. It was odd though that the gardai had made no mention to her of a woman disappearing from her neighbour's house. As old Tom and Nuala came in and they all settled round the table, he became caught up in the domestic conviviality of the family meal, distracted from his broken-glass thoughts.

'Did we tell you the wedding-date's been fixed, Conor?' asked Vaun, putting the big aluminium teapot out on the table. 'In one month Nuala'll be legal. McCarthy's are putting on the spread in some hotel in Galway.'

'Are you not having it here?' asked Conor. 'If the weather was right wouldn't it be perfect out on the grass, trestle-tables, a lamb on a spit, and a fiddler for dancing?'

'I think it would be best leaving it to them,' said Mrs Riordan. 'They've all the facilities at hand in the city.'

Nuala leaned forward. 'I think Conor's right. Why didn't I think of it? We could have a real old-fashioned country wedding. It's the bride's family who should decide. We could have a marquee in case it's wet. I think it's a great idea.' She looked pleadingly at her mother.

'We could,' Mrs Riordan began dubiously. 'Only Mrs McCarthy was anxious that they should arrange it. Which would save us a good bit of expense. But I suppose it would look well here.

We could clear the rubbish and old bits of machinery, give the house a lick of paint, tidy up the thatch.' Her interest began to grow. 'There was an old man from Kilnaboy that was grand on the fiddle, could make a dying man jump off his bed.'

'John Deasy's been dead these five years,' quavered old Tom. 'His fiddle's there on the wall in the bar, gathering dust ever since.'

'There'll be no bother in finding musicians,' said Nuala. 'I know a couple of fellows who play the pipes.'

'How would we roast the lambs?' asked Vaun. 'We'd need spits.'

'I'll make something up,' Conor offered.

'We'd need two lambs, wouldn't we?' asked Nuala. 'I don't fancy killing them myself.'

And there flashed into Conor's mind the picture of the girl in the glen wood crouched over the fire, roasting a leg of lamb. Nel Farrell, the journalist, living rough, hiding from those who wanted to silence her. But how had they managed to find her? Damn them, damn his rotten luck.

'We'll get O'Donnell's to do it, and have them properly dressed,' said Mrs Riordan.

'I'd love a long pink dress,' said Vaun, half-closing her eyes. 'One that'd fly about when I dance.'

Everyone seated round the table was now fired with ideas for the wedding, their enthusiasm taking off like a flock of chattering starlings, sweeping this way and that across the sky. As the meal was eaten, the plates scraped clean, second helpings dished out, plans for the wedding developed almost involuntarily. They included Conor, but he felt himself detached all the time, as if he was seated on the edge of a steep precipice. A cold echoing void which swallowed his thoughts. Here was warm effervescent reality before him, all these pink animated Riordan faces, black-haired, grey-haired, bright-eyed, all his friends and surrogate family that he loved, bubbling and holding forth. But behind was the chill abyss, and in it floated the ghostly features of Nel. He had begun to refer to her as Nel in his thoughts, the other names easily discarded. And he had also begun to assume that she was dead; and the pain was like a great jawful of teeth in the process of ripping him apart.

'I don't know why I never thought of it before,' said Mrs Riordan. 'But it wouldn't be right to let the McCarthys pay for the wedding.'

'Except it might be cheaper,' said Vaun.

They were all too absorbed in the plans to notice his agitation. Half of him wanted to remain there, safe in the cosy womb of the family atmosphere. But the other half, the relentless obeyer of the call of inevitability, was the stronger. 'Thanks for the tea,' he said, getting up. 'I've still a couple of jobs to get done while there's daylight.'

'Did you forget?' wailed Kathy. 'You promised to help me with my homework. Nobody else is any good at figures.'

'Right,' he agreed, half-relieved at being able to stay on.

As they sat down at the big round walnut table in the front room, old Tom came and crumpled into an armchair, threaded his fingers together and leaned his gaunt and practically tooth-less head back, closed eyelids thin as tissue paper, and let his adam's apple wander slowly up and down his wizened throat.

'Show us the problem then,' said Conor.

Sir, Who was the fat-head who first suggested universal education? What governments want is placid herds of amenable workers, not thousands of sharp-witted cleverclogs who can see right through their incompetence. If there has to be a show of education then let it be a load of boring rubbish, taught by the dullest drivellers to make children hate school so they learn nothing. Make them sit and draw teapots, learn endless lists of dates, the amounts of cocoa beans countries produce and lots of religion. The latter as a consolation that whatever their misfortunes in this world, they're bound to improve in the next. Or has it been like this in schools all along? Yours, etc.

When he was leaving, Mrs Riordan looked up at him over her spectacles from the lists she had been writing. 'Make sure you have nothing but sons, Conor. Eileen's safely married, and now here's Nuala about to, but I've still three daughters to go, and I can see I'll be on the dole before they get fixed up.'

As he was about to climb up into the Landrover, Nuala ran out. 'Thanks, Conor,' she said, putting a hand on his arm.

'For what?' He could not remember her ever touching him before.

'Your idea of the wedding here. It's changed Mam completely. Before, she didn't want to accept that I was getting married at all. But now she's thrown herself into it like she's the coach and we're the team with a chance. She's really accepted it. You're a genius.' He almost expected her to kiss him. 'Don't forget Wednesday,' she added.

'Wednesday?' he echoed.

'To sort out the lambs for Thursday's sale.'

As he drove down the road, away from Riordans, he felt he was leaving calm security for the alarming unknown. He approached his yard warily, keeping his head fixed straight ahead, but flicking his eyes over every piece of wall, past every tree trunk, for signs of watchers, a hidden car. He parked in the yard, his skin prickly with anticipation, every sense out on stalks. Belle got up from the doorstep, flagged her tail at him eagerly. Could he trust her reaction? he wondered, opening the Landrover door and stepping down, his whole body tense for some kind of interception. But nothing stirred. Except for the birds everywhere. After the cessation of the rain, a joyful exuberance seemed to have overtaken them and there was a cacophony of sound from all round. Shafts of evening sunshine fell from long silver splits in the clouds. Swallows skimmed over the hazel-tops and the ridge tiles, came chirruping as they dipped through the yard. He could hear one of the sows making gentle soothing grunts as she settled down to feed her bonhams. He felt his apprehension was ridiculous and entered the house forthwith. Nevertheless his heart was still thumping as he searched it . . . just in case.

Of course, they could still be out there, watching, waiting till he had settled and was off his guard, till it was dark. Someone posted up on the bluff could see everything. They could watch him as the ravens did, as he walked along the valley bottom, or if he went up the path through the garden and the hazel groves to the boundary wall. He could take his binoculars up there, he thought, and hide in the hazels and scan the bluff. But this was getting paranoid. If they wanted to search the house again, they'd have no compunction about time, they'd barge in as they had done on poor Nel. His insides revolved in ulcerous self-recrimination as he thought of her terror as they broke in. He kept wondering how they had found out, for how long they must have been watching. He stood about for some time, restless, looking out, but staying well back from the windows.

As darkness fell, he slipped out to the workshops to bring his shot-gun inside. He'd feel safer with that under his bed, he thought. Blow a hole in one of them before they got him. Then he went round and fastened all the windows, locked and bolted the doors. In his bedroom, he drew the curtains. Now was the time to read Nel's papers. He was tingling with trepidation as he lifted them out from the typewriter case, not only in anticipation of what they might reveal, but as if his actions were already alerting "them", and at any moment they would be hammering at the door, bursting in on him. His tension was so great that he found it difficult at first to concentrate on the printed and written words. But gradually, though his hair remained on end, he began to absorb the information.

It began with a detailed list of the principals of an organisation with a solid front of respectability, who appeared to control much of what went on in the country. A kind of Irish Mafia. Many were names he knew, men of reputation, members of the Dail, judges, bankers, a bishop, and of course, prominent businessmen. Against each was a succinct biography of their activities within the organisation, their responsibilities and areas of operation. Its principal source of revenue was drug-trafficking. It controlled many city and town councils, and hence half the development contracts in the country. Its methods were either the infiltration of their own members or the corruption of individuals in key positions by bribes, blackmail or force, and it employed groups of operatives who were often confused with terrorist groups and, indeed, some were staging bank raids and robberies.

Against each of the principals were reference numbers. These referred to the relevant evidence that followed, copies of letters, transactions, statements, documents and interviews with people who might be persuaded to act as witnesses, with notes about their reliability and how best to approach them to ensure their cooperation.

It was difficult to take so much in all in one go. He assumed the most damning evidence must be the letters, mostly photo-stats, and the potential witnesses she had talked to, especially those who had already made statements. What was striking was that she had managed to amass so much without being stopped before, if these people were as ruthless as they appeared. No wonder she had tried to hide.

They must have tracked her across the country, or done a blanket search, simply asking around, following every single female stranger to the district. They could have picked up word through one of the Riordans mentioning that a girl was staying at the old Casey farm in the Caherconnacht valley. Then spied on the place to see if she fitted their description.

He began to read some of the evidence. A judge called Martin figured significantly in a number of cases that were inexplicably dropped, quashed or thrown out of court on technicalities. He remembered the Senator Finnegan case. Gunrunning, about three years earlier. A scandal that nearly toppled the government. Yet the senator and two members of the Dail involved were never brought to trial because, at a preliminary hearing before Judge Martin, most of the evidence was eliminated as trivial and hearsay. Then the weapons themselves, supposedly held in the McKee barracks, disappeared. And the rumour was spread round that there never were any weapons, that it was nothing but a smear campaign against the three politicians. Yet here was a receipt signed by a Commandant Mulvaney, for eight crates of automatic weapons seized from the Dutch fishing vessel Ingrid docking at Killybegs in Co Donegal on the very date mentioned in the original indictment. He felt intoxicated as more and more corroborating facts unrolled. This was indeed dynamite. And it was lying here between his hands. He stood up, suddenly feeling ill. Quickly he folded the papers up and stuffed them back into the lid of the typewriter case. Then, clutching his mouth, ran to the lavatory, and lost all that once delicious Riordan casserole into the pure white void of the bowl. He knelt back on the floor, tears of excruciation smearing his eyes, and turned the handle to restore the cold china to its pristine whiteness. After a while he went into the kitchen for a glass of water to wash away the taste. He felt limp and gutted. Belle rose from her piece of sacking, lay down again, then got up and touched her bowl with her nose as just the slightest hint of reminder, becoming instantly apologetic that she should have assumed he might have forgotten her. He went to the dresser and took out a bag of dog-biscuits. 'Sorry, Belle. Was it . . . Dorothy, who said you were very long suffering?' But she was gratefully crunching, her tail sweeping the floor. He patted her and went to bed.

But he could not sleep. He was no longer afraid. His mind spun silently round and round like an empty turn-table, the pick-up arm returned to its rest, nothing left but echoes of the music it had played. Echoes of a woman he did not know. He could almost feel angry that she had cheated him of knowing her. So how could he feel so much pain and sorrow at losing her? What courage she must have had to root among the monster's lairs. He could not imagine himself taking such risks. Perhaps there was some personal vengeance involved. Maybe she or her family had suffered at the hands of these . . . How could he describe them? No words could describe them without over-emotive ramifications. Evil? No doubt drug-traffickers consider themselves to be doing the addicts a favour. Murderers? They would kill Nel from fear. Fear for their reputations, their ill-gotten riches, fear of their exposure as criminals.

*

In the middle of the night Conor rose, went barefoot into the kitchen for a drink of water. Through the windows he could see the yard lit by the monochrome moon, as still as a black-and-white photograph. The big problem, he thought, was that if he had to get to Dublin, somebody would have to milk the goats.

He stared out into the night shadows. They were bound to have tortured Nel, done something pretty bestial to try and extract the whereabouts of the papers. They wouldn't be too bothered with scruples. Had she blurted out the truth in her agony they would have been back by now. So either they had already killed her, or they had not yet broken her resistance. Therefore she might still be alive. In the moonlit gloom he went back to the bedroom and felt in the lid of the typewriter, took out the wad of papers and returned to the kitchen. He put them in a plastic bag, then felt up inside the chimney where he knew there was a recess behind a loose stone.

It was doing something practical in the face of his powerlessness, he thought as he washed the soot off his hands under the tap. Any small gesture that might help. Because in reality he could do so little, and that hurt and angered him. In the dark hours of the night all other action was suspended. Only his nocturnal imagination could run endlessly like the spring water gushing into the concrete cistern out in the paddocks in the moonlight.

He was up early. He was beyond the glen, searching for a missing heifer on the western slopes when he spied a figure higher up. It was Nuala herding the missing animal back towards a gap in the boundary wall. He went up to meet her, glancing at his watch. 7.30. 'Come back and I'll cook you some breakfast,' he invited her on sudden impulse. 'There's something I need your help with.'

Was he taking a risk involving her, he wondered as she assented. 'You'll find all this difficult to believe,' he began as they returned to the house. He told the story as he cut up bacon, broke eggs to fry, made the coffee, cut bread for toast. She was very attentive and he found himself comparing her with Nel, the times she had stood there in various guises as he talked and cooked. Life was oddly repetitive.

She took it all surprisingly calmly, as if such tales were common as slugs in lettuce. 'Conor,' she said, as he put a plate of hot food before her. 'How can you be sure that what she says is true, since she pretended to be all these different people?'

He went over to the fireplace, reached inside, took out the stone and brought out the plastic bag. He put the papers beside her plate. She was silent as she ate and read, and he was reassured by her frown of concentration, and the occasional amazement in her lifted brows. He had been half-afraid of her dismissal of the whole matter as impossible rubbish, or that it was his concern not hers. How beautiful she was, he thought irrelevantly. What a relief it was to share it all with someone.

'How did she manage to get it all?' she wondered, looking up at him. 'Why have you been keeping all this to yourself all this time, Conor? You never breathed a word to us.'

'While she was here it was like some game she was playing. I never knew what to believe. But I never dreamed she had all these lethal papers with her. But since they took her, it left nothing to go on, nobody to tell, nothing I could do.'

'Except get this stuff to Dublin.'

'You think I should go, then?'

She looked at him, puzzled. 'But of course. It must be made public. They'll have to let her go then.'

He gulped his coffee, wiped his mouth. 'So you think she might still be alive?'

She smiled sympathetically, put a hand across to cover his. 'Poor Conor, it must be terrible for you. You haven't said so, but I fancy you cared for her?'

He nodded.

She helped herself to more coffee, then shivered. 'I'll do the milking and feeding for you. Go now. Drive all the way, or go to Galway and take the train. We both know these people are evil. What good are they doing the country, rotting it with heroin and corruption? It makes a mockery of our lives. When you're up against the intransigence and bigotry of the Brits and the prods, you feel the end justifies the means. But this is ourselves they're sucking the blood from. These sort of people are only interested in lining their pockets.'

'But suppose it's all invented, a put-up job designed to make trouble and stir up scandal?'

'Damn it, Conor,' she cried, exasperated, pushing her chair back and getting up. 'You're the most indecisive person I've ever met. This isn't the time to mess about with doubts. Are you ever going to get off your backside and do something? You've been hiding away here like the world was crawling with maggots. If you won't take these papers, then I'll go.'

He was stung rigid by her accusations. 'I was trying to work out the best thing to do. . . .'

'Which is commonly called sitting on the fence. Or in other words, avoiding becoming involved in anything. You sit here writing letters to the papers, but you never actually do anything. It's like standing on the roof and emptying buckets of water over passers-by. It may annoy them but it doesn't achieve anything.'

He got up trembling, nodding as much in agreement as to shake off the pain of her words.

She softened, touched his arm. 'I shouldn't have said that. I haven't forgotten about the plane-crash and the girl in Australia. But surely you can see that you must do something quickly, for Nel's sake?'

He nodded. 'Of course. I'm glad I told you.'

She hugged him. 'I'm glad too, that you felt you could confide in me. Now that I'm going to be married, I see you in the place of Sean, like you're a brother to me. It's funny, isn't it? We could never talk like this before.'

He was over-conscious that he had never held her before, felt his susceptibilities wavering.

She looked up at him. 'I haven't been able to talk to anyone about Niall. And there I was up there, putting my family in a terrible state, announcing this great turn-round in my life, never dreaming what was going on down here. I did wonder in the back of my mind, will anything happen between Dorothy and you. I was even a little jealous, as if you were our property.' She gave his hands a final squeeze before letting go. 'You mustn't think of the worst. There's a good chance she'll be all right.'

'The sooner I go the better, then.'

'If they're on the look-out to see if someone takes off for Dublin, better use our car, and leave me the Landrover.'

He looked at her quickly, his jaw dropping. 'I shouldn't be involving you. Suppose they come looking for me and find you here?'

'I'll take care of myself, don't you worry.'

'I don't like to do it all the same. . . .'

'If you don't go this minute, I'll go myself,' she exclaimed. 'Maybe it would be better if I did.'

'No, I'll go,' he said, picking up the papers. 'I'll put these in the bottom of a bag with a few clothes I can change into on the train.' His hands were shaking as he covered the papers with a clean shirt, pants and socks, best shoes and his suit carefully folded. He put one of Nel's £100 notes in his wallet.

'There's biscuits in the dresser for Belle in case I don't get back tonight,' he said as they got into the Landrover. 'The sows' meal is ready-mixed in the barn, a bucket each, make sure they've plenty of water, and a bucket for the bonhams in the second shed, and there's grain for the hens. . . .'

'I'll manage,' said Nuala as they drove up to Riordans. 'If you can't get back, just ring and pretend you've decided to spend the night in Galway. I'll tell Mam you went for a dental appointment, so I asked you to take the car and have the brakes relined. She won't notice if they're done or not.'

As he set off up the valley road he felt the red Datsun doubly responsive under his feet compared to the day before, weighed down with Riordans. At least he could shift it if any pursuit appeared. His apprehension was acute over the first few miles, expecting to come across parked cars waiting to pounce at every turning, in every gateway. He kept glancing in the rearview mirror, and nearly suffered heart-failure when a white car nosed out of a road-junction moments after he had passed. But it turned and went the other way. A Toyota. Looked like Donal Smith, the vet's car. But as the miles went by and nothing untoward materialised, his confidence grew a fraction. Of course, some watcher with a radio might have sent word through the ether to intercept him. On impulse he took a left turning for Ballyvaughan. That would fox them. It meant a longer journey, but quicker to the main road, and once on that he should be safe.

The waters of Galway bay were a deep gentian blue, and the distant Connemara hills dark as the notches on a crocodile's tail. Dark-bellied clouds trailed above them. Probably be showers by mid-day, he thought, as he drove along the coast road to Kinvara, sandwiched between a truck laden with orange gas-bottles and a car with German number plates. Not a sign to arouse suspicion anywhere. He wondered whether he'd eluded the watchers, fooled them by taking the Riordans' car, or if they were just figments of his fear, bogeymen of his paranoia. Or perhaps their agents were everywhere, laughing at his complacency as they noted his passing. It could be the inside of the car, the speeding capsule responding obediently to his control, that lulled him into feeling secure. Nobody he passed evinced the slightest interest in him nor seemed to constitute any kind of threat. A boy in shirt-sleeves on a tractor towing a silage harvester, a suited salesman in his Sierra, an elderly priest in a dented Mercedes, a rusty pick-up laden with fish-boxes, two girls on bicycles, legs as bare as uncooked sausages, a petrol-tanker reversing into a garage, awkward as a stranded whale, and young women hurrying home, having delivered their children to school; this was the world going unconcernedly about its business. He swerved round a van parked outside a shop, a woman in curlers arguing with the driver, the two gesticulating like Punch and Judy set in the stage created by the open van doors. Nuala would be milking the goats now, he thought. No problem getting them down off the hills, Belle would do anything for a woman.

As he drove through the suburbs of Galway city, it occurred to him that to leave the car in a garage and actually get the brakes done might not only lend veracity to Nuala's story to Mrs Riordan, it might even improve the car's ability to stop. And it would solve the parking problem. Also, just in case some zealous watcher had recognised the Riordan car, however far-fetched his overworked imagination, leaving it in a garage might divert their suspicions. There was a garage in Eyre street that had fitted a new clutch to the Landrover once. Could they be persuaded to reline a mere Datsun's brakes without an appointment, perhaps as an emergency?

After the wildly optimistic foreman standing in the middle of a pack of cars like a telegraph pole half-submerged in flood waters had promised to see what he could do, it was but a short walk to the railway station. He carried the grip-bag over-conscious of its burden, trying not to keep looking over his shoulder, just glancing everywhere by swivelling his eyes, the back of his neck burning with the certainty of watchers. The first two morning trains had gone. It was now 10.15 and the next one wasn't till two in the afternoon. The booking-clerk magnanimously suggested a coach. It wasn't as quick, of course, and some people didn't care for the motion, but it was very convenient, just outside the door . . . Conor was trying to let his eyes wander casually about, taking in everyone passing, queuing, standing about, pretending nonchalance as he list-ened. The next one should be leaving in about five minutes. Conor nodded his thanks and tried to appear not to be in a hurry. This would fool them, he thought. They'd never expect him to travel by bus.

It was about half-full, mostly young people, students he suspected, or ex-students not yet employed, buzzing with pin-ball repartee and blitzes of laughter. He sat next to an elderly lady, his heart still thumping, slipped his bag behind his calves for protection, wished he had a book to read. They were nearly at Athenry before he realised that the elderly and silent lady beside him was not wearing a headscarf and Dunne's Store's grey cardigan and matching skirt, but was a nun in modern attire. She was reading a Mills & Boon, and rested a plastic lunch box on her knees from which she devoured, despite the early hour, a continuous stream of sandwiches, chocolate biscuits and iced buns. He tried to ignore the appetising smell of food and stared past her munching profile at the passing countryside. Endless small fields, a few cattle up to their bellies in rushes and ragwort, hawthorn hedges heavy with foliage. How luxuriant and under-used is the land, he thought, anxious to take his mind off the burning bulk of the bag behind his feet. The sky darkened and rain slid in diagonals across the windows.

Sir, We little ticks may bleat, nip, prick, and there may be millions of us, but against those thousand-mile Mastodons, the USA and the USSR, we're the proverbial raindrops off a duck's arse. And we hate each other, too. We're Catholic ticks, Protestant ticks, Capitalist ticks, Socialist ticks, and none of us can agree. Could we ever band together like the

151

Lilliputians binding Gulliver, and disarm the USA and the USSR? If we don't, the clock ticks inexorably towards dooms-day. Yours, etc.

'Conor,' his therapist had said to him. 'This tendency to slide off into general discussion about world problems is avoiding the real issue, isn't it?' There was a curious smell in her room, he thought. Could be from her. The sour gas that comes from the bubbles in beer. 'What is the real issue?' he asked. 'You know perfectly well,' she replied: 'You are.' He shook his head. 'I find it hard to be the real issue against the backdrop of all those momentous political intrigues and dramas, the famines and the killings and the disasters going on out there.' 'They're not important,' she said. 'Not at this particular moment. As we speak together, nothing that is happening out there is affecting us.' Could you be described as a psychotherapeutic ostrich? he wondered.

By the time they had reached Athlone, the nun had emptied her lunch-box, the Mills & Boon had fallen shut on her lap, and her head sunk in sleep. They stopped to let passengers off or on or to find a lavatory or a drink. Conor took his bag and changed at frantic speed in the lavatory, then bought a sand-wich and a can of Guinness. The students came back on board clutching clusters of beercans like clips of ammunition. Two of the girls had brightly coloured hair, verging on mauve and emerald, one young man had blond hair waxed into quills, and a thin girl with hair in fifty plaits sat strumming a guitar. Two elderly couples came aboard, their families congregating round the door to say farewell. When the nun came back she smiled at Conor, acknowledging him for the first time. Perhaps it was his suit, he thought, tailoring him to respectability.

'I love a long journey,' she confided, settling back into her seat, her lunch-box restocked. 'It's like a tonic. It can never last too long for me. Are you going to Dublin on business?'

'That's right,' he assented. 'On business.'

Another shower of rain drummed, the bus tyres hissed through the drenched tarmac, the plait-haired girl sang to her guitar, sometimes the other students joined in, sometimes they drowned her with boisterous laughter. Conor ate his sandwich. The long reaches of the main road curved over the undulating miles of Westmeath, the grass verges meeting the asphalt as casually as water.

If only he had managed to arrive at the terms he was now on with Nuala earlier, he thought. Then perhaps the nuptial arrangements now current would have been his. What an irony that Nel, too, had been taken from him. Women were always being snatched from his grasp. Was it because he was too inactive, failed to take the initiative? Somebody had once said to him, perhaps it was his grandmother, for she believed in laissez-faire, the flower you pick for the vase lives half the life of the one left to bloom where it grows. But then there had been that dry summer when half the garden died, and the occasion when some drunken dealer had reversed his horse-box across the flower-beds.

'I'm going up to Drogheda,' said the nun. 'For a refresher course at the Lourdes Hospital in tropical medicine before returning to Africa. I was born up there, south of the Boyne. Near Laytown. D'you know that part of the world?'

Conor shook his head. The nun had sharp bird-like eyes that one moment flicked at him inquisitively, and the next clouded and softened like tea poured into milk.

'I see you have the Atlantic colouring,' she said. 'Fisherman or farmer?'

He laughed, then explained.

'I was brought up on a farm,' she said. 'A lovely farm of land on the Nanny river. We had the Jersey cows. I remember the milking-machine filling the big glass bottles, and the cats sitting waiting in the dairy for their bowl to be filled. My brothers farm there now. They used to play football in the yard and they always made us girls stand in the goal. I preferred to play the piano. My father loved to sing. He had a fine voice, like old John McCormack. And there was always the sea, a few minutes on the bicycle. I loved that strand, so wide and spacious.'

After a while the nun's head nodded into sleep again. And then they were in Dublin, passing Phoenix Park. Conor picked up his bag and went forward to ask the driver to let him off at Wellington Quay.

As the coach drove off, he stood with his bag among the rush and din of traffic and the anonymous citizens, his fear returned. But nobody appeared to be aware of him. He glanced at his watch. 3.30.

In the precincts of the Castle he asked for Stephen Monaghan, and was given directions. He crossed a courtyard and mounted a creaking staircase. These, he realised from the signs, were the Attorney General's offices. A bespectacled girl checked on her intercom. 'Mr Monaghan's at the Four Courts today.'

He did not enjoy the prospect of having to carry the bag out in the streets again, even though it wasn't far to cross the Liffey. The sun was shining now. Gulls squawked and floated over the bridge like windblown sheets of newspaper. The traffic roared. On the steps of the Four Courts a group of men stood talking, one in black gown and barrister's wig. Conor hesitated to interrupt. 'Could anyone tell me how I can find Mr Stephen Monaghan?'

As he stood beneath the great portico of the Courts and spoke the words, his head swam, not so much with foreboding, but with the river in its deep confinement behind him, more a feeling of exposure as if he was standing on a ledge halfway up a precipice.

They all stopped talking, turned to stare at him, momentarily suspicious of a stranger in a fraternal city. Conor blinked to clear his head as a short man with near-white hair looked at him sharply. 'I'm Stephen Monaghan,' he said. Horizontal lines of brows and mouth against vertical lines of nose and jowls made a rectangle of his face.

'Might I have a word?' asked Conor, stepping back.

Monaghan looked at his watch. The other members of the group had returned to their discussion. 'I haven't much time,' he said, taking a few paces along the steps and glancing at the security gardai standing at the entrance.

'A journalist called Nel Farrell asked me to deliver some papers to you.'

'I don't know anybody of that name. What papers? Is it to do with some case?' Monaghan regarded him suspiciously.

'You don't know Nel Farrell?' Conor asked, surprised.

Monaghan frowned impatiently. 'I do not. What's it to do with?'

Conor hesitated, dismayed, 'She works on the Irish Press.'

Monaghan turned as if to dismiss him and return to his colleagues. 'I've never heard of her.'

'It's information she's been working on. About drug-trafficking and arms-deals.'

'Why didn't she bring it herself. Mr . . . ?'

'De Burgh. She was staying in my house. While I was out on

Sunday, she was abducted and the house was ransacked. They must have been looking for this.' He lifted the bag.

Monaghan's impatience disappeared, and he stared at Conor as if trying to assess from his appearance the significance of what he had told him. 'I'd better have a look, then.' He returned to the group, exchanged a few words then turned round and signed for Conor to accompany him.

Monaghan led him up the main staircase, taking precise metronomic steps in his neat dark-blue suit and shiny black shoes. 'Are you in the information business, Mr de Burgh?'

'I'm a farmer. I found this stuff hidden in the lid of my typewriter case with a note asking me to deliver it to you.'

Monaghan nodded gravely as they headed down a long passage. 'They all know me. I'm the official sieve for unsubstantiated rumour. It comes in by the barrow-load, Mr de Burgh. I'm like a popular publisher, every hopeful inundates me with scripts.' He opened a door and ushered him into an office. There were three secretaries at their desks, all paused from their typing to smile as they passed through to an inner office. 'Agnes, dear,' he addressed one of them. 'Could you find us a cup of tea?' The office they entered was small, made even more cramped by stacks of dossiers and papers heaped against bookcases themselves bulging files, like layers of archaeological shards, each labelled and itemised, each grey and undistinguished. He gestured at a chair and sat down behind his desk.

Conor undid the zip of his bag, embarrassed at having to pull out his clothes in order to reach the papers. Monaghan took a case from his top pocket and unfolded a pair of spectacles, perched them on his nose and began to peruse the papers. Conor let his gaze travel round the room and out of the window. Outside was a grey phalanx of Georgian casements, in each were small cameos of office activity, representing hundreds of people immured behind walls of paperwork, processing millions of words. He fell to visualising the secretaries and clerks in their neat blouses and trim skirts, spending their working hours like spotlessly clean miners in tunnels of paperwork, then catching the buses home in the evening to their bed-sits and flats, cooking curried baked-beans on toast, rushing out to meet their boyfriends for a movie, or stepping naked into the shower to wash their hair and then iron their neat white blouses while watching *Dallas* on TV. Monaghan was silently absorbed in his reading, going through sheet after sheet. The door opened and the girl Agnes brought in a tray on which stood a brown teapot, pink milk-jug, yellow sugar-bowl, one white and one pale-blue cup and saucer, together with a plate of biscuits. Monaghan looked over the tops of his spectacles. Agnes had a bow on her blouse, beside it was pinned a marcasite brooch. She had blond hair and dimpled cheeks, and seemed as fresh and clean as a new sheet of typing-paper. 'It's the Earl Grey, Mr Monaghan,' she said. 'We've run out of the Lapsang.'

He reached out a hand and clutched half her black polyester rump, fingers curling with the familiarity of the rugbyman's grasp. 'And we know where it's gone, don't we?' His voice had risen several notes with jocularity. 'This is only my office on the days I'm involved in court, Mr de Burgh.' He released her with a pat, small geraniums of colour on her cheekbones. 'The rest of the week I'm at the Castle. And while the cat's away . . .'

'I'll buy some Jasmine tea from Bewlay's in my lunch-hour tomorrow, Mr Monaghan,' she promised, going to the door. 'Or would you rather the Keemun?'

'What happened to that green tea Deirdre bought last week? That was delicious.'

She shook her head, a lock of blond hair falling across her sudden lascivious smile. 'All gone. . . .'

'The Keemun, then.' He waved back to the papers, resettling his spectacles as she went out. He waved a hand at the tray. 'Help yourself, Mr de Burgh.'

About ten minutes later he stood up, put his spectacles away, rubbed the bridge of his nose as if to remove the ineradicable frown that had appeared on his brows, and came round to pour himself a cup of tea, concentrating on the routine in silence. Conor watched him expectantly.

Monaghan returned to his seat, sat down and rubbed his forehead again, sitting back to savour his tea. 'Tell me, Mr de Burgh, how exactly did you come by these papers?' He listened patiently as Conor explained all that had happened. When the story was finished, he nodded. 'Let us contact the Irish Press.' He reached for the phone. 'To check on Miss Farrell.' He pressed a button. 'Get me Pat Sheehy at the Press.' His eyebrows moved up and wrinkled his now smoothed brow. 'I'm very surprised that this stuff has reached me. Surprised, you understand, that it was allowed to get this far. Either you

156

were very lucky, or they didn't quite appreciate what was in them.' He looked at the phone. 'Hallo, Pat? Fine. And yourself? Is that right? Listen, Pat, I'm interested in a reporter called Nel Farrell. D'you have anyone of that name working for you? Are you sure? You know them all? Not even freelance. Well, it's a big outfit, I didn't expect you to know every mouse in the barn. She could have been some cub in the outer office covering funerals. Sure, maybe it was some other paper. Listen, before you go. There's nobody there who's been off sick recently, or absent on some assignment? No? I'm trying to trace someone and there's not a lot to go on. Fine. Maybe see you at the weekend at Portmarnock.' He put the receiver down and nodded. 'From what you've told me, Mr de Burgh, all the different names she's used, assuming different identities with the speed of a chameleon, there's no reason to expect that Nel Farrell is her real name. She could have had the cards printed to help her undercover identity. In a sense it doesn't matter who she was.' He patted the papers. 'These are what matter.' He got up to pour himself another cup of tea. 'Will you have another cup?'

Conor shook his head.

'Right enough. It's not the real thing.' Monaghan sat down again, sipped his tea.

'You mean the papers are no good?'

Monaghan chuckled. 'No, no. I meant the tea. Earl Grey is a blend for the average palate, Mr de Burgh, it's not for the discerning. I should really apologise for giving it to you, but my girls out there are addicted.' He sighed. 'What you have brought me here puts me in the position of the general who has the responsibility of pressing the button when word comes the enemy missiles are on their way. It's quite stupefying.' He looked at his watch. 'Corruption in high places. It confirms and provides proof of what we've suspected for some time. It's a marvellous piece of investigation. A real scoop.' He stood up and put a hand on the teapot to test if it remained hot enough. 'Did you . . . take copies yourself?'

Conor shook his head.

'Good,' replied Monaghan, pressing a button on his telephone. 'Agnes, my little bundle of gunpowder, ask Despard to come up, will you?' He turned to Conor. 'The fewer traces outside here the better.' He went over to the window, stood looking out with his hands in his pockets. 'I wonder did Miss

Farrell take such precautions as to keep copies herself? What do you think?'

Conor shrugged. 'I knew nothing about the papers till after she'd gone. But I suppose it would make sense if she had.'

Monaghan nodded thoughtfully. 'Just so. The worst that could happen would be if certain daily papers got hold of anything. We don't want anyone alerted.'

'Of course not,' agreed Conor. He wondered if he ought to get up and leave now that delivery had been achieved. It was out of his hands now.

There came a knock at the door. 'Come,' said Monaghan, returning to his desk. Two security guards in unobtrusive dark uniforms entered. Both were armed. Monaghan picked up the papers.' Take these, Despard,' he said, handing them to the first of the two guards. 'To the shredder.'

'Very good, Mr Monaghan,' said Despard, taking the sheaf of papers and turning on his heel.

It was only as the door closed that the significance of Monaghan's words broke into Conor's complacency like a pack of excited dogs. He leaped to his feet. 'The shredder?' he exclaimed. 'What does that mean? You're not going to destroy them?' He lunged towards the door.

Monaghan barred his way. 'Don't make a fool of yourself, Mr de Burgh.' He tried to push him back towards his chair. 'Let me explain.'

'No,' shouted Conor. 'That girl probably died to collect all that information. You can't let them do it.'

'Don't be stupid,' exclaimed Monaghan, as Conor tried to barge him out of the way. 'It's not what you think.'

Conor managed to push him aside, tore open the door and rushed past the astonished typists, out into the passage. There was no sign of the two guards. He sprinted down the passage to the main stairs, ran down, passing people who turned, disapproving of such extravagant indecorum. Halfway down he realised the guards must have gone the other way down the passage, and he raced back up again, his heart beating with anger and fear as he pounded down the shiny lino. He skidded to a stop beside a lift, saw the indicator ascending. He found another stairs, but they went up as well as down. As he hesitated, two barristers came out of a door, stared at him as they passed, talking to each other, voices pattering like descants to the rhythm of their squeaky shoes. A secretary clutching a file came down the stairs. 'Did you see two guards?' he blurted out. She looked at him disdainfully. 'I did not,' she replied. He ran down the stairs, clearing five at a time, swinging round the banisters. At each floor empty passages radiated away, filled with the mouse-murmur of voices emanating from the many rooms either side. 'I can't believe it,' he cursed. 'The bastard. The bloody bastard.'

Uncertain of where he was, he was climbing back up the stairs when he saw Monaghan waiting for him. 'Why?' he shouted at him, almost incoherent with rage. 'Why did you do it? Are you one of them? Are you trying to protect your own kind? I'll go to the newspapers, I'll tell them everything I know.'

Monaghan shook his head. 'They won't print a word without evidence.'

'How do you know I haven't got copies?'

Suddenly Monaghan was angry. 'Listen. I could have let you go back to your farm believing the wheels of retribution were being instantly set in motion. But I chose not to because I wanted you to understand how things operate here.' He turned on his heel and walked rapidly down the passage.

Conor stood panting, sweating, anguished, undecided. But his anger remained. He ran after Monaghan. The outer office was now empty, the desks vacant, the typewriters covered. He found Monaghan standing by the window in the inner office. 'What am I to understand? That you condone drug-pushing and corruption? That you don't give a fig for all these young-sters rotting with heroin addiction?'

Monaghan waved at a chair. 'Sit down, Mr de Burgh. I'm a servant of the government. I'm not a political animal. What I'm concerned about is the stability of the state. Anything that is liable to rock the boat is my prime concern. D'you understand that?'

Conor did not sit down. Still breathing hard, he leaned on the desk. 'That information could save the country millions of pounds.'

'Is that what you're after, Mr de Burgh?' snapped Monaghan. 'Money? You're wanting payment for this information?'

'You know I'm not interested in that,' shouted Conor.

'Then what do you want?' Monaghan swelled like an irate owl. 'People like you have no idea what goes on behind the scenes to keep this island afloat. How d'you think we support half the country on the dole? The sort of scandal that your evidence, or rather Miss Farrell's, to give her her due, could sink us with one belch.'

Conor remained breath-tight with anger. 'You know what I'm talking about. How can you stand there and condone the poisoning of young people with drugs while the pushers get elected to the Dail as honest brokers of the country's interests?'

Monaghan waved a hand dismissively. 'How do we know that stuff was genuine? It could be a massive fabrication to discredit the government.'

Conor snapped his fingers. 'You knew it was good. I saw it in your eyes when you first read it. That girl Nel Farrell, Josephine Grant, Maggie, whatever her real name was, did a really good job.'

Monaghan's face, ragged with rage, suddenly resumed its rectangular shape. 'Josephine Grant? What has she got to do with this?'

'I'm not wasting another ounce of my breath on you,' cried Conor, so angry his mind was incoherent with rage. He seized his bag and ran from the room.

'Wait,' shouted Monaghan. 'Come back. . . .'

Conor did not stop. He was out of the door, through the outer office, along the passage and slapping his feet down the broad marble staircase with furious resolution, the voice of Monaghan calling behind him in the great echoing silence of the empty building. Once outside the din of rush-hour traffic was like the roar of surf pounding rocks, Inns Quay filled with cars. He mingled with people hurrying home along the pavement, turned into Church Street, no idea where he was heading, except to get away. He turned down a side street, saw a pub and plunged through its door into the dark refuge of its vinous cavern.

*

There was the steady clamour of thirty or so people letting off the pressure of a day's work. It was no laminate and vinyl lounge glittering to capture passing trade, but an old pro-fessional drinking den of smoked mahogany counters worn like an old whore's thighs, beerpulls of white Edwardian porcelain and brass measures on the upturned Jamiesons and Powers. He ordered a pint of Guinness from the old woman behind the bar. As he watched her dispassionately filling the fat glass, he could feel his rage inside himself like a furnace contained within its kiln. Onto it he sank the black liquid till the incandescent coals of his burning thoughts settled into a congealed mass.

'I'll take a pint, too, Charlie,' said a voice beside him as he leaned impacted upon the counter. 'Charlie was ten years old,' the voice continued, 'when the Four Courts were under seige in '16, helping her father in here. Curfew or not, if a place has a reputation for never selling a bad pint, people'll crawl up the drainpipes to get in. My grandfather was a judge then. He didn't come home for five days. When he was brought home on a stretcher my grandmother thought he'd been wounded in the shooting, nearly died of fright. Turned out he was near drowned from the inside out. He'd been trapped in here all the while. Charlie remembers him, don't you, Charlie?' Monaghan held up his glass, leaned close and spoke into his ear. 'Tell me about Josephine Grant?'

Conor had no words prepared for such a question. His anger was bitter as ash, but there was still half a glass of soothing liquid in his hand. He was puzzled that Monaghan should have pursued him here.

Monaghan suggested they move across to a small table. 'Let me put the question differently,' he said, bringing his chair close as they sat down. 'Why did you mention Josephine Grant in the same sentence as Nel Farrell?'

'Why d'you want to know?'

Monaghan emptied his glass and ordered two more pints from a passing youth in a white coat, Charlie's assistant. He was plainly struggling to contain his own irritation. He looked round again as if making sure they were not overheard. 'It could be important. It affects the source of the material you brought me.'

The alcohol was beginning to work on Conor's empty stomach. 'What does that matter since you've destroyed it?'

Monaghan frowned. 'If what you told me is true about the abduction of the unfortunate Miss Farrell, connection with those papers has proved a trifle hazardous. These people have many interests, among them the IRA. And you know what a depressingly efficient record they have of eliminating any threats to their interests? I was trying to protect you.'

Conor's anger began to revive. He gulped down more Guinness. 'You mean you haven't destroyed them at all? What the bloody hell are you playing at?'

'It was your assumption,' Monaghan pointed out coldly. 'I never said anything about them being destroyed.'

'You led me to believe it,' snapped Conor hotly.

'Keep your voice down, old man,' said Monaghan, turning to catch the eye of the youth in the white coat.

'It's my turn,' growled Conor, pulling out his wallet, his fingers sliding over the sleek, unused £100 note of Nel Farrell's as he pulled out a fiver. He had to clamp his teeth over an incipient grin, abruptly lightened of the anger he had been carting about for the last hour.

Monaghan sighed. 'Would I have been likely to destroy them?'

'If you'd been working for them?'

Monaghan laughed. 'That's the chance I take, too. There's some truth in what I said in the office, you know. When I was a youngster just passed my law exams and got a job in the Prosecutor's Office, I was bowled over at the cases that poured in, a ton of files a week at times. My God, I thought, this alone'll keep the courts busy till doomsday, what's going to happen tomorrow? But of course most of the stuff was rubbish. What shocked me though as a greenhorn was the number of deserving cases my chief chucked out, never allowing them to reach the Attorney-General's desk. Dirty business afoot, I thought, Stephen's here to see fair play.' He flicked his eyebrows self-deprecatingly as the fresh pints were placed on their table. 'I had my ideals too, you see. But the man who had my job in those days was a real scholar, knew the law like his wife's backside. His explanation for his manipulation was that the Attorney-General was a political appointee. The poor man'd view every case as a chance to make political mileage whatever the consequences to the country. So it was necessary to be mindful of his prejudices and be careful not to overload him. After all, isn't he a very busy man?'

Conor was scandalised. 'You mean the Attorney-General might suppress those papers anyway?'

Monaghan shrugged. 'Could be. So I'll have to be very careful how I handle it. But you keep that to yourself, now.'

They were into their fourth pints and Charlie had brought them each a ham roll. She was surprisingly deft and confident for someone of eighty, Conor thought. She was quicker than her youthful assistant, though with forearms thin as broomhandles and fingers like pencils she hardly seemed to have the strength to lift a full pint, so that she appeared to move with studied grace, each movement careful and deliberate, a faint twist of amusement on her dried chilli lips, her glass-pale eyes never looking directly at anyone who might be looking at her. He was beginning to feel relaxed, if not a little drunk.

'Which brings me back to Josephine Grant,' said Monaghan.

'That bloody terrorist,' exclaimed Conor.

'Did Nel Farrell talk about her?' asked Monaghan.

'She pretended to be her at one stage,' said Conor, and he explained about the series of transformations.

Monaghan listened with interest. 'Tell me about the abduction.'

Conor described what had happened. 'I'd got pretty fond of her.' He was feeling very befuddled, unused to so much drink. 'I wish I could get her back. But she's probably dead by now.' All of a sudden his eyes filled with tears.

Monaghan nodded. 'I'm sorry, old man. It doesn't look too good. Unless she's managed to hold out.'

The bar and all the drinkers rolled out of focus when Conor shook his head to clear his eyes. 'Where d'you think they might have taken her?'

Monaghan put a brotherly arm round his shoulder. 'It'd be like looking for a wave in the ocean.'

'And so many false names,' groaned Conor. 'I've no idea what she's called.'

'She had to cover her tracks,' said Monaghan.

'I hate feeling so helpless,' swore Conor.

'Listen,' said Monaghan. 'You leave it to me. I'll put out a few discreet enquiries through our contacts.' His eyes narrowed and he looked round the bar. 'We might be able to do something. If it isn't too late.'

Charlie brought two more pints over to them. 'Threepence in your grandfather's day, Mr Monaghan. Not many of the gentlemen drank porter then.'

Conor knew he was drinking too much, that the drunker he became the thirstier he grew. Eventually a stiffness came into his arm to act like a brake, slowing him down, but by then he was finding it difficult to keep abreast of what people were saying, since now there seemed to be more than just he and

Monaghan, acquaintances, perhaps. Later they all left, he could remember clambering into the back of a car, and arriving somewhere else, trying to walk very stiffly so that he would not appear to be drunk. Sometime he was sick into a lavatory, that old familiar head-down-in-the-bowl, like those who have been guillotined once would dejectedly recognise it the next time should it happen. At some stage he must have passed into unconsciousness.

*

He was woken by the most appalling din, as if a great herd of cattle were stampeding over him, a million hooves clattering through his skull. Through cracks in his shrivelled eyes he found himself crouched on a bench at a large railway station, no sign of his bag, and hundreds of commuters hurrying past, coats and brief-cases all but brushing his face. He felt terrible. His head was splitting, his mouth was rancid, and he was shaking. After sitting for a while in a semi-coma as the human tide rushed past, his mind an ugly blank, he got up and dragged himself across to the news-stand. At least his wallet was still intact. He bought some aspirin then went across to the coffee-bar. It was Connolly station, that was the only information he felt able to assimilate.

After a while the combination of coffee and aspirin raised him to a state of ashen reflection. All that had been said the night before lingered in his memory in a incomprehensible muddle. They must have brought him here in the middle of the night, left him to catch the first train.

Leave it to me, Monaghan had said. But what could he do? How could he believe a word the man had said? For all he knew Monaghan might already have tipped them off. But he felt too ill to care what might happen to him as a result. All he wanted to do was return home, to get away from it all.

Time settled rather than passed. He caught a train, sat rigid in a corner-seat clutching a bundle of daily papers, unconvinced that death might not be preferable.

He slept fitfully, flesh sweating beneath cold skin, stomach like the maggoty corpse of a long-dead seagull. Only as the train rumbled over the Shannon into Athlone station did an interest in the world reassert itself, and he began to read his papers. There had been a particular if only half-conscious motivation that had made him buy them in the first place. Body of a tourist, a young man from Hartlepool, taken from the river at Rooskey. A mother and two young children burned in a house in Finglas. Two elderly sisters killed outside Slane when their Morris 1000 was demolished by two tons of Mercedes driven by a director of a well-known brewery. Despite evidence of inebriation, verdict at the inquest was death by misadventure. That follows, he thought. The Gardai were treating as murder the discovery of the body of a man believed to have INLA connections, in a caravan near Carlingford. At the inquest on Eileen Maquire in Kilkenny, the coroner said that to ride a horse on the road without wearing a cap was like diving off the top-board into an empty swimming-pool. The deceased left five orphaned children. No mention of a young woman anywhere, at least, he thought. But they would have buried her in some secret place. His eye was then caught by an article about the social ghettoes where heroin addiction flourished and the unemployed sub-culture thrived on violence to finance its distraction from the despair of no prospects. Back to Dickens. But he felt tense with anticipation as he read. Was Monaghan likely to act, or was he part of the conniving? Or had he, himself, failed to understand the whole point of the exercise? God, if only he didn't feel so ill.

Sir, How is it that with all the resources and ingenuity of man's enquiring mind that nobody has yet invented a liquid that gives all the pleasure but none of the poison of alcohol? What an opportunity lies waiting for the genius who creates the nectar that will allow us to get drunk without wishing the next morning we were dead. Yours, etc.

It was raining in Galway City. He ran most of the way to the garage, but was still well-soaked. 'The brakes were like paper,' said the foreman, picking black lumps from under his fingernails. He was a prospectively dapper man with his neat hair and smart white coat, except that he could never refrain from getting right inside and underneath the problems people brought him, so that he was always smudged with grease. 'I'd say you were lucky to get the yoke here in one piece. But she'll stop like a cat now. The bill's in the office.'
The rain had stopped but the roads were too wet to test the brakes. Conor stopped at a supermarket to buy some stores.

He was feeling better. Perhaps it was the dash through the rain. Perhaps it was the proximity of home, the valley, the wild stony landscape he was addicted to, that lay across the bay, dark blue backs of geological leviathans asleep beneath the grey rain sponges. Odd, he thought as he left the city, how he felt as if the Riordans were more his own family than his own father and mother.

As he turned off the Gort road for Kinvara, his imagination awoke a neglected consideration. What might have been happening in his absence? He drove faster, fantasising a dozen terrible alternatives. He took the last stretch down the twisting valley road like a hawk coursing the land, backwards and forwards, nearing the cluster of roofs that were Riordans. His own were invisible, hidden behind the ridge that divided the two farms. As he swung into the driveway, already expecting the worst, he saw the two older girls. They were dragging the cutter-bar from a shed towards their old tractor. Thank God, he thought, sighing with relief.

'The wanderer returns,' hailed Vaun, peering in at him. 'You look like an escaped convict, a suit but no tie, and unshaven.'

In reflex action he put a hand to his chin and looked down at himself, aware for the first time that he had completely forgotten his appearance. Then he remembered he was supposed to have rung Nuala to pretend he couldn't get back from Galway. 'I met a couple of friends,' he explained. 'We had a bit of a wild night.'

'After the wild Galway whores, I'll bet,' said Vaun.

'I got the brakes on the car done,' he said, ignoring her. 'You'll find them a bit fierce.'

'Must have a go,' said Vaun, dropping her end of the cutter-bar.

'Just you be careful, Vaun,' Nuala shouted after her, as she turned to him. 'How did it go?'

As Conor began to explain Vaun was already halfway down the drive, slamming on the brakes and making the tyres roar and stones fly. 'Nobody'd ever heard of Nel Farrell. I thought at first Monaghan was going to have the papers destroyed, he was on about the balance of power being a juggling act.'

Nuala shook her head as if it was difficult to digest such news. 'Was he the right man at all?'

Vaun brought the Datsun back. 'Instead of stepping on

sponges and praying, it's like hammers nailing you to the road.'

'What is the child up to?' said Mrs Riordan, joining them. 'You look like the end of a wild night, Conor.' She glanced from him to Nuala as if trying to assess what might have been going on that she ought to know about. 'Nuala was over at yours feeding and milking at all hours.'

'I'm really grateful to her,' he said, avoiding her eyes.

'You're just back in time to help fix the mowing-bar,' said Mrs Riordan.

'We can manage,' said Nuala.

'You're never going to cut hay in this weather?' asked Conor.

Vaun pointed at him. 'Listen to the man. You'd think he'd been farming all his life. He'd probably teach his grandmother to give birth, let alone suck eggs.'

*

It was good to be back, he thought, driving into his yard. Belle rose from the doorstep riddled with guilt at her pleasure to see him. He allowed her one lick of his face. But once inside the house, moving about the interior, re-absorbing its familiarity, smelling its atmosphere, it did not feel so good. Nothing but a stone box to keep his few necessities in.

When he looked around at the traces of damage, the broken pictures still leaning against the wall, the scars, the ripped sofa, they seemed trivial against the loss of . . . someone whom at the time he had not appreciated as important.

He could not bear to remain inside another moment and rushed out of the house. He set off down the old track along the bottom of the valley. There had been another shower, and the grass was gleaming as if freshly cellulosed with green, and the leaves of hazels and hawthorns dripped droplets of jewelled water. Every tree, every stone, every blade of grass was sharply focused and intricately hued with detail. All the living creatures of the valley were about their business, filled it with their noise. Bumblebees bullied the soaked cranesbills and swallows skimmed over the paddocks like small black boomerangs. The bulky rain-soaked cattle all grazed pointing in the same direction like yachts moored in an estuary. A calf called, a lamb bleated. A raven rose from the topmost ash trees and lifted over the bluff with scarcely a quiver of its outstretched pinions.

Now is the time I shall fly again, he thought, coming to a sudden decision. Complete the wings, make them work. In this world where I am so powerless to affect my own destiny, it will be some achievement to gain another dimension. And if they work, I'll use them to search for her, a silent aerial survey.

*

But the wings were put out of his mind over the next few days as he and the Riordans combined forces to select batches of lambs for the Kilfenora Livestock market. He shovelled weeds and firewood out of his four-wheel trailer, put on the creels, hitched it to the Landrover and made two runs to the town with twenty strong lambs in each. The market pens were set up close to the ancient High Crosses of the old Kilfenora cathedral, and a large crowd of farmers and dealers had gathered, milling in and out of the nearby bar, conversing in groups under its big tree, pressing round the auctioneer as he disposed of batch after batch of anxious, panting fat lambs under a blue Atlantic sky.

Mrs Riordan, her round red face glossy with sweat, was with a group of widows like herself, farm matriarchs pitched into taking charge, like Eithen Lawlor left with seven children all under ten when her husband was treated for 'flu till it was found out too late that the symptoms were from tetanus contracted from a nail through his gumboot. Another was Aileen Cahill whose husband Jerry stepped down off his tractor in Gort into the path of a speeding car. She had five children, the eldest of whom, Sharon, aged eighteen, was a severely-disabled spastic, a fifteen-stone virtually nine-month-old baby whom she coped with at home along with everything else. They were indomitable women well able to surmount adversity, however much time they spent complaining about it. The market was one of their social meeting-grounds.

Nuala had remained at home, at work in her weaving-shed, but Vaun had come with a friend called Carol Blayney, face as pale as dough, fly-blown with freckles and a frizzy nest of red hair, a complete contrast to the dark Vaun. Both girls were in cotton dresses, for the market was also a festive occasion.

This could not be further from Dublin, thought Conor, swept along in the current of interest around the auctioneer in an atmosphere rich with crushed sheep droppings. He too was with a friend, a young man with a thin, hawk-nosed face the colour of smoked ham rind, Terry Dillon-Smith. Terry, like him, was not a local. 'Just when you get the little beauties to the peak of physical perfection you have to sell them. It's a funny business. No different I suppose from painting away at a picture till you feel you have it just right, and then you put it in an exhibition and some bugger comes along and buys it.' Terry was also an artist.

'But we take the money all the same,' said Conor.

'Lot 29,' called the auctioneer. 'Ten Galway-cross fat lambs the property of Mrs Sheila Riordan. Straight off the land. What'll you give me now . . . ?'

'I'm not entirely a hypocrite,' said Terry. 'Because it's the human condition to appreciate irony. Otherwise I'd be a veg-etarian. But it's my belief these are the last decades of the meat-eating era. In a hundred years people'll look back and shake their heads, and wonder how we could do it. My kids'll end up vegetarian, I'm sure. They're already into saving every slug and fly. Lucky for them fishfingers don't look as if they were ever alive.'

Conor laughed. 'I find it hard to identify a slice of ham with a pig.'

The auctioneer slapped his clip-board to denote another sale.

'Prices are good this year,' remarked Terry. 'At least I shall be able to afford some new brushes.'

As they leaned on the rail looking down on the lambs in the next pen, there came into Conor's mind a sudden image: the woolly body of a blood-smeared lamb, a girl crouched beside a fire beneath a canopy of trees, her startled frightened gaze from brown caramelised eyes, the glistening roast leg on its makeshift spit, the smells of cooking meat and woodsmoke. 'I'll buy you a pint.'

He had suddenly decided to confide in Terry. With Nuala now entirely absorbed in the forthcoming wedding, he was left feeling isolated, alone with his imagination. And since Sean had died, Terry was his only real male friend.

They found a corner bench in the pub. Terry's eyes were of a shade of blue that in summer was paler than his leathery tan, but grew darker by December than his winter pallor. They remained continually in contact as Conor told him all that had happened over the last few weeks.

'I wonder why she pretended to be Josephine Grant,' he

mused afterwards. 'Perhaps Josephine Grant herself is not whom she is thought to be. Did you ever find that notebook again?'

Conor shook his head. 'Not a sign of it.'

Terry frowned. 'D'you think she might have tried all this to implicate you, in revenge for what you did to her when you first met? No, don't answer, that wouldn't make sense. But suppose she faked the ransacking herself so that she could hide her tracks and disappear again?'

'But what about the tyre marks? Somebody else was there as well.'

Terry sipped his pint. 'Unless she had confederates. But no, who would she be trying to fool? So if we accept she was abducted, it was obviously bungled, since they failed to find the papers. If I'd been them I'd have set fire to your house.'

'Thanks, just what I need.'

'No, but you see what I mean. Those papers sound to be damning evidence that could put an end to a few people's careers, not to mention their incomes. They should have been desperate to destroy them. So why didn't they come back?'

'Either because they assumed the papers weren't here or by now they know it's too late.'

Terry nodded. 'Either way the girl could be dead or alive. It might depend on who took her. We've always suspected there are big fish behind the IRA, who pretend to be respectable, feed them guns and use them for their own schemes. But suppose the IRA wanted to get their hands on the papers for their own advantage? She might be more use to them alive then.' He narrowed his eyes. 'Were you and she . . . ?'

Before Conor could reply there emerged through the crush of drinkers the floundering figure of Vaun like some dark-haired Alice-in-Wonderland in her cotton dress. She seized his arm. 'I've been looking for you everywhere. Your first lambs made the best price so far. The next lot's coming up now.'

He allowed himself to be dragged from the cool darkness of the pub into the brilliant sunshine. 'They were top weight,' she said. 'You should have entered them in the fatstock show. How d'you do it, Conor?'

'I just talk to them,' he replied as the bidding rose.

'Why d'you never take me seriously?' she demanded.

He looked at her in surprise. 'What d'you mean?'

She was scowling, her cheeks red as poppies, and he was

reminded of Nuala's old expression of exasperation. 'I'm just a child to you, aren't I? I make stupid trivial remarks, I crack jokes, so I'm not worth any credit, am I?'

They both turned as his second batch of lambs were knocked down to a dealer for the highest figure yet to a gasp of appreciation and burst of comments from the surrounding farmers. 'Is there something in the grass down there in the hidden valley?' Vaun asked. 'Or are you an exceptionally good man with livestock, Conor? Don't bother to tell me, I'm only a child, I wouldn't understand.' She seemed to choke a little as she jerked round and pushed through the crowd, leaving him hemmed in by walls of farmers, amazed at her outburst.

'What did I do to deserve that?' he asked Terry.

'You'd best mind your Ps and Qs there. I'd say she's a soft spot for you.'

In the early evening Conor and Mrs Riordan drove home alone, the creels on the empty trailer rattling behind them. Vaun had gone off with Carol Blayney to a ceilidh, and would be dropped back later.

'How does it feel to get top price after only four years a farmer, Conor?' Mrs Riordan asked, her basket of groceries on the seat between them.

'It's good to be lucky in something.'

'Give yourself a bit of credit, Conor,' she laughed. 'You're a good man with stock. You've the patience. Not like many you see. There's too many who hate their lives, and they take it out on the dumb animals, especially the men. Maybe we women expect a bit of suffering.'

They bumped up on the verge to squeeze past an oncoming car. 'I've been thinking maybe I should sell the place,' she said. 'It'll be near impossible to manage without Nuala. She had the energy of ten. And I've a fancy for a bungalow in Salthill, to look at these hills from across the bay.'

'What about taking on some help?'

'It's a big drain finding wages. But you remember my cousins Seamus and Cassie Flynn over near Ballyvaughan? They've a lad, Machra, their third boy, weren't they the lucky ones to be blessed with males? He's just left school and they haven't the work for him. It's a possibility.' She sighed. 'It's my regret I never matched you and Nuala.'

Conor found the remark unsettling, as if fastidious of the conjecture now that Nuala was someone else's. Absently he

171

turned his vision aside over the loose stone walls they were driving between, like a bird taking flight; out over the neolithic landscape, over the limestone slabs that protruded from the grass and the hazel trees like the bones of a long dead world . . . this week, he promised himself, he would complete the wings. Nel was out there somewhere . . . .

*

Next day he cleared out the barn to make maximum space to set up the wings.

His urge to fly was cyclical. The last time, about two years ago, he had got as far as running down the glen holding them above his head. Suddenly he found himself airborne. Cold with fear he adjusted his hold to grip the mechanism that tilted and flapped the wings, and realised it was too feeble, and that he had no control whatsoever. Luckily he came down fifty yards across the next paddock, narrowly missing a wall. As he unstrapped the harness, his heart beating with both fright and exultation, he knew he had achieved one positive step. These wings could fly. He had achieved a reasonable proportion of wingspan to weight. So he had taken them back to the barn and spent hours redesigning the mechanism that should allow his arms to flap them. He had utilised handgrips from spade-handles, a system of reciprocating coil-springs, and compensated for the extra weight by dispensing with the support harness, realigning the central struts so that he could lie inside them. At this stage, unable to obtain some vital lightweight materials locally, his enthusiasm had waned. So perhaps some of the revival of his urge to fly was due to the recent note from the hardware merchants in Gort, stating that the high-tensile aluminium wire he had ordered had at last arrived.

Another factor was the appearance of a dealer who had bought the litter of bonhams weaned earlier. Adding the wad of notes to the cheque for the lambs, the actual arrival of money itself, however large his debts, it always lightened him, made him feel free and energetic. Though he was sad to see the plump, fit little bonhams taken away, reminded of his conversation with Terry. They were such confident, bright-eyed, contented little creatures, cheeky and playful, pink and sleek. They went away in the dealer's truck, squealing in anxiety and alarm. What haunted him most was their little human eyes reproaching him for his betrayal, for selling them for thirty pieces of silver. They reminded him of an early girlfriend who passively allowed him to fuck her, and then disparaged him with bitter eyes for his 'animal needs' as she called them.

His therapist had a new wristwatch, a miniature calculator on a black band. Her surreptitious habit of glancing at her old watch had been like those who pick their nostrils and pretend to be rubbing their noses. But now, unfamiliar with recognising time from a digital read-out, she would stare at it annoyed that it required her attention so blatantly. 'Do you find yourself uncomfortable in the presence of women? I was interested that you mentioned how certain parts alarmed you, like jowls, fat elbows and thick ankles, double chins . . .' Conor saw that she had described his grandmother. 'Too many ideals conjured from too many movies, and disliking expressing love in clichés, all those pat phrases. So one . . . sorry . . . so I took refuge in their appearances, disappointed by their minds.' The therapist was now practising a new gesture that enabled her to stare at her wristwatch by sliding the back of her hand slowly across her mouth. Unfortunately this gave the impression she was hiding a yawn. 'What do you find disappointing about women's minds?' He wished he had not mentioned this. 'Their self-insufficiency,' he exclaimed. 'Their emotional dependence. I wanted too much perfection.' 'The dreamer,' she said. 'Perhaps that's why you long to fly.'

One problem in flexing the wings was the reliability of the joints. Lightweight materials lack the strength of steel. Nothing could quite deputise for muscle and bone. All he had was aluminium castings and nylon cord. He would work late into every evening, the wings spread out on their armature right across the floorspace of the barn, as if waiting inertly like an assembly of bird parts for the avian Baron Frankenstein to imbue them with life.

His entire mental function became obsessed with the task. Even when invited for a meal at Riordans, drawn into discussions over the wedding or the future of the farm, even while lending a hand with the stock or helping Kathy with her numeracy homework, his concentration would slip back to the barn and the current problem. He had cut some aluminium pulleys on his lathe, but under test the shafts had sheered, the metal too soft. He had substituted instead a shaft made of bone, tough and slippery. Would it be strong enough?

'Conor, you're sitting there like a man who's wet himself and hopes nobody'll notice,' said Vaun at tea that evening.

'Maybe he's something on his mind,' said Nuala, catching his eye.

'You're not sickening, are you, Conor?' asked Mrs Riordan.

'Probably thinking of ways of spending all that money,' said Vaun. 'Top lamb prices two weeks in a row. You could buy yourself an aeroplane.'

'I know,' said Kathy. 'He's sitting there writing letters in his head.'

'Kathy, have you done your homework?' asked her mother.

'I hate school,' groaned Kathy.

'I thought you loved it,' exclaimed Conor.

'Not since our class-teacher Mrs McClintock left to have her baby. Sister Gabriel's not interested in poetry, she doesn't like projects, she won't allow discussions, she won't let us go out anywhere or do any drama, she's more like a prison wardress standing over us till our sentence is served.'

Sir, When a girl becomes capable of bearing a child and a boy able to father one, they have another five years ahead of them of being treated like children themselves. An artificial postponement of maturity. What would happen if we were to scrap adolescence? Yours, etc.

Searching for the correct tensile springs, he had to discard conventional types because of their size and rigidity. Instead he incorporated sets of maximum strength chest-expanders, sewn in plastic sheaths. But on the first test in the yard, several of the limited-movement joints cracked and the nylon cord stretched. It took him several days to design a new joint, larger than his knuckles, manufacturing laminated sections for them.

Often while at work the image of Nel would mingle with the shapes he was measuring, cutting and filing. Generally he found his thoughts of her were tinged with regret, as of someone who is dead. But he still savoured hope.

Engaged in a precision task one evening, he did not hear the barn-door opening.

'Holy crows,' exclaimed Vaun. 'This must be Batman's secret hide-out. No, that can't be right, he only had a cloak. It must

174

be the den of Count Dracula. Nuala said you had an old pair of wings in the barn, but these are fantastic. Are you trying to escape from your rural exile, Conor, like Daedalus and Icarus?'

Conor was silent with mingled irritation at being discovered and surprise at Vaun's erudition. She came round the wings to the work bench where he was making one of the laminate sections of a knuckle-joint. There was a completed and assembled joint nearby, and he could see her rapidly taking in what he was doing. 'Sly old Conor, beavering away in your workshop while all the rest of the males I know are pissing themselves in the pubs or sprawling like codfish in front of the tele. And we never knew in all these years you were a birdman. I thought it was just aeroplanes you flew.' She walked round the wings, peering underneath. 'If they work can I try them, too?'

This was not the reaction he had expected. Mockery and sarcasm, if not outright laughter. 'I didn't think you were interested in flying?'

'When you've a body like mine, flying looks a good answer,' she said lurching about as if to emphasise her ungainliness. 'The sight of a bird skipping through the air always makes me think, lucky little bastard. I hate feeling so heavy.'

'You're not all that heavy . . .' he began, instantly regretting the innuendo.

'Why don't you say it? A great lump of lard.' She was suddenly bitter. 'I know what you think of me.' And she turned and stumbled over a cable as she headed for the door.

'Vaun,' he called after her. 'Did you come down for something in particular?'

'Holy Mother, the wings put it out of my mind. Have you any mastitis cream? The black cow has an udder like a brick.'

'Middle shelf on the dresser.'

She's very sensitive these days, he thought. And it's true, I didn't notice before, but she's not as heavy as she used to be.

The following week he took the wings out on to the slope on the glen, to test the new knuckles and spring mechanism. He intended to run down the slope, become sufficiently airborne to flex the wings and assess the effect, before coming down again. If all went well, he'd extend the trial a little further each day, but only after careful examination of all working parts and the frame. The cattle and sheep eyed his approach warily. He thought he might have to herd them into the paddocks behind the old farmhouse, but they backed and ran away, alarmed as the apparition drew nearer.

He had been ready the day before, but it had been windy and raining. Today was sunny with only a light breeze, almost ideal conditions, he thought. The weight on his shoulders was not much more than that of the hand-spray with full tank. It was only their extreme width that was cumbersome and tended to overbalance him.

The moment he began his run, his feet pounding heavily through the grass, pushing the wings forward, the lack of balance disappeared. All of a sudden he was running in air. His chest and throat were constricted with fear and excitement. The air was rushing over his face. Cautiously he pulled on the handles, slacked them, pulled them. He shot upwards, alarmingly. The sensation of lift vibrated through his bones, felt as if his stomach was hollow. Not intending to, but carried away by exhilaration overcoming caution, he pulled on the handles again. And shot even higher. He must be fifty feet up, he thought, frightened now at the distance of the paddocks below. This was enough, he'd proved the mechanism and the wings worked. They felt stable and firm in the air as if they gripped it, as if they were in their element. Now he must come down and check that nothing was strained.

But he could not make himself descend. He was nervous of moving his body lest he upset the trim and capsize in the air. He had constructed the wings so that by pressing upwards with one elbow and down with the other he exerted a slight twist. This enabled him to bank. But as he circled over his house, he rose higher. Gingerly he tried lowering his legs to introduce some drag, but this tilted the wings, and afraid of stalling, he desisted. Each time he tried to consider some movement or shifted his body, the act of gripping the handles and their automatic spring release meant the wings flapped again. And he rose higher. To his horror and consternation he was now flying level with the bluff, 200 feet above the floor of the valley. He was soaked with sweat, yet chilled by the air rushing past. He must remain calm, he thought. There must be some way of going down. Birds, of course, did not have such rigid wings, they could put them into a thousand different positions in order to manoeuvre through the air as they wished. Perhaps he could turn over the bluff and land on the high level. So he banked carefully, trying to keep his hands still.

Which was difficult as he had no other grip. But by the time he was approaching the ring-fort, he was fifty feet above it. And still rising. The entire countryside was now stretched out beneath him. Each time panic assailed him, a convulsive grip of the handles would pump him higher. He closed his eyes, desperately trying to calm himself, to think.

This was absurd, he had been a pilot, he knew how to fly an aircraft. But these wings were not like any part of any plane he had ever flown, they were more like a cross between walking a tightrope and being hoist by a balloon. He thought enviously of the planes he had flown, of their easy response to controls, to throttles, ailerons, flaps and rudders. Except once. Not that again, he groaned. At least nobody else was involved this time.

This was like a fledgling bird on its first trial flight, able to get into the air, but unable to complete its instinct and find a way back to land. He could capsize and plummet like a stone, of course. If he couldn't find some way he would soon soar too far, like Icarus. Though he was more likely to be frozen to death in the high icy wastes, than scorched to death by the sun.

As he floated, almost tranquilly, air hissing through the cords and springs, cold on his face, he was looking down at what he had imagined in his dreams and fantasies. The hidden valley, the stone hills and limestone pavements, hazel groves and stone-walled fields laid out in intricate pattern beneath him. It was unique, like nothing in all his experience as a flier. It was so silent, so vast, so still, he seemed to be barely moving, just the rippling of materials, his shirt and some of the wing fabric. He could see five ring-forts, like craters made in a world of stone. Already he could make out a seam of Atlantic between land in the west and the sky. He was caught between exaltation and terror.

He could see every aspect of the Riordans' farm, neat as a set of models, nobody about. Then as he looked down at his own farmhouse, a group of boxes at the bow end of the boat-shaped valley, he saw a white car like a small aphid drive up the lane and turn into his yard, stop beside the Landrover. A door opened and a dot of a figure emerged, walked towards the house. Although far too far up to see, he sensed that Belle wagged her tail at this visitor. Was it a woman? He felt sure it was. Whoever it was had gone inside. Could it possibly be . . . ? Frantically he exerted himself to descend. But each time the effort pushed his legs down rather than the wings, which resulted in a drag effect, tilting the wings upwards, threatening a stall, and he would have to level himself quickly. He saw the figure emerge from the house and head towards the pig sheds. Desperate to attract their attention he began to shout. The figure went round the back of the house to the garden, then returned and went into the barn. He wrenched at the wings, raging that he could not make them obey him. The figure had returned to the car. He screamed and shouted till he was hoarse, but could not seem to attract their attention. As the figure got back into the car, he wept with vexation, pinned so helplessly in the sky. The car reversed out of the yard and drove slowly away down the lane, turning into the road and heading back towards the village. It might have been nobody important, he thought. Might have been a sales rep. And even if he had attracted their attention what could they have done? He was stuck up here, and still rising. He was doomed to leave the world unnoticed, like a soul departing into outer space.

Suddenly he felt enraged. 'I don't want to die,' he shouted. 'You're not going to win this time. I'm going to get down, you bastards.'

Unexpectedly a gust of wind rushed at him, heeled the wings up on end, and he was struggling to retain control in a whirling force of air. To prevent the wings side-slipping like a knife, he had to flap them faster than he had thought himself capable. The thrusting violence of the air made it seem as if he was not more than a small boat being tossed about by great invisible waves. But the frenzied muscular effort he had to make to save himself, to try to maintain some kind of equilibrium, seemed to unite him far more with the wings. Suddenly he found he was able to master the rushing wind, fly through it, dive and soar at will. Hurray, he was saved, he had control. He'd been too timid before, just hanging on. He needed to be part of the wings, to throw himself muscle and sinew into their power. In order to descend all he had to do was drive downwards. If only he had thought of it before.

In a series of swoops and wafts he brought himself back down into the valley with dramatic speed, and in the calmer air glided to a landing in the paddock beside the yard, scattering sheep and collapsing with a bang on the grass. He lay there exhausted, the muscles of his back and arms throbbing and aching, his hands hot and sore. How marvellously solid and stationary was the ground, he thought, though his head spun as if he was still a thousand feet up. He lay cradled in the grass for nearly half-an-hour, feeling himself impacted with the earth, so that he was not so much lying on his back gazing upwards, but was pinned to a wall and looking outwards. He had but to step forwards and he would become detached from the world and be out in space again.

He was so spent the wings seemed to weigh a ton when he tried to lift them up, to carry them back to the barn. It was only when he was mounting the step to the door of the house that he remembered the visitor, and hurried inside.

There on the table was a copy of *The Irish Times*, spread out to catch his eye. Someone had drawn a black arrow to point at a particular headline.

JUDGE FOUND DEAD.

Judge Murrough Martin was found dead at his house in Stillorgan from gunshot wounds in the head. Foul play is not suspected. A spokesman from the Attorney General's Office stated that there was no truth to the rumour that the judge was about to be suspended from office to face certain allegations . . .

Conor stood gripping the table, his body turned to stone, his mind racing. Had Monaghan acted? If Nel was still alive, would this finish her off?

Shaking, he went and filled the kettle. Who could have brought the paper? Someone who knew. Terry. Of course, the white car, his old BMW. Pity he hadn't looked up and seen him. But the real disappointment was that it hadn't been Nel. But then how could it have been? He made a pot of tea. While he drank it he slumped in a chair and reread the article. Monaghan had said he might be able to do something. Was this part of it?

Despite his excitement, physical exhaustion began to overpower him, and he dragged himself over to the sofa, thinking as he lay down of that first day, of Maggie as she was then, curled up asleep there, barefoot, an ear poking through her hair.

He fell into a deep sleep. He was dreaming of a naked flying woman he could not catch when he awoke with a huge erection. Belle was looking in through the door. He could hear the shuffling and bleating of the assembly in the yard. He put a hand on Belle's head, looking into her anxious brown eyes. 'What a clever and remarkable girl. How can I ever reward you? No, not that.'

He was halfway through the milking when Nuala drove in to collect his churn. 'It's not like you to be so behind, Conor.'

'Go inside and have a look at the paper on the table while I finish off,' he said. 'There's a piece of news you should see.'

She came back out, holding the paper. 'That was quick.'

'Maybe not quick enough for Nel.'

She put the paper down on the step and picked up a bucket to help. 'It's a strange way they went about it.' She looked at him across the back of a goat. 'There's nothing you can do, Conor.'

'I know. She's probably dead all along.'

They milked in silence for a while.

'Wouldn't it make a grand distraction,' she said. 'to have the bride in her gown squatting down and milking the goats in the middle of the wedding?'

'It's all arranged. Kathy, Vaun and I'll get it done while everyone's dancing. You'll have to say goodbye to all this. Only two more days now.'

'I'll miss the feel of their lovely soft bags, and the glassy stare of their ancient Greek eyes. There's a similarity between milking and weaving, the sliding of the fingers, the threads of milk . . . .'

'I never thought of you as sentimental, Nuala.'

'Piss on you,' she grinned, flipping milk at him.

'Things won't be the same without you,' he said. 'Did your mother make arrangements about your cousin coming?'

'Machra'll be here tomorrow. He's hardly the brightest. Goes around with his ears plugged into pop-music, leaves gates open and drives tractors over buckets. That was the first thing he wanted to know. What kind of tractor did we have?'

'I'll miss you too, you know,' she said as they filled the churn. 'I'll come out here often. What a city has is energy. I'm not like you, Conor, contented to admire life. I want to change it, improve it. This is a snail's world here.'

He was discomforted by her remark. Was that how she saw him? As a snail? He had been about to mention that he'd seen someone deliver the paper earlier. But how could he say that he had been unable to descend from 1,000 feet above to find out who they were? He was reluctant to mention his flight to anyone. It was something very private.

*

From then on all available time was taken up with the wedding preparations. Deliveries poured in, boxes full of glasses and plates, and an immense quantity of food. Trestle tables and benches arrived, the marquee was erected. Three lambs were taken in to be slaughtered and dressed. Conor spent hours manufacturing three spits to cook them on. It was as if they were arranging a festival, an open-air extravaganza, Riordans' farm the theatre itself. Mrs Riordan took on unusual energy as she directed operations. Perspiring and red-faced, she was like the Red Queen in Alice in Wonderland, ruthless and extravagant. Her daughters Maire and Eileen had arrived, spent their time fitting costumes and cooking, the air heavily flavoured with smells from the kitchen. Even old Tom joined in the fervour, staggering about collecting fuel for the spits. On the last evening a van delivered kegs of Guinness and ale, and crates of champagne and wine. A friend of Niall's brought a carload of flowers, chrysanthemums, roses and carnations. Conor had collected the dressed lambs, which now hung in the dairy, brushed with rosemary and sunflower oil. 'I'll kill it if it rains tomorrow,' exclaimed Mrs Riordan, glistening like a sticky bun as she rearranged furniture in the front room to have as many people as possible seated round the walls should the weather turn bad. 'No, Tom,' she cried as the old man tried to restore a chair to where it used to be. 'You'll have to sit in the kitchen. Nuala,' she exclaimed, going into the parlour where the wedding presents were displayed. 'There are a million and one things to be done and here you are sitting on your backside reading a book.'

Nuala looked up unabashed. 'It's about the best designs in the world, furniture, fabrics, fashion, delft, everything. I don't know how Conor knew it was what I wanted. I could never afford it before. Maybe I should have married him.'

Mrs Riordan shook her head, speechless with regret.

'We would never have been suited, Mam,' she exclaimed, jumping up. 'But we're friends now, as we never were before. He's very understanding is Conor. But he stands back, lets life go by. Niall isn't like that. He's always thinking up something

181

new. That's what I like in a man. Someone who can take decisions and act on them. I never know what he'll do next. It's very exciting.'

'I don't think his parents cared overmuch for us taking the wedding out of their hands and having it out here.'

Nuala put her arms round her mother. 'It's the greatest idea, and I'm ever so grateful.'

'And it was Conor's idea in the first place,' sighed Mrs Riordan. 'Mam,' said Eileen, coming in, swathed in an apron, her arms white with flour. 'We seem to have used up all the eggs. Can we squeeze the hens or something?' She was the biggest of all the Riordans, a strong young woman who wore her dark hair shoulder length, her ruddy complexion crimson from working in the kitchen. She had come with her husband Tony, at present detailed to look after their baby daughter, Rosceen.

'What do you need eggs for?' asked Mrs Riordan. 'Haven't we food enough for a Sermon on the Mount?'

'I'm making a quiche for our supper.'

'Such grand food,' exclaimed Mrs Riordan. 'You'd best ask Conor.'

A tractor clattered up towing a trailer piled high with chairs lashed together with a long rope. They had been borrowed from the parochial hall. Mrs Riordan hurried out to organise their distribution. Nuala and Vaun rushed off to milk the goats. The telephone rang. It was answered by Maire, who had been altering Kathy's bridesmaid's dress as the hem was so long she trod on it. It was Niall's mother, very agitated. The cake had been delivered to her house instead of out to Riordans.

Kathy appeared with a basket of eggs raided from Conor's fridge and his Leghorns. 'He sent up a pound of rashers, too,' she said as her elder sister gave her a bowl to break the eggs in. 'He'll bring up the spits when he's finished milking.'

'What would we do without Conor?' asked Eileen, rolling out more pastry. 'I thought it would be him Nuala would marry. He was very struck on her.'

Maire came in lugging two huge plastic bags full of bread-rolls. 'Mam's ordered enough to feed the entire country.'

As soon as he had finished milking Conor was out on the grass before the marquee hammering stanchions into the ground to hold the spits. Old Tom dumped a load of kindling beside him. 'We'll be in the poor-house after this expense.

182

Sheila hasn't had a new coat in forty years. I remember De Valera promising prosperity. But I never saw it yet.'

Tony, Eileen's husband, a thin, bespectacled accountant with Dublin Corporation, was leading his tiny, tottering daughter across the grass. 'The woman at the post office said a couple of English tourists saw a vulture over here a couple of days ago. Must have heard about the lambs being slaughtered.'

A large beige Ford Granada drove up and a young man wearing medalions, bracelets and earrings, shirt open to this belt, and a young woman with hair sticking out like fibre matting got out and looked around. 'It's the musicians,' said Mrs Riordan hurrying back to Conor. 'They want to know if we can run a cable out for their amplifier.'

After they had gone she returned to Conor. 'I'm worried about the toilet. Just the one to cater for two hundred people.'

'Conor,' called Vaun, humping a churn of milk. 'Who's turn to deliver?'

'I'll do it,' he replied, wiping sweat off his brow.

'Would you let me drive? I've only two weeks to my test.'

It was a relief to get away from the pandemonium and pressure of the preparations. After hours of Nuala's tutelage, Vaun was a reasonable driver, and Conor had no qualms as they set off.

'D'you think Niall'll turn up tomorrow?' she asked. 'Isn't all this great expense tempting fate?'

'How d'you come to be such a cynic, Vaun? Of course he'll be there. Nuala's a big investment.'

'Now who's the cynic?'

'Vaun, when you come to do your test, don't drive so fast. Show them you're careful. Examiners are only concerned that you obey the rules.'

After delivering the milk and heading back, Vaun suddenly slowed and turned into an old grassed-over laneway, started to drive down it. 'Where are you going?' he asked, surprised.

When they were enclosed by dense hazel groves, she switched off the engine and turned to him. 'Would you give me a kiss, Conor?'

'You little schemer . . .' he began.

'Please, Conor, just for once,' she exclaimed, her voice shaking.

He saw this was one time where rejection would seem insulting. 'All right.'

183

Funny to find the usually shameless Vaun reduced to such nervousness, he thought as she leaned towards him. She put a hand on his arm. 'The real thing now. Don't be fobbing me off.'

At first he thought she was play-acting ignorance, so lifeless were her lips, like bits of cloth through which protruded the small buttons of her teeth. Then he realised he was going to have to teach her, that she really was inexperienced.

She began to respond to his nibbling and kneading, and quite soon her lips came alive, began to press back eagerly. He could feel her body trembling in his arms, stirring a forgotten lust. So he drew back, afraid of his own enjoyment and the controls melting. Her eyes were shining, her mouth ajar like a foxglove.

He was about to suggest they ought to be getting back when there was a click and with a jerk they fell backwards, he on top of her. She lay trembling violently and pushing her jeans down. 'Please, Conor,' she pleaded.

'For God's sake, Vaun,' he hissed, annoyed at her for letting the seat-back down. But as her soft hips emerged gleaming white as immature chestnuts from their green shells, he lost his head. If this is what she wants, he thought angrily. This is what she shall bloody well have. But he asked her about the time of the month, hoping that might save him.

'My period finished two days ago,' she whispered, shaking uncontrollably as if realising now that it was really going to happen.

He pulled her jeans, shoes and knickers off, surprised by the grace of her youthful thighs, expecting them to be gross. She was shaking with a wild mixture of fear and excitement. He shed enough of his own clothes to cradle her against his skin, stroking her gently. Portions of the seat jabbed uncomfortably, they were very cramped. 'Let's get out on to the grass,' he said.

In front of the car she lay down on the rough sward and her thighs fell open like a book. Christ, he thought as the tip of his penis penetrated, I forgot she's a virgin. But his momentum and the moistness made him slap in like an electric plug into its socket before he could stop. The effect, shock or pain, he could not tell which, made her legs clamp across his back like a vice. 'God,' she groaned, her eyes tight shut. For a while he lay like a bomb disposal expert embracing an unexploded mine.

Sir, What is it that the Church has against sex? A good fuck ought to be one of the most salutary therapies available. It releases tensions, makes people forget their mortality and their debts. It's a great liberating experience. It should be freely encouraged, lovingly given, happily received. It's probably the most positive act most people are capable of. If there really was a God, He would promote it. Yours, etc.

'You mentioned that you sometimes found sex dirty,' said his therapist, knitting her fingers together. 'The taint of guilt,' he replied. 'It's imprinted on our genes. Don't mothers still slap their little sons and say, don't play with that, it's dirty? Everything begins when we're little.' The therapist waved a hand. 'Why hide behind people in general? Why don't you talk about yourself?' He shrugged. 'I feel my desire to fuck is so overridingly basic, so primitive, so selfish. It is just the urge to grab hold of a woman and lay seeds in her, it is not the urge to love her. Inside me I want to love her most of all because she is a person, not a tactile receptacle for the continuation of the species. Somehow it seems to diminish her womanhood, her importance as a person, this animal thrust from my loins.' The therapist nodded thoughtfully. 'Perhaps you idealise women, hoping for something unattainable. Were you disappointed by your mother, let down by her?' He laughed. 'But she was so big, when I was small. How is that I have forgotten that when she lay sunbathing in the summer, it took me ten paces to go from her feet to her head?'

Upon his axle thrust into Vaun's moist centre he revolved like a wheel, limbs outspread like spokes. What am I up to? he asked himself. What am I doing to this girl I do not love? Should I be doing this to her? She's not much more than a child. Am I taking advantage of her? Or is she taking advantage of me?

Pay attention that man at the back wanking away like a baboon in the bushes, what have I been talking about? Taking advantage. You'll be a dead duck in two slaps of a barmaid's arse if you let one little Irish barbarian take advantage of you. We happen to have the honour to wear her Majesty's uniform and badges, so they can see us coming. Which means you don't come when they expect you, you don't appear where they're waiting, because you're going to take advantage of them. Something that should be clear as the stain on the sheet after a virgin's first night. You're going to take advantage of them. You're not going to be the one who wanders like a Christmas dinner straight into the oven.

Corporal House reporting, sir. Patrol in at 0800 hours. Two strikes. Both certified by RUC MO. Carrying a PRL.

Russian?

Homemade, sir.

A homemade rocket-launcher?

Just a drainpipe, sir.

And rockets?

None, sir.

What age were the targets?

Fourteen/fifteen, sir. Ignored all routine warnings.

I see. Army murders two children. Piece of pipe thought to be dangerous weapon.

Sir! Trooper Cramm was killed three weeks ago outside Crossmaglen by a thirteen-year-old boy with an Armalite. D platoon brought him in, not more than seven-stone, freckles, skin like a girl, a fine-looking lad any father'd be proud of, murderous little runt.

Vaun was stirring, easing herself around the pole in her middle, gaining confidence that she had not been mortally impaled by a spear and that her life's blood would not gush out should she move. Come on, he urged, stroking her, kissing her, for each stir drew his climax nearer.

523,109,321 sperm lined up in his vas deferens, poised to descend into the vagina of Vaun Carmel Riordan, seventeen-year no-longer-virgin spinster, whose plump body lay crushing two hundred blades and seedheads of cocksfoot, fescue and timothy, five dandelions, two docks, a ragwort, thirteen daisies, six speedwell, three ribworts, a dog violet, two bugles, seven clovers and two milk-worts, not to mention countless small spiders, beetles, aphids and ants.

She was beginning to respond to his touch like a sleeper awakening, moving her hips hungrily. I can't keep it back much longer, he thought. 'You're so young and soft, Vaun,' he murmured distractedly. 'At this moment you're the most beautiful girl in the world.'

But when she dug her nails into him, he could hold back no

longer. 'I felt something,' she whispered, opening her eyes. 'Far away inside me.' She wriggled, pulsed, then gradually settled, as if accepting that his limp inertia must signify completion.

He thought the therapist an unfuckable concept of woman-hood, a squat Buddha-figure whose breasts hung like draining cheeses and whose orifice was as remote as a drain-hole in a swimming-pool. 'Sex is no fun if your partner is not going to enjoy it as much,' he said. 'Otherwise it's like wanking with a dummy. But foreplay can sometimes be like a ham-radio freak twiddling his knobs in the middle of the night, trying to make contact through crackling interference with someone ten thousand miles away. What I'm trying to say is that lust gets in the way too often. It cripples normal communication. Why must it only be stimulating to talk with an attractive woman because the lower half of you longs to fuck her?' The therapist casually guided her watch past her face. 'Women have their desires, too. Don't you think many suffer something similar? It's difficult for them, too, knowing men only see them as sex objects.' 'That's what I mean,' exclaimed Conor. 'There are times when I'd like to cut it off.' The therapist frowned. 'Do you ever fantasise about being a woman?'

Wish I'd managed it better, he thought as he lay face down, cheek pillowed in Vaun's shoulder, mouth wet on her clavicle, body slumped, limbs crashed, organ limp and slipping out. A blackbird landing in a nearby hazel, called in alarm as it saw them. Or were they cackles of mirth as it flew away?

The need to return roused them. Across Vaun's back and plump buttocks was etched a complete and perfect pattern of all the plants she had lain on. Once clothed, all that had happened seemed wiped clean, they were restored to an earlier state as if nothing had occurred. 'You'd best drive,' she said. It concerned him to observe that she walked very gingerly round to the passenger door, as if trying to move her legs as little as possible.

With the boot-lid up for the milk-churns, he had to hang out of the door to reverse back down the overgrown lane, the churns clanking together as they bumped over potholes. Vaun sat curled up beside him, head back on the seat, silent, the expression on her soft features as inscrutable as whipped cream. But as they drove up past the marquee in front of the house, she sat up and clutched his arm. 'If I said, sorry we're late but Conor and I stopped on the way back to have a good fuck, they'd think I was joking, wouldn't they?' And she gave a strangled laugh, struggling to reassert the old Vaun, but not quite succeeding. As she got out of the car she turned back, looked at him almost dewy-eyed. 'Have I a lot to learn?'

With the hurly-burly of the wedding preparations everyone was far too distracted to notice their lateness. Tea had been delayed because half a dozen minor contingencies had interceded, and Conor sat down, squeezing among the numbers round the big kitchen table, with some of his guilt abated. Except when Mrs Riordan caught his eye. 'What time will you start the lambs, Conor? We don't want you to miss the church.'

He couldn't help visualising her shock if she knew what he had been up to with her younger daughter. 'I'd best stay with the spits, Mrs Riordan. The meat'll take a couple of hours. I don't mind missing the service. Remember I'm only a heathen.'

'We could do it in shifts,' said Eileen. 'It seems a shame to miss the service even if you are a bloody heathen, Conor.'

'To think he's not even a protestant,' commented Nuala, flushed with inner excitement, taking over the wise-cracking from the silent Vaun. 'Tending the fires'll get him into practice for when he's sent down to hell.'

They all laughed, since nobody liked to disbelieve in hell entirely.

I hope no one is noticing how silent Vaun is, he thought. I wish I'd never done it. Whatever came over me? Damn her, damn lust. Could I have ruptured her? She's very pale. She swore it was safe, but does she really understand? Suppose she blurts it all out as she joked of doing? He took a deep breath. I must stop flapping about like a moth at a windowpane.

He carried the debate on within himself driving back to the farm in the dusk for an early night ready for tomorrow. A wash of pink was purpling the indigo sky. It's going to be a fine day, he thought.

He parked the Landrover, peering round cautiously, ever since the ransacking never quite certain someone mightn't be waiting, his skin prickling with fear as it had never used to. He patted Belle and went into the barn to have a look at his wings. Because of the wedding preparations all thought of them had been driven out of his mind. But now excitement came surging back. He was the first real flying man, he thought. The first to fly like a bird. The first since the mythical Icarus. Not even Leonardo had succeeded. Nobody so far in *The Guinness Book of Records*. I've actually done it. Little me up there with the condors. Christ walked on the waters, Conor flew in the air. I am Conor de Birdman. If only Nel had been here to see it.

*

In the early misty morning he was up feeding and milking, then after breakfast he delivered the milk before returning to spit the lambs and start the fires. By half-past ten the sun dangled high in a silver-blue sky as three limousines drove up and gaily dressed and behatted Riordans emerged, hurrying about making last minute checks, correcting each other's costumes. Old Tom appeared in an ancient swallow-tail coat, reeking of mothballs. Maire, Vaun and Kathy were long-frocked bridesmaids in traditional white, coroneted with flowers, clutching bouquets. Vaun did not look at Conor. He was already soaked with sweat, the combined heat of the fires and sun more than he had anticipated. When the first two cars had gone, Nuala came out holding her train over one arm, tripped across the grass to him, while old Tom stood waiting by the beribboned limousine. She shook her head at Conor. 'Grass fell out of Vaun's clothes last night. I got out of her what happened.' She was about to turn for the car. 'Her head's screwed on more than you or Mam realise. You'll see.' Then she smiled. 'I'm sorry you'll not be in the church, dear Conor. Thanks for everything.'

By midday the three fires were small red furnaces, the lambs cooking darkly, and Conor, all alone, was now shirtless as he went from one to the other, revolving the spits, stoking the fires, pouring dollops of Maire's marinade over the meat, so that the air was aromatic with the scents of woodsmoke, rosemary, marjoram, garlic and olive oil.

He felt as if he was roasting himself and was reminded again of the incident over a month ago now, of discovering the girl crouched over the fire in the wood, the leg of lamb cooking on the makeshift spit, his rage and the thrashing he had given her. Was he angry now? he wondered, backing away from the intense heat, leaping in to rake down a fire where it was too hot and scorching the meat. Was he still angry that Nuala was

189

marrying Niall? Was he angry with Nel Farrell for never telling him whom she really was? He felt like a devil in Hades torturing wrongdoers as he revolved the roasting carcasses. Was he angry with Vaun for making him become the beast he resented? Was he angry with all women for luring him on and ultimately rejecting him?

Afraid the meat was cooking too fast, he raked the fires to the outside, becoming even hotter. So he took everything off except an indecently small pair of briefs. His feet got burned so he restored his shoes, then hot fat spat on to his stomach, so he ran to the house to find an apron. In a drawer he found a chef's hat that Sean had once brought home as a joke. On the way back he found the marquee like an oven and rolled the sides up to let air in. The lambs were nearly cooked, and there were fifteen minutes before the guests arrived. Still too hot he took the apron off and fashioned it into a loincloth.

The first sight the arriving guests saw was the smoke haze, then an all but naked figure in a white chef's hat, a figure as darkened and glistening as the roasting lamb carcases he was dancing round. The appetising smells that smote their nostrils made everyone instantly ravenous, and queues formed, plate in one hand, glass in the other, as the pagan Indian figure in his loincloth wielded carving knife and fork, dispensing meat. There was a great clamour of voices resounding like surf in this normally quiet landscape, laughter and hubbub rose in waves. There were cars parked for nearly a mile along the valley road. People sat at tables, eating and talking, drinking and laughing, and the queues kept coming for more lamb. Eileen and Maire brought out the reserve bowls of rice and potato salads. Somebody brought Conor a tumbler of wine. The combination of heat and drink made everything a little blurred.

As the afternoon drew on the music of the band began to thread through the hubbub and people discarded hats and coats and started to dance. An air of bacchanalia surreptitiously took over. Conor, a roast rib in one hand, found himself dancing with Nuala.

'Everyone's enjoying themselves,' she said. 'It's your doing, you heathen. D'you think there were weddings like this here hundreds of years ago?'

When the band took a rest, and the panting, sweating dancers threw themselves on to the grass to rest among those too full of food to move, the opportunity was taken for

190

speeches. Old Tom, like most of the old men there, refusing to be parted from a single garment, stood up and banged on a table with an empty bottle.

While some young cousins from Gort deputed to carry round bottles of champagne, went round filling everyone's glasses, old Tom began a rambling dissertation about the number of children his grandfather and father had had in places like Chicago and Perth. 'God knows what all that was about,' muttered Mrs Riordan after she had persuaded him to finish. 'But he insisted on having his say.'

Then Niall's father in shirt-sleeves, cravat and braces, spoke. He was a stout man, thick-jowled, what his son would be like in twenty years, thought Conor.

After Niall had responded on behalf of the bride, raising much laughter, Conor, not entirely aware of what he was doing, managed to stand on a chair as Mrs Riordan's health was being drunk. 'And now for a change of precedent,' he exclaimed. 'Since this is female country, let the bride herself speak.'

'Speech, Nuala, speech,' everyone cried.

'I'll deal with you later, Conor,' exclaimed Nuala, emptying her glass of wine over his head as he got down.

In the midst of the cheering after her speech Conor wobbled back on to the chair. 'A hundred years ago this party was unthinkable. Our ancestors were starving. Maybe the old landlords have been replaced by the banks, but at least they're interested in keeping us fit to keep them fat . . . .'

'You're not writing letters to the papers now, Conor,' shouted Terry.

'It's your turn now, Mrs Riordan,' called Conor, as he fell off the chair.

Mrs Riordan, never one to refuse a challenge, rose up, her face aflame, resplendent in blue hat and blue floral dress with a ruffled collar that made her as high-busted as a pigeon.

As the cheers rose again after her speech, Conor attempted to mount the chair again, but Terry pulled him off. Father Devenney took the centre. 'These fine young people on the threshold of life . . .' he began sententiously.

Conor turned to Terry. 'Thanks for the paper . . . .'

'How did you know . . . ?'

'I was a thousand feet above . . . .'

'Up on the bluff, were you . . . ?'

Conor was poised to mention his flight, for Terry was good to talk to, and there was so much he wanted to discuss, like screwing the virgin Vaun, but the words jammed in his throat.

'Orna was passing,' said Terry, referring to his wife. 'I thought you'd be interested.'

So I was right, thought Conor. It was a woman in the yard. 'Nuala thinks it's a warning shot to whoever's holding Nel Farrell. Because there's been nothing more than rumours since.'

'Could be,' agreed Terry.

'But then she's probably dead long since,' sighed Conor.

'Don't say that,' said Terry, gripping his arm. 'Hope is not to be despised.'

A round of clapping announced the end of Father Devenney's speech. It was followed by the best man with a profile not unlike a puffin, reading messages from absent well-wishers. Then everyone began to gather round to watch the rosy bride and the gold-knuckled groom cut the cake that had been brought out from the marquee. Under the hot afternoon sun the band began its tinkling rhythms of pipe and fiddle, and soon the young were dancing again, while their elders sprawled at the tables, eating meringues and slices of cake, washing them down with glasses of wine, Guinness and beer. Already there was an established queue outside the backdoor to use the lavatory.

Conor forced himself with what he felt was an iron will to walk about with iron legs. He danced with Maire. She was light and nimble, smiled at him short-sightedly without her spectacles, the only Riordan to wear them. 'Are you jealous?' he asked. 'To see your younger sister marry before you?'

'I've had my chances. The rational me says it's not a race. Aren't you hurt that she didn't accept you?'

Touché, he thought. And he felt girdled up with his secrets of Nel Farrell and of lying with Maire's other sister, her taste still in his throat like a yesterday's memorable meal.

He saw Vaun sail past, dancing with the puffin-nosed best-man, who arched his back and bent his legs to bring his face close to hers dutifully attentive or lecherously inclined. Vaun was skipping youthfully with that approximate coordination that has a curious attraction. When she caught his glance she looked away. He saw his jealousy already in employment, writhe captive in his transparent subconscious, and felt amused by it.

Later he came upon her with her friend Carol Blaney, sitting at a table, cleaning up a plate of cream and meringues. Conor touched her on the shoulder.

'Aren't you going to dance with me?'

She whirled round. 'You're disgusting, Conor, dressed like that. I'd rather dance with a pig.'

'So you shall,' he exclaimed, grabbing her round the waist and heaving her clean off the bench, surprised even himself that he'd managed to lift so big a girl so easily. Before she could resist he whirled her among the dancers. 'So you won't dance with me, eh?'

'What's got into you, Conor? Why are you making this exhibition of yourself? People are saying it's because you didn't get Nuala.'

Conor was shocked by this evaluation, suddenly made aware of his lack of garb, the resin and grime of smoke and lamb fat on his skin. 'I must have got affected by the heat of the fires and the sun when I was cooking.'

Her expression softened and her voice grew concerned. 'Shouldn't you sit down and take it easy, then?'

Kathy ran up to them. 'Nuala's nearly ready. They've to leave now. It's after five and the plane leaves Shannon at half seven.'

As Vaun ran after her into the house, Conor felt cheated of that moment of tenderness. Terry took him by the elbow. 'You need some of this,' he said, leading him over to a table laden with teapots and jugs of coffee. He handed him a mug of black coffee.

'Have I been behaving badly, Terry?'

'I'd be disappointed in you if I thought you hadn't. Look at everyone. Isn't it the natural instinct of the Irish to have a good time? Even Father Devenney is flutered, see how muddled up his legs are. And there's old Agnes Geraghty from the village bar remembering steps she hasn't danced since she was a girl.'

'But it all goes so quickly, Terry. Tomorrow all this'll be gone, we'll be clearing up the débris, the celebration over. Time runs away downhill, out of control.'

'Your trouble is you're always worrying about tomorrow.'

Nuala and Niall came out of the house in their going-away clothes, Vaun behind carrying a suitcase, Mrs Riordan with another. As they loaded up Niall's waiting Mercedes, the guests crowded round, cheering, wishing them well, and throwing

193

clouds of hoarded confetti. There were last embraces then amidst a flamingo flock of waving arms and clamour of farewells the car drove through the throng, dipped down into the road and turned away, so festooned with aerosol decorations it was not unlike a wedding-cake itself.

The departure was only a temporary hitch in the festivities. Soon the band was playing again, its style continually altering as the musicians became interchangeable, coming and going, passing out, being replaced by substitutes bursting to display their skills.

Conor left to milk his goats. He found Belle had already brought them in. Practical reality was not easy to cope with when drunk. He leaned his head against their soft flanks, observed each dart of milk leave their soft carrot teats and spurt into the gleaming metal bucket that he watched with remote anticipation lest it topple over. All while he could hear the throb of the band playing in the still evening air, and voices coming over the hill like a distant football crowd. The goats stared at him with their haricot-bean eyes, knowing full well he was nothing but an intoxicated reveller pretending to know what he was doing. 'You're very indulgent, my pagan beasts,' he praised them. 'You wag your little beards because you've seen it all before.'

Afterwards he fed the sows, then went and changed into a pair of trousers and a shirt. When he came back out into the yard the goats had left. He stood in the emptiness listening to the contented grunts from the sow sheds, the gurgling of pigeons in the hazels, the song of a blackbird, the faint music from over the hill. He looked up at the sky, its blue clarity hazed like breath on a windowpane. It's as if Nel Farrell never existed, he thought sadly. She's forgotten already.

Then he walked back to help Kathy and Vaun milk their goats in the haggard. 'Couldn't find a sign of that skiver Machra to give us a hand,' grumbled Vaun. She seemed glad to see him. 'Are you all right?' she asked.

As the dusk dimmed the bright sky and the cool of evening dampened the ground, he collected wood and shovelled the few embers from the cooking fires to make one large blaze. The music had reduced to a solitary fiddler and a girl playing an accordion. But there were still plenty dancing as night fell.

Old Tom reeled out of the darkness, clutching a half-full glass of beer, his remaining ragged molars glistening like two pebbles in his grin. He pointed towards the wall beyond the sheds. The firelight was just enough to illuminate a row of horns above pairs of eyes gleaming like fireflies. A line of ghostly goats standing on their hindlegs to watch the festivities. 'Damn billy drank half me glass.' He cackled with laughter. 'More fool me to leave it out of my hand. Been called an old fool a few times today. Anytime I made mention of the big bird that was over yours. Did you not see it? Big as an eagle. Could easily take a lamb. Old fool, they said. In his cups, going senile.' He snorted and spat. 'I'd take the gun out and show them, only my hands are no good. Did you not see it at all?'

Conor shook his head. 'I must keep a look out for it.' He could see the old man was disappointed, hoping for his endorsement. He wondered how many other people had seen 'it'.

There was nobody dancing now, people were sitting round the band listening or clustered about the fire, baking potatoes. His night's work had become scrounging for wood to keep the fire going. He had taken a flashlight from the kitchen. Wherever he went there were young couples seeking privacy, and he grew embarrassed at what he might disturb next. He wondered if he might come across Vaun, for he had not seen her for some time. He did find a young girl crying, clutching a bloody handkerchief round her foot. She had cut it on a broken glass while dancing. He carried her into the house to look for a plaster. He found to his surprise that the house was packed with people, every chair filled, some talking, others asleep. He had thought Mrs Riordan deep in some discussion, but she came bustling into the kitchen as he washed and bound the girl's cut. 'It's near two in the morning. You'd think people'd know it's time to go home. There's most of them dying for their beds and still they won't go. It's ridiculous.' But she laughed all the same. 'I daresay half of them'll still be here for breakfast. Though Lord knows what we'll give them. There isn't a crust in the place.'

Quite soon after that he decided to go home himself. The fire was still burning well, a group of four, accordion, flute, fiddle and drum were playing an intricate jig, pale faces around them in the dark, drinking and listening, a few points of cigarettes glowing. He drifted along the path under the indigo nightsky, propelling his fatigue before him like a prisoner. Crossing the style in the boundary wall, he could see the glow from his yard-light reflecting on the roofs of the barn and the pig-sheds through gaps in the hazels. The music behind was a faint but busy sound.

The million-mile upon million-mile blackness above was filled with stillness, not a movement among the scattered diamonds. Up in the glen a tawny owl hooted. The whole weight of space was suspended above his head in a measureless vault. Now was the time to fly, he thought. When darkness obscured the primary distractions. Somewhere out on the road a car engine started, and a flare of headlights lit up walls and trees and distant slopes of ancient limestone. He felt quite alone.

Entering his yard he heard a sow snort as she suckled her piglets. He turned and went into the barn, turned on the lights. There lay the great wings, stretched right across the floor, evocative and dramatic. Now that they were proven, it seemed as if they had always been able to fly, that they were real, part of some actual flying creature. He longed to try them again, was already mentally designing a skirt of plastic that he could wear to act as a tail.

He had no idea how long he had been standing there when he heard the door open behind him and the sound of a footstep.

Vaun was still in her bridesmaid's dress, somewhat dishevelled after the long day's wear. She looked from him to the wings, and her eyebrows slowly lifted. 'Was it you uncle Tom saw the day before yesterday?'

He nodded.

'Fantastic,' she cried, wide-eyed. 'Why didn't you tell us?'

He explained how the flight had nearly been disastrous.

'You'll be famous,' she exclaimed. 'People'll come from all over the world to see you. And you'll be booked for enormous fees to perform, the amazing birdman, the Icarus of Ireland.'

He stared at her enthusiasm, aghast. 'But I don't want that. I don't want to become a performer, showing off in front of people. I don't want crowds coming here, swarming all over the place.'

'You could patent them, then, set up a factory and build kits for people to buy. They'd sell like fried chickens.'

He remained shocked. 'But it's my own personal pleasure, not to make money out of.'

'But you should share your pleasure. Let other people enjoy flying, too.'

He sighed. 'I hadn't thought about all this, you know.'

196

'How can you keep it to yourself, Conor? I'll bet a few more than uncle Tom saw you. There's always tourists crawling over the country with great big binoculars. And if nobody else saw you the first time you can bet your last pair of knickers someone'll see you the next time. Then what happens when the papers get hold of it? You may as well accept the inevitable.'

He sat down. 'I suppose you're right. It never occurred to me.'

Vaun shook her head at him. 'I don't know how you could go about all day keeping it to yourself. I'd have been over the moon, rushing round boring everyone to death with it. I'd have flown into the wedding.'

'I've a few repairs to do first. Anyway it wouldn't have been fair on Nuala. It was her day.'

'A good many thought you were acting the maggot because you were losing her.'

'Is that why you were avoiding me?'

She chewed at her lips, looked away. 'I didn't know what you'd think of me after yesterday.'

He suddenly realised that he had not given the inevitability of this moment a second's thought all day. It was like stepping out on to a wide-open space in the dawn, clear of all obstacles to the horizon, nowhere to run to, the place empty save for this one white figure of retribution.

She glanced at him, her face loose with uncertainty. 'I didn't know whether to come or not.'

He didn't know what to say.

She searched his eyes for reassurance. 'I didn't know what would happen next.' She was trembling again as she had been in the car, then made a determined effort to check herself. 'I've been like a child again today, dressed in this virginal bridesmaid's gear . . . .'

A part of him wanted her, wanted to turn out the light and lead her into the house. The sky was already brightening with the onset of dawn.

She stood twisting her fingers, waiting for him to speak. 'Is it . . . different now, between you and me?'

However half-expected, the question shocked him. 'But I'm over thirty. You're just beginning . . . .'

'I knew you'd say that.' Her face had crumpled. 'I'm still a child to you.'

'You're not a child. It's just that you've had so little experience of life. Wait till you've been to college . . . .'

'I get the message,' she cried. 'You don't want me . . . .' And she flounced round in a flurry of white petticoats and ran, crying, out into the darkness.

He stood cemented to the floor. A few days back and this would have seemed inconceivable, utterly incongruous. How could she imagine him taking up with a girl of seventeen? He'd never even thought of Vaun in such terms. He was fond of her, he had to admit, but . . . He went into the house. It smelled of wet soap on the flagstones and Belle's bed of old sacks, a tinge of sour goat's milk and a slight woodlike aroma of ground coffee-beans. Suppose she was pregnant already? It would be fine for him to become a father, he'd quite like to have children. But he'd have to marry her and marriage wouldn't be fair on her at her age.

'You've mentioned that you find some things about women threatening?' The therapist had discovered a more discreet manner of observing the time. She had taken her watch off and laid it on the arm of the chair, angling her body so that she sat directly above it. 'Indications of mortality,' he replied. 'From a pimple to a double-chin. By such is their insubstantiality further undermined. Even a woman's cunt is alarming. From out of this jumble of veal fillets babies, such as I was once, emerge. Should I stuff my pee-stick down where I came from?' The therapist frowned, glancing out of habit at her empty wrist. 'I think you're being philosophical. I'd prefer an emotional reaction.' There was a balcony behind the therapist's chair. Through the glass-panelled door could be seen a large marijuana plant. He had watched it grow. 'How can anyone have a purely emotional reaction? Every feeling is clouded by the circumspection of our conditioning. How to behave, how to have regard for other people, all the little rules of social interplay that have to be observed. Inside each of us is an editor, constantly chopping out bits, pasting in additions, an automatic compensating mechanism that keeps us on the level. You talk about emotional reaction. I was brought up that if in a situation that is terrifying me, an inner voice is shouting, but you're not supposed to be afraid, you're a man, where are your guts? Another voice is saying, they'll despise you, if they see you're scared. And there's a third voice getting angry, how dare they do this to me, who the fucking hell do they think they are, I'll bloodywell kill them. Emotional reaction indeed. I had a girl-friend who, when I cuddled her and spoke in a playful voice, said severely, I'm not your mother, stop playing the child role, it's demeaning. But when I put on a forceful manner, she cried, stop, you're not my father, I don't want you in the parent role.' 'These damned roles,' exclaimed the therapist, throwing herself back in her chair with unusual violence. 'It's this ideal of perfection. So many men discard their women because they don't live up to expectation.' There were tears in her eyes. 'My husband left me for a young woman with a slender body and fresh complexion because he said I was grotesque.' And she began to sob loudly, pounding the chair arm so that her watch fell off. 'We never learn. Nobody's perfect. The next one'll have flaws too. We're all so dreadfully selfish.'

*

He felt awkward going up to Riordans the next day to help clear up. 'Vaun's taken to her bed,' complained her mother. 'Says she's ill. Too much drink, the stupid girl.'

Double guilt assailed him. If only he could talk to her, he thought. Try and explain. Give herself time, give them both time, maybe. He saw that she was out helping with the milking that evening, but he stayed clear. Later she drove the car with her mother beside her to deliver the churns.

Perhaps it was the subconscious desire to escape this influx of confused responses that made him return to the wings. He worked solidly for three days, built a replacement knuckle-joint, and made a tail from strong hessian sewn into an old pair of jeans. He had rejected the idea of a skirt, as it could ride up his legs, whereas the jeans kept the fabric down to his ankles and gave his legs more control to reduce the tail or fan out or twist diagonally.

When there came a fine evening with just a light breeze, he could not resist the opportunity to try the wings out again, even though there were still a few minor repairs to be done.

This time the cattle's curiosity overcame their trepidation and they swarmed round, so that he had to chase them away to make a clear run. There was always a current of air running down the valley, but the ease with which he achieved lift still amazed him. As soon as he reached about fifty feet, he propelled himself round the end of the valley, over his yard, and turned, wobbling as he tried to keep his legs straight, then on the return run he beat up a good speed to try out the tail. The increase in manoeuvrability was breathtaking. If he'd had the tail the last time he would never have become trapped in a thermal. He could bank much sharper now and came down low to try a landing, but the cattle were in the way, so he lifted up and turned over his yard, seeing Belle flee for cover. He beat down low over the cattle, scattering them out of the way, swept up over the glen again and returned in a long glide. The moment he fanned his tail down wide, tilting the wings back, slowing to the point of stalling was rapid. The miscalculation was that this should coincide with his feet touching the ground, whereas he was still three feet up, so he collapsed backwards on to the ground. He sat on the grass, breathing heavily, wedged in the wings. The cattle regarded him from a safe distance with wide-eyed unease. As soon as he'd got his breath back, he thought, he'd have one more flight and try to judge the landing better.

He flew higher, circling the valley. As he came close to the topmost ash trees beneath the bluff, two hundred feet up, a pair of ravens mobbed him, far more aerobatic than he, striking the wings with their claws and beaks, uttering deep shrieks of rage, not giving up till he was over the ruined farmhouse in the glen. He felt quite pleased that they'd mistaken him for a real bird. He flew back along the northern ridge of hazels and alders, just high enough to see the roofs of Riordans. On the return he kept out in the centre of the valley.

The evening sun ahead seemed to be eye to eye with him, beckoning him on, when there was a sudden crack and one wing shot upwards, pulling its handle clean out of his grasp. There was nothing he would do but hold on to the frame as he began to gyrate and plummet downwards.

Sir, It is said that in the last moments of life as a man falls, his past flashed before his eyes. I can vouchsafe from sad experience that all that passes are the flavours of his last meal: in my case a leg of chicken, boiled potatoes, lettuce, a Starking apple and a glass of Guinness. In haste, yours, etc.

Seconds before he hit the ground, he heard a voice calling. Then his feet struck like hammers, knees buckling, hips folding like a book snapped shut, the weight of the wings crushing him down, a sharp pain in his chest before he lost consciousness.

*

Occasionally he was aware of a neat, geometric world of ceilings and windows. Sometimes a bell tinkled in the distance, angelus or telephone. Footsteps approached, then receded. Phases of time passed like pages of drawing paper pulled away before he had time to make a mark on them. Women with distinctive eyebrows and mouths, hair encased in white caps, loomed over him while their invisible hands shoved against remote boundaries of his consciousness. He could never catch a glimpse of their hands, only their faces hanging above him like decorated balloons. He had the impression that this consciousness that was himself was now constructed differently. Once there had been men in green masks whom he knew were smiling as they spoke to him.

Then he was sitting up in bed with a meal spread out before him on a tray, a meal he was uncertain what to do with. It seemed quite alien that he was supposed to eat it. It sat there like the prospect of a new learning experience, especially as he only had one usable hand. The other was like a dewclaw growing out of his chest. The dishes seemed more like toy food. Each portion perfectly painted. Neat brown edges to the roast potatoes, matching slices of meat glossily varnished, peas like green ball-bearings. Surely none of it intended to be eaten?

It surprised him to find how much it actually tasted like food, how many memories it brought back.

He looked round at the five other occupants in their beds, most of them lying back after finishing their lunch. There were no greetings. When a patient came through the swing door, there was just a nod of the head as if he was an old acquaintance. But he had the feeling that he had never come through the door himself, had arrived through the depths of the bed.

When Mrs Riordan and Vaun came in, dressed and made-up as if they were going to Mass, the sense of being caught in the unlikelihood of a dream remained.

Mrs Riordan's face was glossy with perspiration. 'How're they looking after you, Conor? Are they feeding you properly? We brought you a pie and some cakes. What a terrible thing to happen. Isn't it just our luck, one thing after another?'

'Stop moaning, Mam,' said Vaun. 'Everything's fine. There's no real work running your place, Conor. All this talk about you being the hard worker. It's Belle does it all. I got Machra to help me put your wings back in the barn. They don't look too bad.'

'How long have I been here?' he asked, his voice grating with disuse.

'It must be a week now,' said Mrs Riordan. 'Your poor head. Isn't it lucky you weren't killed? And how's your poor shoulder? And your leg?'

Stiff and aching all over, he was still uncertain what exactly was wrong with him. 'How did I get here?'

'You didn't fly, that's for sure,' said Vaun. 'If only you'd waited till today, I could have brought you myself, I passed my test yesterday.'

'Clever girl,' he said.

She grinned. 'It was lucky I saw you. Falling out of the sky like a giant sycamore seed. I thought you were dead when you hit the ground. Cried my heart out. But Uncle Tom said we should get the ambulance, you were still breathing. He wouldn't believe you'd been flying the wings, said it wasn't possible, but I told him I saw you.'

Conor looked down at himself, waved his good hand. 'What did they say was wrong with me?'

'Can't you tell? I expect your brain's been affected. You've a broken wrist and collar-bone, broken ankle and I think your skull was fractured . . .' Vaun scratched her head. 'Hang on while I ask the sister.' She ran out through the swing doors.

'I never knew Vaun had it in her,' confided Mrs Riordan while she was away. 'There was I thinking the place would become a tinker's camp after Nuala left, but she's been running from ours to yours and back as if it was from the sink to the cooker. I'd say she's lost a stone already, and no harm to that. She has Machra working so fast he doesn't have time for the mud to stick to his boots. She has Kathy milking goats at such a rate the milk's near turned to cheese before it's delivered to the factory. We had a calf yesterday morning coming the wrong way and she pulled it out herself before I could find Tom. She's a new wonder, I can tell you. Goes to show some good can come out of bad.'

Vaun came in, breathless, threw herself in the chair. 'You'll never guess? They were wheeling a case down the corridor, a woman, and she smiled at me. I didn't recognise her, but there was something familiar. I'll swear now it was Dorothy. But she looked terrible, like she'd been in a fire or something. Maybe it wasn't her.'

A pulse started up in Conor's temple before he could recollect who Dorothy was, and the little mental bells rang. He frowned to disguise his excitement. 'Maybe you should find out if it is her?'

Vaun nodded. 'I will. I should have asked.' She hurried off again.

'Didn't Dorothy go back to Australia?' asked Mrs Riordan.

Could it really be her? he wondered, forgotten recollections starting to spill into his mind's eye. Had she really survived? 'I haven't heard from her,' he replied. Which was the truth, he thought. He closed his eyes the clearer to view his memories.

'I hope this'll warn you not to go in the face of gravity, Conor,' Mrs Riordan admonished. 'You were very secretive about these wings you had there. Vaun was telling me she wanted you into business making them. Would there be any money in it, d'you think?'

But Conor had fallen asleep.

When he woke the Riordans had gone. Through the fishtank glass partition he could see a dark figure standing outside, looking in. The door swung open. It was a hatless garda carrying a clip-board. Interest rustled through the other patients like a sudden breeze.

'Are you fit for a few questions? Mr de Burgh?' he asked, pulling up a chair.

It must be about the flying, Conor thought nervously. Should he have had a licence?

The garda was a young man in his twenties, with curly black hair. 'I was talking to a young lady earlier. Miss Riordan. A friend of yours?'

Conor nodded.

'She asked about a patient. We happen to be making enquiries about this patient, a Miss Rachel Martin.'

'Rachel Martin?' echoed Conor, panged with disappointment. 'It must be the wrong person. That wasn't her name.'

The garda frowned. 'That's what Miss Riordan said. But she felt she recognised her. It's important that we try to trace anyone who might know Miss Martin or have seen her in the last few weeks?'

'Why?'

'We have reason to believe . . .'

There was a rapping on the glass partition. Outside a grizzled sergeant was beckoning to the garda. 'Excuse me a minute,' he said, getting up.

While the two dark figures were conversing outside, Conor tilted himself over till he was in danger of toppling out of bed. His good hand could just reach the clipboard left on the chair and swivel it round.

RACHEL MARTIN

Anonymous phonecall, 4th July.

Injured woman in ruined farmhouse near Letterfrack. Caller identified her by name.

Found unconscious. Brought by ambulance to Galway Regional Hospital. No other identification. Only clothing a ragged dress without labels, no jewellery.

All attempts to trace family, friends, or group failed to date.

Medical report indicates severe undernourishment, large numbers of bruises about the body consistent with heavy blows, hair pulled out, several burn points suggestive of electrodes, many punctures in arms indicating use of hypodermics. Body also covered in sores due to septicaemia from critical overdoses of drugs. Indications would suggest these drugs were not self-inflicted.

Patient too ill to interview.

Conor sat back, his skin prickling. It must be her, he thought. Alive. Vaun's recognition confirmed it. Rachel Martin another identity. Wasn't Martin the name of that judge? What had the bastards done to her, poor girl? What amazing luck that she was alive! This was the best news of his life. What fate that they should both end up in the same hospital. But how was he going to make contact cemented to the bed with all this white concrete round his body?

The garda came back and retrieved his clip-board. 'I have to go now Mr de Burgh. I'll call back and see you another time.'

After he had gone, Conor's neighbour rolled over in his bed. 'Was it about your injuries?'

Conor thought it best to agree.

'You should get a good few bob for that lot,' commented the man.

A short dark-haired nurse who walked with a thrust of her hips came in with a tray of pill cups. A friendly cheerful girl, the sort any man would take advantage of, Conor thought. 'Could you ever do me a favour, nurse?' he asked as she handed him his pills.

'What would I get in return?' she quipped.

'If I didn't know you were spoken for, you could have my favours anytime. I need a piece of paper and a pen, and would you take a note to a patient for me?'

She grinned. 'What favours? You'd look great at a disco, wouldn't you? Back in about half-an-hour.'

He lay impatient, afraid she would forget, or get distracted by other calls. But she came. 'Now,' she said, taking a sheet of paper from her pocket and handing him her pen. 'Will you be long writing?'

'Not if you hold it steady for me,' he replied, and scribbled— IS IT YOU? CONOR. 'There,' he said, folding the sheet and writing RACHEL MARTIN on it.

'Which ward is she in?'

'I don't know. Is there any way of finding out?'

She sighed. 'I wouldn't run errands just for anybody, you know. Is it very important?'

If he had hoped for a reply that evening, none came. It was difficult to contain his disappointment. At night they gave him sedatives to help overcome the ache of the setting bones and discomfort of his restriction. But it was a long time before he fell asleep, thinking about her, hoping it really was her, visualizing their reunion.

Next morning at about eleven a nurse he had never seen before entered the ward. She was middle-aged and large, with fat cheeks and small eyes. 'Mr de Burgh?' she asked looking at him. She handed him a note.

Inside was one word, scrawled large—YES. He could not restrain the width of his smile, stringing the banner of his joy from ear to ear. 'Thanks. Which ward is she in?'

'Grainne. Third floor.' When the nurse smiled, affected by his response, deep dimples appeared in her round cheeks. 'She wanted me to put her in a wheelchair to come and see you. But she's not well enough.'

'Could I get to her?'

She hesitated. 'It'd be good for her to see someone. I'll see what I can arrange. It mayn't be till tomorrow, though. I'm Nurse Dunne.'

The pace of hospital routine dragged with frustrating slowness, the indignities of bedpans, the stodgy meals, the throat-clogging pills, the patronising doctors and the endless hours when the ward was like an abandoned attic, all activity sealed off the other side of the fishtank partition, figures hurrying down the arterial corridor, but none peeling off to enter the ward. He cursed his inoperative body.

The following afternoon the ample form of Nurse Dunne appeared, together with the cheerful little Nurse Egan. She was pushing a wheelchair. Between them, with much heaving, grunting and some laughter, they lifted him into it. 'Mind you behave yourself now,' Nurse Egan called after him as Nurse Dunne wheeled him away.

It was a long smooth glide down the vinyl passages. 'She's looking forward to seeing you,' said Nurse Dunne.

Me too, he thought, his chest so tight with anticipation he was nearly breathless.

They came to a small ward with three beds.

As Nurse Dunne left him by the only occupied bed, his first thought was, this is a terrible mistake, it isn't her, and he half-turned in panic to call the nurse back.

How could this emaciated, hairless, scabby figure be her? This woman looked all of sixty. She was skeletally thin, her skin was smudged with blue and grey bruises, there were sores around her mouth and on the bald patches in her scant hair. Her mouth was like a tear in a paperbag, spilling teeth.

A bandaged wrist reached out towards him, matchstick fingers groped in greeting. 'Hallo, Conor.'

Only her eyes were as he remembered, brown and bright, lighting up for him. When they filled with tears he could not tell if it was from emotion at seeing him again or because she read the rejection in his shocked expression.

'I wish you could get into bed with me,' she said with a note of lustful regret. It was so reminiscent of her old self that he should have laughed, but now it only disgusted him.

'Are you really Rachel Martin? Is that your real name?'

The expressions on her ravaged face were hard to determine. It took a few seconds each time to realise that her grimaces were smiles. Her voice had shrunk to a croak. 'Thanks, Conor . . . for getting those papers to Dublin.'

Her hand clutched his with the strength of tiny claws.

'It was no problem.' He told her of Stephen Monaghan's reaction, the business about the shredder, and them getting drunk together. She seemed to find it difficult to speak, wincing and moistening her lips. He thought her face was like a crust and that she was stuck underneath it like an unmetamorphosed butterfly trapped inside its chrysalis. He could gauge nothing from her expression, save the sort of contentment at his presence that a dog might show in its eyes. 'Monaghan said he'd never heard of Nel Farrell,' he added. 'Though he got very interested when I mentioned Josephine Grant.'

She nodded then, her fingers tightening their grip on his arm as she struggled to speak. But her voice was so faint that however close he leaned he could not catch their gist. 'Surely you weren't Josephine Grant?' he exclaimed.

But the effort had been too much for her, her lips ceased trying to move, and her eyelids fell like closing cockles. He became anxious, held on to her hand. He looked round as a nurse came in.

'Dropped off, has she?' She checked her pulse. 'It's the medication, makes them drowsy. I'll find someone to take you back.'

His head whirled as he was returned to his own ward. He was in a state of shock. He was so scared of his own feelings he dared not think; the bloom of his expectations so violently crushed underfoot. He did not notice what they brought him for supper.

He found he was trembling as he lay on his bed, as if his body could not tolerate his reactions. Gradually an incredulity took hold of him. Of course it wasn't that bad. She had seemed worse because it was so unexpected. He must get back to see her again.

The minutes crawled next day while he waited for Nurse Dunne to come. He slashed through the pages of magazines, good leg hanging out of the bed. His eye sardonically observed the black-stockinged calves of passing nurses, lifted up to follow their rustling haunches, their white necks. Their shoes always seemed to have a slight squeak. The other men in the ward slouched in their beds in neanderthal contemplation or hid behind screens of newspapers. One wandered about aimlessly like a prisoner, another stood staring out of the windows. Visitors arrived and sat huddled round beds, whispering. Vaun came on her own.

She seemed obscenely healthy with her vibrant Riordan colouring and full cheeks tinged red as apples. He had never seen her look so lean and sharp, almost beautiful.

'I've been to up to see her,' she said.

'Wasn't it lucky you recognised her that first time? Otherwise she and I would have been lying in the same hospital and never known.'

She narrowed her eyes. 'Conor, you're sitting there like a bandaged parcel. I know you. You know what happened to her, don't you?'

'It's a long story.'

All he omitted in the telling was his feelings for Rachel, and the sex.

'Holy shit,' Vaun exclaimed, after he had finished. 'Why did you never tell us any of this before?' Her voice grew resentful. 'You told Nuala?'

'The fewer people who knew the better. It wasn't safe to know.'

She made a face. 'What bastards could do that to anyone?' She looked at him. 'I bet you slept with her?'

He nodded before he realised what he was doing.

She bit her lip. 'I don't suppose you fancy her now. Poor girl.' She frowned. 'What about the gardai? Did you tell them.'

'One started to question me, but he went away. I keep expecting him to come back.'

After Vaun had gone he lay thinking, disturbed by her perception. But how could he say to himself that Rachel now disgusted him? The fat figure of his therapist loomed in his mind as she had wept over her husband's rejection of her. He pushed her away. He was not going to be like that.

At last Nurse Dunne arrived with the wheelchair. They found Rachel asleep, her frail body submerged in bedding like someone floating in water. As he sat waiting for her to wake, gazing at her scabbed face and baldness, her sunken grey flesh, he could not prevent a wave of disgust saturating him. It was impossible to believe she was the same person, any of them for that matter. Except of course, she had been none of them. Or had she been one of them in particular? Surely she couldn't be that terrorist woman? Half a busload of dead schoolchildren against her name? He was deep in the distaste of his conjectures when her hand reached out and touched him.

However emaciated and brutalised her features, her eyes remained bright and liquid as fresh-made tea. He hung on to them, for they seemed the only connection with the person he remembered. 'Tell me you're not Josephine Grant?'

Her brow folded, not so much into a frown as trying with the patience of a photographer to frame her focus of him.

He felt that with his arm strapped across his chest he should make some passionate avowal. 'As soon as I get home I'll get the place cleaned up for you to come and convalesce.' He grinned. 'My low-grade guesthouse has gone downhill since you were last there.'

Her head was sunk low in the pillow like a brooch in its padded box. 'You don't need me, Conor.' Her voice was a whisper. 'You should marry Vaun and fill your paradise with babies.'

For a moment he felt a surge of relief that she was releasing him, that he would not have to struggle to find feelings for this feeble wreck.

He was aware that Nurse Dunne had come in to take him back. There came a rushing noise in his head, prickling across his scalp. He heaved himself up and leaned down to kiss Rachel's scabs. 'I'm going to get a bath and pipe it in for when you come.'

He lay in his bed that night once more disgusted with himself that he should have felt so repelled by her appearance. Was it the outward manifestation of a person that made the bond, rather than the character inside? Wouldn't the wounds heal and she be restored?

A different nurse came to see him the next afternoon. She was young and brisk, with short boyish hair. 'It's Margaret Dunne's day off. I promised her I'd call down and see you. Rachel's been moved back into intensive care, so you'll have to give her a miss for a few days.'

'Why?' he asked anxiously.

'It's just to monitor her more closely. This is one of the troubles of severe drug addiction.' The young nurse was full of self-importance. 'It reduces the capacity of the body's defence systems to cope with ordinary infections. The septicaemia is difficult to control. If only people appreciated the danger they put themselves in.'

'But she wasn't an addict.'

The nurse looked at him. 'It's on her diagnosis. Besides, the symptoms are typical. Unfortunately we're getting more and more of these cases.'

He was angry, but knew he would gain nothing by arguing. It must be some mistake, he thought.

He became riddled with self-recrimination that Rachel's relapse was due to him, that it was because he had not told her that he still loved her, and so imbued her with determination.

He lay in his bed, conscious only of his helplessness. He should be sitting beside her, whispering to her, pressing her sleeping hand, urging her to fight.

Margaret Dunne came to see him the next afternoon.

'Any change?' he asked.

'It'll take time. We're all praying for her.'

'Did you know they think she's an addict?'

She nodded, her small eyes sunk beneath her frown. 'I can't believe it's just administrative convenience.'

'What d'you mean?'

'It's like someone has taken the deliberate decision that the sores on her body are from septicaemia, not from burns. That since she took the overdose herself, the bruises are from falls.'

'But why?' he exclaimed angrily.

Margaret Dunne shrugged. 'I heard the gardai and the doctors when she was first brought in. They knew it was torture. Any fool could tell from the evidence. I saw the reports. Whoever those people were that did it to her, the devil's handymen, they tried everything. They were probably at it for weeks, starving her and pumping her full of lethal drugs. What did they care? The normal resistance of her body was paralysed. That's why septicaemia set in. Her blood awash with toxins, abscesses on her heart and kidneys.'

Conor nodded. 'So why have the doctors changed their minds?'

'You know as much as I do. Have the gardai been back to question you?'

He shook his head.

'Wouldn't you think they'd want to find out everything about her? But they've closed the case, no more enquiries. Yet there's no contact with any family or friends.' She patted his arm. 'It's like me saying to you, all that nonsense about flying. Didn't you break your bones falling off a ladder?'

She nodded at his expression. 'Yes, I know about your accident. I was there when young Vaun was talking with Rachel. She told her why you were here, that she had a birdman now to come back to. She's a nice girl. I'd say she was fond of you, too.'

Conor did not want to think of Vaun. He lay sunk in gloom. He felt tied up in his husk of bandages, one-armed and a leg in a boot of plaster. Comfort was impossible, and though the pills they gave him should have helped him to sleep, sleep was a tangle of dozing among the writhings of his conscience. He could not even banter with Nurse Egan, and turned away from all attempts by his fellow patients to engage him in conversation,

Sir, You realise that really I am writing to God. To plead with him to exist. Because I need him. I want somebody, something to be effectual, to control what I want. To uphold what is right. To enact justice. To show me truth. To give me something to measure myself against. To explain why someone who has so courageously uncovered corruption, suffered horrific torture, should lose her life? Yours, etc.

In the days that followed he was unstrapped so that he had freedom to move the arm with the broken wrist, the cast now with a hook on it so that he could use a pair of crutches. The surgeon was particularly impressed by the progress of his fractured skull. 'You've a nut like a cannon-ball. We'll let you home soon.'

Conor felt guilty at the prospect of leaving the building where Rachel lay so ill and alone. That day he struggled on his crutches up to the intensive-care ward.

A nurse at a desk dominated by a closed-circuit TV relay system asked him if he was a relative. Voices whispered from behind closed doors in his mind, mocked him with cock-crows. He was allowed to look through a window. Rachel was barely visible. Just her head like a book on the pillow. There was a festoon of wires and tubes attaching her to bottles and a cabinet of winking diodes and cathode indicators. He felt awash with pity. What relationship did he have with all that?

It was a dark overcast morning that he saw Margaret Dunne appear outside the glass partition and hesitate to enter. In that gesture he recognized instinctively an unwilling messenger.

When she stood there and slowly shook her head he was all but sick on the spot. She came and stood by the bed. He leaned against her and wept.

He had never in his life shed such tears. They were not so much the bursting of an accumulation of a lifetime, the emptying of archives of grief as if only now he had finally given in and ceased to dam up what should flow naturally. Nor were they as if his unconscious was at last accepting that none of what he wanted could be preserved. They were release.

'Lord, I pray justice catches up with those that did it to her,' said Margaret Dunne. 'She surely didn't deserve it.'

A few days later Vaun came to collect him. Mrs Riordan had insisted he stay with them, and had prepared Sean's old room for him.

Conor might have appeared to be over-affecting the role of stricken mourner. But it was a refuge. He was in a state of shock rather than grief, through the unexpected reunion with Rachel followed so quickly by the irony of her death. He hid within this state of numbness as if he did not know where else to put himself. Everyone behaved with deference to his condition, not difficult since he was so physically handicapped by his plasters. Vaun in particular, was considerate.

Vaun was a changed person. She was no longer the outrage-tongued child. She could hardly blatantly lust after him. But since she could have discerned what had probably been the cause of his earlier rejection of her, namely another woman who was now removed, this might mean her chances were restored. But that was only his conjecture, cynicism growing wild in his depleted state of mind. He had imagined she would lunge clumsily after him. But she behaved with consistent restraint, concerned only with his well-being. Had he wanted her to behave in a manner to gain his respect, this was how he would have liked her to be. But then he had no particular wish that she should. Or so he told himself.

Some weeks later, after the autopsy and inquest, Vaun took him to the funeral. She drove him in the Landrover since the Datsun had a flat tyre. She was wearing the navy-blue suit she had been bursting out of at Sean's Requiem Mass. Now she was loose inside it like a pestle in a mortar. But she was never one to keep silence and regaled him with the story of her driving-test.

'The examiner was an old fellow. Sat huddled in a corner of

his seat as if scared it was his last drive. Or maybe he didn't care for women. He clutched his notepad against his chest like it was a shield and each time he wanted me to take a left or right turn he'd jerk out an arm like he was fencing. And everytime we'd near a junction he'd grab the doorhandle. Then a dog runs out in front of us and I have to dive for the brakes. So he flings his arms up over his face. That'll do for the emergency stop, he shrieks. I didn't think I had a cat's whisker of a chance. At the end when he was asking a few questions, he gabbled them so fast I couldn't hear. What was that? I asked politely. "You've passed," he shouts, flinging himself out of the door. I don't know how a man like that could do that sort of job. He must be hanging by a cotton thread from a nervous breakdown. Funny how Belle refuses to do a thing for Machra, isn't it? Yet she'll fly like a bird for me or Kathy. She even growls at him, a thing she never does. Poor Machra. You never saw anyone tire so easily. It takes him ten minutes to recover from smoking a fag. Maybe his energy goes into making all those spots on his face, poor boy. At least we've persuaded him to take a bath. Or maybe it's because he wants to impress Kathy. That gaping moony look that comes over his face whenever he sees her. And she just treats him like a mouldy apple.'

The funeral was taking place at a small churchyard at Moycullen, outside Galway city on the road to Oughterard. Conor had imagined Rachel would have been brought back to Dublin by her relatives. But it seemed that nobody had claimed her, as if it was still not known exactly who she was.

It was a breezy, leaf-gushing day. Clouds clung to the hills, grey-bearded the sun. Pigeons beat in and out of the beech trees, swallows swerved among the lichen-covered labels to other people's passing. The air was redolent with scent lifted from the wreaths, lilies and chrysanthemums, their myriad petals white as teeth gnashing the breeze.

The priest's thin hair blew like smoke off his scalp. He read the burial service quickly, a daily chore for him. As the coffin was lowered into its deep hole, Conor thought how such a tightly clamped varnished box was an apt container to hold the mysteries of its occupant. It was already difficult to recall her exactly, there were so many conflicting voices in his head, each with a faceful of different expressions. So many memories in so short a time. What a talent ended. He felt the tears burn in his eyes with anger rather than grief as he stood there leaning on a stick.

Vaun was openly crying. Beside her stood Margaret Dunne, her heavy cheeks glistening. There were a few others from the hospital, and among them a white-haired man in a charcoal-grey suit.

Stephen Monaghan came up to him after the ceremony. 'She was saved yet lost. They couldn't have done anymore.'

Conor could only nod.

Monaghan gripped his arm gently. 'I have to ask you something. I'd prefer if you told no one.'

'I've already told the Riordans.'

'Then tell no one else . . .'

'So it was you who suppressed the enquiries?' cried Conor. 'Can't she even get credit for what she's done?'

Monaghan raised a hand placatingly. 'I understand your feelings, old man. But I think it's what she would have wanted. Not to jeopardise what she's achieved.'

They walked among the gravestones, Conor limping, leaning heavily on his stick. 'If it appears that a young woman has died of heroin addiction,' Monaghan continued, 'nobody's going to ask what else she was up to.'

'It's the bloody state again,' Conor exclaimed disgustedly. 'Mustn't rock the boat.'

Monaghan stood staring into the distance, at the cloud-shadowed hills. He shook his head. 'She was one in a million. The best we ever had.'

Conor looked at him. 'So who exactly was she?'

Monaghan turned to him. 'Are you going to keep your flying secret?'

'How did you . . . ?'

Monaghan smiled, put an arm around his shoulder. 'Come on, now, Conor . . .'

*

When they were driving home later, Conor saw that there were still traces of tears in Vaun's eyes. He felt more moved by her grief than his own. Across the bay the stone leviathan hills of the Burren lay impeturbable beneath a wash of rainclouds pressing down upon their craniums.

Vaun rested a hand upon his knee in a gesture of comfort. He placed his hand on top of hers, in companionship.

All the women he had loved eluded him, he reflected. 'I seem to be unlucky with women,' he said.

Vaun smiled. 'Are you going to give up, then?' she asked, retrieving her hand to change gear.

BENEDICT KIELY

Nothing Happens in Carmincross

Benedict Kiely's latest novel tells the story of a journey to his childhood home undertaken by Mervyn Kavanagh, a man in middle age who has been living and teaching in America. The wedding of a favourite niece takes him travelling back across the Atlantic and Ireland to Carmincross, the small town in Ulster where he was born. As he journeys towards this family celebration he repeatedly encounters people and events from his own and his country's past, while the constant flow of news of contemporary acts of terrorism and counter-terrorism invades his consciousness more and more insistently. Somewhere, it seems, the past and the present are bound to collide. . . .

'Written with zest and grace, humour and irony in a style that is totally individual . . . It must be read by everyone interested in Irish writing and the peculiar tragedy of the Irish situation.'
Kevin Casey *Irish Times*

'Richly, grimly funny . . . At its best this is a remarkable study of a man struggling to come to terms with the country he thought he'd left behind him and with his own complicity in the troubles.' Margaret Walters *The Observer*

'I have been waiting for a novel as full of rage about contemporary Ireland as this one. And this is the book I have been waiting for.'
Frank Delaney *BBC World Service*

'[A] dark and compellingly troubled meditation on our contemporary situation. Read it.'
Terence Brown *Sunday Independent*

BENEDICT KIELY

A Letter to Peachtree

'A masterly collection of new stories' *Irish Press*

Benedict Kiely is one of those rare writers who can portray the unexpected, the comic and the tragic sides of life, often in the same person and in the same moment of hilarity and doubt. In this, his fourth collection of stories, he teases his readers as happily and as wickedly as ever.

'There are fine things all over this collection, lives to brood about and glorious gallops down every interesting looking diversion ... There are so many Irish people who write short stories, and so few who are real storytellers. Ben Kiely is one, and he should be preserved in aspic or crowned high king or just bought in huge numbers.'
Sunday Independent

'This is a splendid collection, confirming Kiely as a master of the oral tradition.' *Irish Press*

'They are as much occasions of sin as any Ben Kiely story ever was' *Irish Independent*

'The stories are full of the sort of verve you would expect from Ben Kiely, overflowing with wit, erudition, a sense of the absurd, a tenderness for beauty, whether of people or places' *Evening Press*

'Sheer magic'
Dominic Behan, *Dublin Evening Herald*

'Stylish, gabby, using language like a fallen angel, he mixes his feelings with a true storyteller's verve that looks like superb skill but is in fact something better. Call it instinct.'
Norman Shrapnell, *Guardian*

MICHAEL SCOTT and GLORIA GAGHAN

Navigator: The Voyage of Saint Brendan

Brendan of Erin is driven by his quest – to find the Isles of Promise. Obsessed with stories of a paradise to be found on a mysterious, floating island, he gathers a crew of fourteen men – monks like himself – who together build a craft that will take them on their fantastic travels.

It is to be a journey of mythical proportions, to islands of great peril and awful temptations, to the dwellings of demons and nymphs, of fabulous and fearful beasts. But like Jason or Odysseus, Brendan is true to his destiny, and will not deviate from his obsession to find Paradise. . . .

Here, brilliantly told in fictional form, is one of the West's greatest myths, which inspired Columbus to look for the route to the Indies, the tale of Brendan the Navigator and his spiritual and fantastical voyage.

URSULA HOLDEN

The Cloud Catchers

In the squalor of a decaying, broken-down Irish farm, Eve's life revolves around her family. Her mother is worn and nervous, her father is frightening, and her brother, Maxie, an epileptic who is in need of constant care. And then there is Eileen. Abandoned by her mother as a young child, she is Eve's cousin, protector and only friend.

Through infancy and childhood Eve and Eileen are each other's strength, but as they grow into maturity so does their discontent. Eileen sets off for the bright lights of Dublin at the first opportunity, leaving timid Eve to village life and her dreams of Matthew, the English boy who held her close under the big tree one summer. But Eve is destined to leave the farm too. It is the beginning of her journey which takes her from Dublin to London in search of Eileen, and of herself. . . .

'Ursula Holden has nothing to fear from inevitable comparisons with Edna O'Brien because she has written a fresh and joyful book that rests firmly on its own happy achievement'
Lesley Garner *Cosmopolitan*

'She's a natural writer with an ear and an eye that would be sharp in a stoat . . . Ursula Holden is here to stay' *New York Times Book Review*

'Ursula Holden is one of the most seriously radiant new English writers' *The Times*

MAEVE KELLY

Necessary Treasons

When Eve Gleeson joins the women's movement in Limerick, she finds it is a largely disregarded concern. Young, naïve but grimly independent, she begins to work for a battered wives' refuge, and her increasing anger and pain at women's lot – especially among the ill-educated poor – is matched only by her growing frustration at the movement's limited resources and support.

Set against this is her relationship with Hugh. Twenty years her senior, he clearly sees in Eve the chaste and tender bride he has always wanted, and is baffled by her more 'modern' side and her growing resentment. To complicate things there are also his four possessive sisters and lonely ancestral home; and the attractions of unthinking, rigid matronhood begin to dwindle considerably while what Hugh calls Eve's 'hobby' becomes an issue of central importance.

'Maeve Kelly writes with a kind of bitter elegance . . . Her descriptions of modern Limerick with its shoddy affluence and its comfortable contempt for "social" issues are vivid and accurate.' *The Listener*

'Ms Kelly's insights . . . are shrewd, her style incisive . . . A fine, provocative first novel from a writer already noted for her sharply individual short stories.' *Sunday Independent*

BARBARA COMYNS

Mr Fox

Mr Fox is a spiv – a dealer in second-hand cars and black-market food, a man skilled in bending the law. When Caroline Seymore and her young daughter Jenny are deserted at the beginning of World War II, he offers them a roof over their heads, advice on evading creditors and a shared – if dubious – future. . . .

'I recommend it for its hilariously accurate descriptions of war . . . Barbara Comyns had me by the throat in that chokey state between laughter and tears given us by all too few writers'
Mary Wesley, *London Daily News*

'An extremely funny book' *Literary Review*

'It has great charm' *The Times*

'I enjoyed her story . . . for its innocence, its straightforwardness, its charming lack of guile.'
Nina Bawden, *Daily Telegraph*

'Delicate poignancy wrapped up in beautifully elegant prose' *Women's Review*

'A minor classic . . . hunt down *Mr Fox* forthwith for its peerless evocation of an era' *Daily Mail*

MAUREEN DUFFY

Change

'[Maureen Duffy] shows at once broad and deep understanding of what the war of 1939–45 meant for ordinary English men and women, both in and out of uniform: a delight to read.' M. R. D. Foot

To different people in Britain in 1939 the coming of war meant different things. To Hilary at a London grammar school it meant her father joining the Home Guard and later, her school moving to the country and reaching adulthood in a dangerous and exciting world. To Alan it meant learning to fly and risk his life nightly, as well as trying to respond with his poetry to the challenges of new experience. To Daphne it meant separation from her army officer husband and making a new life for herself as an ambulance driver in the Blitz. . . .

'It's as if our parents' and grandparents' treasured photograph albums had been tossed in the air and their snapshots, frozen moments in time, had landed heaped and entwined. Maureen Duffy has picked through these fragments of life and fitted them into the mosaic of *Change*.' *Time Out*

'In *Change* Maureen Duffy demonstrates her ability to be simultaneously involved and yet distanced. It is this merging of the implicated and prophetic voice that makes her writing continually and unpredictably challenging.'
Fiction Magazine

'The telling is vivid, very readable.'
Financial Times

'An experienced, prolific novelist; nothing she writes can fail.' *Daily Telegraph*

Methuen Modern Fiction

While every effort is made to keep prices low, it is sometimes necessary to increase prices at short notice. Methuen Paperbacks reserves the right to show new retail prices on covers which may differ from those previously advertised in the text or elsewhere.

The prices shown below were correct at the time of going to press.

☐	413 52310 1	**Silence Among the Weapons**	John Arden	£2.50
☐	413 52890 1	**Collected Short Stories**	Bertolt Brecht	£3.95
☐	413 53090 6	**Scenes From Provincial Life**	William Cooper	£2.95
☐	413 59970 1	**The Complete Stories**	Noël Coward	£4.50
☐	413 54660 8	**Londoners**	Maureen Duffy	£2.95
☐	413 41620 8	**Genesis**	Eduardo Galeano	£3.95
☐	413 42400 6	**Slow Homecoming**	Peter Handke	£3.95
☐	413 42250 X	**Mr Norris Changes Trains**	Christopher Isherwood	£3.50
☐	413 59630 3	**A Single Man**	Christopher Isherwood	£3.50
☐	413 56110 0	**Prater Violet**	Christopher Isherwood	£2.50
☐	413 41590 2	**Nothing Happens in Carmincross**	Benedict Kiely	£3.50
☐	413 58920 X	**The German Lesson**	Siegfried Lenz	£3.95
☐	413 60230 3	**Non-Combatants and Others**	Rose Macaulay	£3.95
☐	413 54210 6	**Entry Into Jerusalem**	Stanley Middleton	£2.95
☐	413 59230 8	**Linden Hills**	Gloria Naylor	£3.95
☐	413 55230 6	**The Wild Girl**	Michèle Roberts	£2.95
☐	413 57890 9	**Betsey Brown**	Ntozake Shange	£3.50
☐	413 51970 8	**Sassafrass, Cypress & Indigo**	Ntozake Shange	£2.95
☐	413 53360 3	**The Erl-King**	Michel Tournier	£4.50
☐	413 57600 0	**Gemini**	Michel Tournier	£4.50
☐	413 14710 X	**The Women's Decameron**	Julia Voznesenskaya	£3.95
☐	413 59720 2	**Revolutionary Road**	Richard Yates	£4.50

All these books are available at your bookshop or newsagent, or can be ordered direct from the publisher. Just tick the titles you want and fill in the form below.

Methuen Paperbacks, Cash Sales Department, PO Box 11, Falmouth, Cornwall TR10 10⁣9EN.

Please send cheque or postal order, no currency, for purchase price quoted and allow the following for postage and packing:

UK 60p for the first book, 25p for the second book and 15p for each additional book ordered to a maximum charge of £1.90.

BFPO and Eire 60p for the first book, 25p for the second book and 15p for each next seven books, thereafter 9p per book.

Overseas Customers £1.25 for the first book, 75p for the second book and 28p for each subsequent title ordered.

NAME (Block Letters) ....

ADDRESS..

....